CW00550766

LANE

TIM THOMAS

Copyright © 2024 by Tim Thomas

The right of Tim Thomas to be identified as the author of the work
has been asserted by him in accordance with the Copyright, Designs and
Patents Act 1988

Cover design by Sedge Swatton

ISBN 978-1-9160987-9-4

All rights reserved. No part of this publication may be reproduced,
stored in a retrieval system, or transmitted in any form or by any means
without the prior written permission of the publisher, nor be otherwise
circulated in any form of binding or cover other than that in which it is
published and without a similar condition being imposed on the subsequent
purchaser

This book is a work of fiction. All names, characters, organisations, places and incidents
are either imaginative or are used entirely fictitiously. Any resemblance to actual persons
(alive or dead), organisations, locations or events is purely coincidental.

acuteANGLE books
London

To my mum (love you)
and dad (miss you)

by the same author

THE CENTURY CLUB
THEN THERE WAS HOPE

Both available as ebooks

1.

1990

Harry Lane stared at his reflection in the barber's mirror and took in the contours of his face. He was about to reach a milestone. He was turning sixty years of age next week.

The bright blue eyes he had inherited from his father stared back at him. He could see himself that his looks were a mixture of both his mother Molly's and his father Stan's. He was five feet nine inches of stocky build. At least that was always the description on his police records. Handsome, in a rugged sense, and still fit, he was a well-built man with an aura, stature and a reputation. He was well-known in his community, the recipient of respectful nods, waves and admiration from his peers and the general population.

Harry knew the years had been kind to him compared to his contemporaries and had carried himself with a level of confidence only a man held in such high regard could. Within the area the name Lane was one to be respected and, by some, feared. If Harry's name alone wasn't enough, then the mention of his sons, Ray Lane and Denny Lane, particularly Denny, was enough to strike fear into any man.

Harry was snapped from his reverie by the barber, Angelo.

"Usual, Mr Lane?"

"Yeah, go on Angelo. Tidy the old sod up."

"Old? Never, Mr Lane. And with looks like that, with such a full head of hair and your sense of style, you could grace any red carpet function."

Harry laughed. "Well, I trust that you will be at my little birthday gathering with the family, Angelo."

Harry loved Angelo and the whole Vital family. They had run this little barber shop for as long as he could remember. And like many local businesses, this one had been passed down through the family. The Vitals also ran Valentines café, just up the road, another local institution. Although both in their early seventies, Angelo's parents, Antonio and Maria, both still laboured all day long amongst the steam and the dishes, serving the locals traditional Italian dishes (based on secret family recipes, at least that's what Papa Antonio would tell his customers with a wry wink and a smile) as well as the usual full English, sandwiches, cakes, tea and coffee. They were ably supported by their two daughters, Valentine and Anna. The café was primarily Maria's, as the food expertise ran in her side of the family, and the barber shop was Antonio's although he had long since left it to Angelo to run so that he could help his wife with Valentines café, named after their first daughter.

Harry relaxed in the barber's chair and allowed himself to take in both his reflection and the retro décor of the shop that had hardly changed over the years. The sound of *The Platters'* soothing tones emanating from the Gold radio station added to the atmosphere. Coming here always triggered memories of past times for Harry. As he relaxed more, the radio's gentle music faded into the distance, as did his awareness of his present surroundings, and his mind drifted into a lingering day dream.

His thoughts turned to a cold early December evening back in 1955, when a twenty-five-year-old Harry stepped from a car onto the pavement outside Antonio's shop, one half of a cohort of two men flanking George Parker. He on one side, Ronny Piper on the other.

As the three men approached the door to the barber's, Harry caught sight of a young PC, known to him as Burt Roswell, heading towards them at a brisk pace, slightly hunched over and quite clearly frozen. Although he was wearing a heavy coat and thick gloves, the hours pounding his beat in the bitterly cold weather were clearly taking their toll. Seeing this sorry sight, Harry couldn't help but laugh. "Blimey, look at Rudolph over here, lads. Big red hooter on that."

Burt looked at the smiling Harry, then at Ronny Piper before catching the eye of George Parker, who had stopped right in front of the door. George took a final puff of his cigar then arrogantly dropped it on the floor, stamping on it as he held Burt's gaze a few more seconds before nonchalantly entering the shop.

As Ronny followed George, Harry turned around. He removed a note from his wallet and went to hand it to Burt.

"There you go, you look perished. Go and get yourself a cuppa across the road in the cafe."

Burt looked at Harry's outstretched hand then looked up at his grinning face and replied, "That's exactly where I'm heading for a nice warm cup of Bovril." With that, he removed his right glove and pulled out a luncheon voucher from his overcoat pocket before turning on his heal and heading towards the opposite side of the road, mumbling under his breath.

Harry stepped into the shop and as George flipped the sign on the door over to "Closed", Harry just caught sight of Burt through the glass, standing across the road, staring at the barber's, before he turned and disappeared into the cafe.

As George settled into the barber's chair, Harry looked at the back of his head with evil intent. It was hard to believe that as a teenager he had looked at this man as some kind of a hero. And of course, to a boy from a normal but somewhat impoverished family, the money, the cars, the women and what he had perceived as an exciting lifestyle had drawn a young Harry into Parker's world, much to the distain of his straight parents.

He had learnt the trade of the underworld from Parker, but over the years Parker's arrogance and bullying behaviour had grown out of control. As had Harry's confidence and ambition. Parker's greedy ways had slowly eroded the feelings of fealty among many in the outfit and his pointless violence towards others, particularly straight people whose lives had no bearing on their world, was becoming a liability to the business and an embarrassing daily occurrence. Every time Harry witnessed one of Parker's outbursts somehow increased his desire to take charge and run this firm himself.

"You just nicked my ear with that razor, you skinny little wop bastard," Parker barked at Antonio.

"Here we go again," Ronny Piper mumbled under his breath to Harry. "Never went near his poxy ear. I was watching. Everywhere we go now that wanker has to start."

Harry glanced at Ronny in exasperated acknowledgement then calmly looked back towards Parker and the now terrified Antonio.

"You come over to my country, set up shop, you Italian spaghetti-munching bastard, and start hacking bits of my ear off when I only wanted a haircut."

Parker turned to Harry, laughing, and said, "You're up next. You better put some ear muffs on."

Harry could feel the anger rise inside him. He had always been respectfully cautious of Parker, even in awe of him up until a few years ago. But not anymore. Now he saw him as nothing but a bully and a barricade to his future.

Suddenly, Parker swung around in an explosion of rage, lashing out with a backhand across Antonio's face, his huge emerald ring cutting this harmless, gentle man's face. Antonio staggered back into the display cabinet then slumped into the chair next to Parker's.

Anger and courage filled Harry at the sight of this liberty. He felt calm but confident as he launched himself at Parker. Parker had flicked open his cutthroat razor and was about to slash it across Antonio's hand-covered face as Harry crashed into him, sending them both to the floor and the blade out of Parker's hand.

The two men exchanged blows and verbal insults as they battered at each other on the floor. Slowly, Harry started to get the better of the spitting and snarling Parker, punching him and then mounting him, pinning his arms down with his knees.

Harry felt across the floor for the switch blade with an outstretched hand, as the struggling Parker, eyes bulging, screamed with rage. Harry found the handle, grabbed it and in a split second, with as much force as he could muster, pulled the blade across Parker's throat.

It was all over in a few seconds. Harry sat astride the motionless, blood-soaked man, staring at him in shock. His hand slowly uncurled as he dropped the blade and sat back in exhaustion. Then he looked up at his friend Ronny.

No words were exchanged as their eyes locked, but the two men mutually registered the fact that they were entering a new era.

"Penny for your thoughts, Mr Lane," Angelo said, smiling at Harry as he held the mirror up behind his head. "You were miles away then. I hope it was somewhere nice."

Harry returned the smile and replied, "I was thinking of a time a long time ago when me and your lovely old man became firm friends. In this very room, funnily enough."

2.

1961

Katherine Kane arrived at Nightingales Dance Hall driven by her boyfriend Derrick. As they pulled up outside, she noticed Harry Lane's Jaguar parked in its usual spot. This instantly cheered her up as she had been feeling particularly agitated by Derrick and bored of life with him lately.

Hers was a life that she had been perfectly content with up until six months ago when she had been taken on as a warm up act at Nightingales. Both Derrick and Katherine were only twenty-one, but since she had stepped through those doors and entered the world of Harry Lane, she had begun to feel like she was out-growing Derrick.

And also secretly falling in love with Harry.

She cared deeply for Derrick and had been happy with her life with him, enjoying her day job in an office typing pool. She was a talented pub singer, but she had never seriously dreamed of making a full-time career with singing. But since taking the job at Nightingales, Harry had made her feel like a star, plying her with constant encouragement and playful, flirtatious comments with references to the big time. He told her he was billing her as Kathy Kane as it made her sound more like a star. She would normally brush such complements off, had they come from anyone else, but such was her crush on him, any contact was enough to excite her and make her day.

Going back home to Derrick now seemed dull, which filled her with guilt. He really was a lovely man who cared for her deeply. He was attentive, had a good, stable job and her parents loved him. She knew she was lucky to have Derrick but she was so excited by Harry.

She craved his attention, much like others who came under his spell. He oozed sex appeal, confidence and style. She had watched him endlessly over the past six months. He could charm women and men alike and she suspected her fantasy of a life with this man, nine years her senior and happily married, was just that. A fantasy. She knew he flirted with everybody, it was in his nature and part of his working day. But she observed him with others and was convinced he held his gaze much longer with her.

She had noticed him watching her from time to time with those beautiful blue eyes with much more interest than others. Her female intuition had told her he wanted her as much as she wanted him. But then she would tell herself not to be so silly. He could have anyone and probably had. He was a successful businessman with plenty of admirers. Why would he be interested in her?

As Katherine walked in to the club, she spotted Harry standing next to the bar with his usual entourage. She was instantly aware of his gaze and tried to look as calm and reassured as she could as she strode elegantly across the dance floor, hoping she didn't look painfully obvious and over the top.

"Here she is, ladies and gentlemen," she heard Harry announce, "the next big attraction to hit the West End. A Lane production." He turned to the man next to him, big Tony Parish, bouncer, enforcer and one of Harry's trusted firm. "Drum roll, please." Big Tony proceeded to gesture an imaginary drum roll, as Harry pronounced, "Miss Kathy Kane."

Katherine looked at the two men as she felt her face redden and she let out a little giggle as she approached them.

"West End? Chance would be a fine thing," she declared, still smiling.

Harry deliberately held her gaze. "Well, stick with me, Kiddo, and we'll take you all the way to the top. Ain't that right, Big Tony?"

"One hundred percent, H. She won't speak to us then, when she is dining with the Rat Pack."

She burst out laughing at Tony's remark but could feel herself flushing as Harry's eyes locked on to hers again. He was dressed immaculately, as always, and so handsome. She became aware of herself daydreaming as she took in the contours of his face and deliberately turned away slightly.

"Could you knock at my office after your set, please Kathy? I want to discuss you taking on top spot on a Friday night. Your apprenticeship is over. The crowd love you, the band love working your set and most importantly…" He leaned across and grabbed Tony's cheek. "…Big Tony here loves you too."

Katherine felt elated, not only by her promotion, but also by Harry's attention.

Elation was again replaced by a slight feeling of guilt as Harry continued. "I know your boyfriend picks you up to take you home so come see me straight away so you are not keeping him waiting. He is a good lad, looking after my staff like that."

She suddenly felt embarrassed and flat again as he addressed her as staff and Derrick as a lad. As she went to reply, a voice from across the room shouted, "H" and he had turned away, his attention gone again.

Always exciting, but just so short-lived. God, she wanted all of his attention, not just a few moments. She felt alone and uncared for as she headed off to her dressing room.

Her mood lifted again as she added some final touches to her make up in her dressing room. My own headlining show? Just wait until I tell Derrick, she thought to herself. She smiled at her reflection in her dressing room mirror and spoke to herself. "Top of the bill, Miss Kane, you clever girl." Her self-confidence had grown over the months, as had her voice and stage presence. She loved performing and hearing the audience's reaction to her. She loved this job and she loved this venue, although she knew much of this new-found confidence was bought on by Harry's encouragement and her desire to please and impress him.

She ran the lipstick over her lips, giggled slightly to herself and puckered them again before speaking softly to her reflection. "Right, Kathy Kane, you're the main attraction here now so let's show them all what you've got."

She thought of Derrick and felt a rush of excitement at the thought of telling him her fantastic news. He had been so supportive of her and she now hoped this news would be the start of a brighter, more interesting future.

Kathy was startled from her daydream by the sound of someone knocking at her door. As she called out, "Come in," the sight of Harry entering the room put an end to her thoughts of both West End stages and indeed her Derrick.

As Harry confidently strode across the room, stopping right behind her, she felt the usual emotions he invoked in her again, trying her very best to remain unfazed and every bit the sophisticated main star of Nightingale's she was expected to be.

She stared up at the man behind her, feeling his light breath on the back of her neck and her nostrils picked up his unique manly smell, a smell so different to Derrick. As her gaze became lost in his deep blue eyes reflected in the mirror, Harry had equally become silenced by her own lovely reflection, accentuated by the bright light of the bulbs that surrounded the mirror.

"Just wanted to give you a quick knock, Kathy. I've been called out on other business, so may not finish it in time to catch you tonight," he said.

She was disappointed at his words, as she always was if his attention was elsewhere, especially when she was up on stage performing. She also knew how busy and elusive he could be, which added to his mystery and allure. It made these little moments of attention feel even more special.

"If I'm not back tonight, your wages will be behind the bar." He smiled, then turned to walk away. He stopped at the door and as he opened it, he turned around. "Don't forget, you're top spot as of next week." He smiled at her and she waited, hoping for a compliment on her looks. As he said, "Your boyfriend will be pleased with your news," she inwardly cringed. Boyfriend sounded like they were school children, she thought, and again she felt that brief moment had all just been fun to him. Perhaps he did only see her as a child?

As she went to answer, she heard a voice in the corridor.

"Harry, phone."

He rolled his eyes and smiled. "No rest for old Harry Lane." He winked at her. "Go knock 'em dead, kid."

The door clicked shut and he was gone. She turned round and looked back in her mirror.

"Right, Kathy, let's go do what the man said!"

3.

Harry sat in his office in quiet contemplation. Two wage snatches in the last week, smoothly operated, with no real drama, money divided up amongst the team and fingers firmly pointing elsewhere.

"Good old Bradshaw," Harry said to himself. He smiled as he poured himself a large scotch, raised his glass and said out loud to an empty office, "To jobs well executed. To corrupt Old Bill. May you keep your greedy little palms on my pay roll and me outside of prison walls."

He checked his appearance in his office mirror, straightened his tie and hummed along to Dean Martin's smooth voice coming from his radio. Downing his scotch in one gulp, he looked at his reflection one last time, then headed out to Nightingales' main hall.

Nightingales had been in the area for as long as Harry could remember. In fact, it was built in 1914 as a picture palace. Harry had spent a large part of his childhood there and it had been here that he spent his very first date with his first love and now wife, Christine. Christine's maiden name was Nightingale so it was only apt that when he acquired the building from a local business man, who had converted it to a dance hall in 1957, that he renamed it after her.

It had been a great deal. The owner had mounting debts to all the wrong people and after endless sleepless nights, Harry had told him he was taking the place on at a non-negotiable price. A price which would clear his debts and keep the people he owed off his back. And of course, Harry had made it quite clear that if his generous offer was foolishly refused, it would be seen as a major insult and would result in one final night of permanent sleep for this gentleman. Of course, Harry had no intention of carrying out such a threat, as he already knew this man's situation and his offer would no doubt be seen as a relief, not a threat.

Harry headed into the ballroom and across the sprung maple dance floor towards the bar. He noted Kathy's eyes following his passage as her dusky tones filled the packed auditorium and acknowledged her with a cheeky smile and a wink which no doubt raised Kathy's pulse, judging by the seductive purr of her voice.

Harry smiled to himself. He couldn't deny he liked the effect he had on Kathy and other women. He was very flattered but equally never played up to it beyond flirtatious banter. There had only ever been one woman for Harry, his childhood sweetheart and ultimate soulmate, Chrissy. But as he walked past this alluring singer with her gorgeous, oval brown eyes, he inwardly admitted he was extremely attracted to her. But his love for Chrissy was much too deep to ever jeopardise.

The smile and wink was, of course, duly noted by Chrissy, whose figure had been obscured from Harry's vision by the enormous frame of Big Tony. As Harry caught sight of his wife, he signalled to the barman to send the usual to his table.

"Nice voice," Chrissy said as she sat down next to her husband.

"She certainly has, that's why I gave her a headline spot," Harry replied.

"Very attractive as well," she countered.

"Well, what do you expect in the best music venue in north London, soon to be the best in the whole of London? Can't have any old rubbish in here, not when my beautiful wife's name adorns the building."

She smiled at him and looked across the crowded dance hall at the exotic, luxurious décor with its red velvet flock wallpaper, chandeliers and two giant glitter balls in a barrel vaulted, coffered ceiling, then returned her gaze again to the stage and Kathy. "I'm not staying long, Harry. Just a quick drink. I was on route to Molly and Stan's, thought I would drop in."

Just as Harry was about to reply, the barman arrived with their drinks. He also noted the change in the music which signalled a short break for Kathy while the band continued solo to keep the crowd dancing. "Thanks Paul, you are a good lad. Do me a favour, ask Kathy to grab her drink and come over. I want her to meet Mrs Lane."

"Of course, Mr Lane," Paul replied while removing the drinks from the tray and placing them on their respective coasters, each emblazoned with the word Nightingales in diamond-coloured stylised writing. Looking suddenly concerned, Paul said, "Hope you don't mind, Mr Lane, while you are sitting with Mrs Lane, but I was asked to tell you Vince Street is here with two other men."

Harry smiled at Paul, noting his obvious concern. "That's fine son, I spotted them coming in earlier."

Harry pulled out his wallet and flicked through a substantial pile of notes. Taking one and handing it to Paul, he said, "Stick that in your bin, son. Take your girlfriend somewhere nice."

Paul's face reddened slightly as he thanked Harry, which made Chrissy smile.

"Ah, bless him. Looks like he is shitting himself just talking to you." She laughed as Harry looked across the room at Vince Street and his little gathering. "Trouble?" she asked, leaning across to give him a gentle kiss on the cheek.

He tilted his head to meet her lips and tenderly kissed her, wrapping his arm round her waist and lightly squeezing her. "Nah, no problem, they're OK. Just inclined to forget their manners from time to time, especially our Mr Street when he has had too many tonics. The lads will keep them in check."

She kissed him again and playfully grabbed his cheek. "Ah, my big bad strong Bubba, if only the lads knew what a little softy you really are."

Harry laughed at her. "Oh, trust me, they know full well you're the hard case out of the two of us. They're all terrified to come round the house unless I'm with you."

She laughed at the thought and kissed him again. "Love you, Harry Lane."

"Love you too, Chrissy Lane," he said, pulling away from their embrace as he sensed they were being watched. Kathy had approached and was standing by their table, drink in hand.

Harry looked up at Kathy and smiled.

Chrissy looked her up and down. She was gorgeous. Petite, slim-framed, perfectly formed breasts, shoulder-length blonde hair, radiating youthful excitement and obviously totally besotted with her Harry. She remarked to herself how painfully obvious it was that this young woman couldn't contain her attraction to her husband. But she was used to this when out with him and such was their bond that it had never worried her before. Yet somehow there was something about this woman, and Harry's reaction to her that made her feel uneasy and she did not like that feeling one bit.

Harry introduced Chrissy to Kathy.

"Hello, Mrs Lane, so lovely to finally meet you," Kathy said, smiling coyly.

"You too, sweetheart. You certainly have a strong voice for a young girl. I was very surprised when I heard you. Such a dainty little thing filling the room like that." Chrissy knew from Kathy's reaction her sentiment had had the desired effect of making Kathy feel both young and inferior to her power without it sounding so obvious that Harry would have noticed.

Kathy looked directly at Chrissy and felt the powerful presence of this woman, realising there and then she would never get to be with Harry. Chrissy was older, more confident in her stature, her clothing, her style and her voice. She commanded respect and had indeed made her feel like a silly school kid with a crush on an older man. She reluctantly had to admit that they looked perfectly suited to each other. It stood out, too. They just looked different to all the other couples in the hall. Sophisticated, intriguing and powerful.

"Yes," Harry interjected, breaking Chrissy's intense, scrutinizing stare. "Told her she is going all the way to the very top," he said to Chrissy, smiling. "Stick with me, kid." He laughed and winked at Kathy who also laughed and held her gaze with Harry for too long.

Chrissy cut in. "We going into the music talent business now, are we darling?"

"Yeah, why not? Let's expand, Chrissy." He laughed.

Kathy took in his handsome smile and then looked at Chrissy and again felt uneasy. "That's my sign to get back on stage," she said as the song changed pace.

"I'll walk back with you, darling. I'm off now, anyway." Chrissy embraced her husband, saying, "See you tonight, lover." This made Kathy feel out of place and she tugged at her dress almost like a nervous little girl waiting for instructions from her parents. "Come on then, Kathy, let's get you back on that stage and make you our first big star, shall we?"

Chrissy took hold of Kathy's hand and lead her away, a look of utter horror and embarrassment on the young woman's face, as Harry looked on, smiling.

As the pair walked away from Harry's earshot, Chrissy turned to Kathy, still smiling so as not to draw any attention to them from the crowd who she knew would be gazing at them, fascinated by their looks and glamour. She tightened her grip on Kathy's hand. "See that stage, little lady? That's your domain and my husband and I pay you to entertain. Keep your mouth on that microphone, your eyes on the audience and both well away from my old man or I'll make sure another note never comes from that trap again, you got it?" she snarled while squeezing even tighter on Kathy's hand.

Kathy looked at her, heart racing with fear and suddenly unable to use her voice to reply. She just nodded.

Releasing her grip, Chrissy quickly scanned the room, acknowledging another couple with a smile and a wave before turning back to Kathy. Under her breath, with an aggressive tone while still smiling innocuously, she said, "Now get that scrawny little arse back up on that stage and do what me and my husband pay you for."

4.

As Harry headed in the direction of the bar his journey was punctuated by handshakes and pats on the back from the men and smiles from the women. He returned each one with a smile, inwardly feeling a strong sense of contentment. Nightingales was packed with happy punters eager to fill his tills and dance the night away. A legitimate earner that was complimenting his many other illegal affairs very nicely.

Once at the bar, Harry was met by DI Eric Bradshaw, supposedly a local up-holder of the law, but most definitely one of the most corrupt. As Harry outstretched his hand to Bradshaw, he diverted his eyes to the man standing next to him, sergeant Burt Roswell.

Roswell was that rare commodity in Harry and Bradshaw's world; clean-cut, smart, uncorruptible. A copper that could not be lured by the prospect of a substantial increase in their wage packet, totally career-driven and duty-bound to uphold the law regardless of the financial struggles of being a working police officer.

"Eric, nice to see you, as always. What's the pleasure?" Harry turned to shake Roswell's hand. "Evening, PC Roswell."

Roswell declined Harry's hand and scowled as Bradshaw interjected. "It's Sergeant now, Harry."

"Oh yes, of course it is. Sorry, Burt, I always forget you're with the big boys now. So used to seeing you on the beat in your cute little uniform and pointed hat."

Both Harry and Eric shared a little laugh, but Burt never responded to Harry's mockery, instead inwardly seething as he remained stone-faced.

"Honestly, Eric, he was a lovely little bobby. Smart and conscientious. Nothing was too much for him and our community."

With that, Roswell finally snapped. "Bollocks, Lane, you flash prick."

"Right, that's enough now, you two," said a grinning Bradshaw as he eyed Harry with a small shake of his head, trying to bring it down.

Harry smiled. "I'm only playing with you, Burt. What's your poison, you two? Have a drink on me."

"Not for us, but I would like a quick word in private, please Harry," Eric said, and then looked at Burt. "I just want a word with Mr Lane, Burt. Go wait in the car. I'll be out in five."

Harry noted the obvious annoyance on Burt's face as he glared at the pair of them before slowly turning around and walking out of the hall. "Night, PC Roswell. Do come again. Don't be a stranger, will you? Go make Robert Peel proud," he shouted.

"Keep it going, you arrogant bastard," Burt muttered under his breath as he turned to leave.

"Sorry, Burt, you say something?" Harry said, but Burt didn't acknowledge him, and carried on walking to the door.

Harry shrugged, handed Eric his usual and led him to a table. "Get that down ya, now laughing boy is gone," he said. As they sat down, he gestured to a couple of his men to keep an eye on Vince Street and his two mates who seemed to be exchanging heated words with one of his bar staff.

"Yeah, I spotted Street when I arrived, Harry. You're not involved with him and the South London Quinn firm, are you?"

"No chance, Eric. Them lot have nothing I want, but Jamie and Johnny Quinn obviously think I have something they want as that lowlife errand boy has been in here a few times. I'll pull him later."

"Good. Don't spoil things, Harry. Keep things tight with your operation. Don't start getting in with other firms. There is only so much I can contain, especially with young Roswell out there. That's ambition personified, and he is as sharp as a nail and totally unbendable. I don't want anything or anyone spoiling my pension pot."

"No, and I don't want my future plans jeopardised by any unfortunate lodgings with Her Majesty, so keep his beak out of my business."

Eric took a long swig of his drink and stood up. "Right, I'd better go and see Dixon of Dock Green. Thanks for the drink."

Harry smiled. "Your money is in the usual place, Eric. Keep on your toes. That Roswell is far too keen."

The men parted, Harry in the direction of Vince Street and Bradshaw out into the night air.

Harry waved and smiled up at Kathy who was on top form tonight and doing an encore for a very appreciative audience as he approached a very animated Vince Street having words with Ronny Piper.

"Everything OK there, Ronny?" Harry's words were loud enough and his presence impressive enough to break the exchange between the two men.

"Here he is, the main man. About time you said hello instead of me having to exchange niceties with your secretary, here." Vince looked straight at Harry as Harry threw Ronny a little wink.

"Grab yourself a drink, Ron, and one for Vince and the lads. Let's all cool down here, shall we? So, what brings you boys over the water then?" Harry said, looking directly into Street's eyes.

"We was in the area, picking up and dropping off, so thought we would drop in and slum it for a drink at yours," Street replied arrogantly.

Harry felt his heart rate rising and adrenaline starting to flow but the last thing he needed was an altercation with this idiot or unnecessary needle with Jamie and Johnny Quinn. "Well, I hope your pick up and drop off were personal and not business on my manor, Vince, as that needs to be run through me first."

Street laughed at Harry. "My business is my business and nothing to do with you, Lane. And you were looking very cosy with that copper earlier, so maybe you are not to be trusted."

"Drink your drinks, Vince, then take your cheer leaders with you or you will get the same treatment I gave you in Fairhurst nick."

Harry turned to walk away with a look of utter contempt on his face. "See these gentlemen out, lads. They have overstayed their welcome."

Ronny and two others from Harry's firm stepped forward, with big Tony Parish heading across the room towards the now obvious scene. Street launched his glass at the departing Harry, missing him by inches, but landing on Kathy who was heading back to her dressing room, spraying its contents over her dress and face.

Harry turned in disgust as a snarling Street was being dragged forcefully out towards the fire escape.

"You slag, Lane! You're nothing!"

Harry's desire to take Street and his mates downstairs and punish them was overridden by both the sight of a clearly frightened and tearful Kathy and also the staring customers. He needed to avoid any unnecessary bad press for him and Nightingales. He also knew his lads would be taking care of business. Instead, he quickly led Kathy back to his office, rather than to her dressing room.

Harry sat Kathy down on the chair in his office. Tears were streaming down her face as the shock of the event and the drink-stained dress slowly sank in. Harry took out an embroidered H.L handkerchief from his jacket pocket and slowly wiped her tears away. She stared into his eyes and he took in her sweet, innocent gaze.

Suddenly Kathy kissed Harry and then apologised and looked down, slightly embarrassed. Harry gently lifted her chin up and kissed her.

He felt her totally release herself to him, and in a moment of carnal lust, fuelled by anger and adrenaline from the Vince Street incident and a need to feel this woman's extreme femininity and softness, he carried her across to the sofa on the other side of the office and made love to her.

Kathy sat in the passenger seat of Derrick's car, the emotions of desire and passion she had felt only minutes ago were now replaced by shame, guilt and disappointment. She tugged at the stained dress as Derrick spoke to Harry through the car window.

"Your Kathy has had a bit of a shock tonight, Derrick. Little accident with a drunk."

She felt mortified as Harry addressed Derrick like a little boy. Harry opened his wallet and pulled a wad of crisp bank notes out, licked his finger and flicked through them.

"Take this. Get this dress cleaned and buy Kathy a new one. Plus, a nice little drink for you. My wife and I value your Kathy very much, as do all our staff."

Kathy felt her heart sink as Harry leaned across and stuck the pile of notes in Derrick's top pocket.

"Good lad. Get yourselves home and take good care of her."

5.

Kathy listened pensively as Derrick nervously explained to her that he had been offered a promotion at work. It was a significant step up with substantial prospects and financial remuneration.

"I've not said yes yet, obviously, Kathy. I know just how much you love this area. But Surrey really isn't that far if we wanted to visit our families. And it is beautiful."

Kathy's mind began to race. She had been about to break her own news to him. And tell him the biggest lie she would ever tell.

She was pregnant with Harry's baby. She was one hundred percent sure of that. She was also sure that telling Derrick the truth would destroy him and both of their families. She had reasoned that she had no possible life with Harry, even if she came clean and revealed the true identity of the father of her unborn child.

Derrick noticed Kathy's blank expression and took it that she was thinking about her job at Nightingales. "I know how much you love your singing job, love. But you're so talented, you will be able to get a singing job in Surrey."

Kathy could hear the desperation in his voice and also felt a sense of relief as she realised Derrick's career move could be a godsend. It would give her a legitimate reason to leave both the club and the area without raising any suspicions.

She had also finally realised that her fantasy of Harry had been just that: a fantasy. And that she did love Derrick in her own way. The fantasy she had built in her mind of a life with Harry had ended in rushed, lust-filled sex in his office. Now she was carrying the baby of a man she knew had no interest in her. And the truth would lead to the kind of repercussions she could never risk.

Kathy smiled nervously at Derrick as she prepared to make her announcement. And a lie she had already decided she would take to her grave. "I'm so proud of you, Derrick. And this is not the only change in our lives. In fact, your news could not have come at a better time for us, because we will need all the money we can get when I leave the club and the house behind."

Derrick looked relieved. "So, shall I tell them yes, love? I do want the job."

"Yes Derrick, my darling. Tell them you'll take the job and while you are at it, tell them you are going to be a father."

She watched as Derrick registered the revelation. Her heart raced, waiting for his reaction. As it dawned on him, a beaming smile lit his face up as he proudly announced, "I've done it! I'm going to be a dad!"

He kissed Kathy and embraced her. His obvious joy made her fill up with emotion. A mix of both the shared elation and also the guilt. She was going to knowingly allow him to raise her child, thinking it was his. She wanted this baby and she knew her and her baby's lives would be safe and secure with him. She burst into tears in the warm, caring arms of Derrick.

Chrissy sat opposite Molly and Stan Lane, Harry's parents. Ever since Chrissy had become serious with Harry, she had always referred to them as mum and dad. Her own parents had been killed during a particularly heavy bombing campaign during the second world war. The raid had wiped out the whole East End street where they had lived. She had been evacuated to a family in Caxton, a small village in the Cambridgeshire countryside. The rest of her childhood, if you could call it that, for the loss of her parents had caused her to grow up very quickly, had been spent living with close friends of her family who ran a pub in north London. It was while working at this pub that she had met the confident, older and very popular (especially with the local ladies) Harry Lane. She had known very early on that this man would fill the void in her life left by the loss of her parents.

When the couple she lived with decided to emigrate to New Zealand, the streetwise and headstrong and already deeply in love Chrissy had no intensions of joining them and was intent on staying behind to start her own journey with her new man.

Chrissy loved Molly and Stan dearly and could not wait to tell them her wonderful news. She smiled to herself as she looked at Molly's ball of knitting and patterns. Molly was always knitting something or other while Stan was either reading the paper or tormenting their cat, sticking things on its tail or wiping coal dust on its fur after stoking up the fire. He derived great personal pleasure watching the cat's face licking the coal off in disgust, or nearly climbing up its own arse chasing its tail. If Stan wasn't catching up on the news or aggravating their long-suffering cat, he was whiling away the hours on his train set. Funny, she thought that while Stan played with his trains, Harry was probably ambushing and robbing real ones.

"What you smiling at then, Chrissy?" Molly asked, noting her daughter-in-law's cheerful manner.

"Well, mum, I was just wondering if you were any good at knitting baby clothes," she said with the broadest smile in Great Britain.

Molly leapt up, knocking her tea cup and a plate of her homemade cake flying in Stan's direction.

"What the bleeding hell's going on, you nutcase?" Stan screamed as warm tea and cake landed on him.

"Shut up and put that poxy paper down, you grumpy old sod and give your Chrissy a kiss. You are going to be a grandad!" Molly wrapped her arms around the elated Chrissy. "What does his lordship have to say on the matter, then?" she enquired.

"I've phoned the club to see if he is there and I was on my way over. I couldn't wait until tonight to tell him. I only just got my positive results, but I just had to stop on the way and tell you both."

"Just what that boy needs to slow him down, a child and responsibilities. That will stop his bleeding old gallop," Stan stated.

Chrissy laughed at Molly and Stan. They were such a lovely couple, she thought. God only knew how Harry ended up a criminal because Stan was a proper old softy and Molly was the salt of the earth, share her last pound and help anybody type.

As Kathy knocked on the door of Harry's office, she could hear the sound of raised, joyous voices before Harry shouted, "Come in."

She opened the door to be greeted by the sight of Harry, Chrissy and a few of Harry's men all looking very merry, an assortment of open champagne bottles and glasses on the table.

"Kathy, sweetheart, come in and join us," Harry said warmly with a beaming smile.

"Grab a flute, darling, and celebrate our great news," Chrissy added with a genuine, warm smile, which surprised Kathy considering the friction the last time they had met.

Kathy took in the enormity of Harry's words as he stated cheerfully that his wife was expecting their first child. She composed herself quickly and mustered up her best feigned impression of joy while her heart sank. She looked into Harry's sparkling eyes, knowing that he could never know he was in fact in the room with two women carrying a child of his.

It was obvious to Kathy, looking at them both now, how much love they had for each other. She realised there and then that her decision to lie to poor, lovely Derrick and to move away from the area for a complete fresh start with him had been the right one.

There was nothing here for her now. Of that, she was sure.

6.

1962

Harry held his son proudly, studying his tiny features.

Chrissy looked at them both with a beaming smile. "Look at my boys. Oh, look at him, Harry. He is just adorable and he has your beautiful eyes."

"How can he have my eyes? I wouldn't be able to see anything," Harry replied, not taking his gaze away from his son. "I'd like to call him Ray, after my dad, if that's OK, Harry."

Harry glanced up at his wife. "Of course you can, love. Ray Lane sounds fine to me. He looked down at his baby. "Hello, young Ray. What do you think of that, son? Ray, after your mum's dad. I'd have named you after her mum. That would have toughened you up a bit sharpish." He laughed.

"Stop it, you leave my little man alone." She laughed too. "My Ray will be a lover, not a fighter. I've got enough on my plate with you."

"Oh, bit like his old man, then," Harry said, grinning. "I mean, look at him, Chrissy. No mistake he is a cut from my cloth." Harry cupped little Ray in his arms as Chrissy set the timer on their camera and hurried back to stand next to her husband. Harry smiled broadly as he announced proudly, "My family, the Lanes."

The camera shutter clicked and recorded the moment.

Harry sat at his favourite table in Nightingales surrounded by his trusted friends and, he hoped, allies. He snipped the base off an expensive Cuban cigar, his favourite. He was only a smoker on special occasions, and this was certainly one. He flashed the lighter up and rolled the cigar expertly around over the heat before taking a large puff as he eyed the others at the table.

"Let's drink a toast to the new addition to the Lane family. Ray Lane."

Everyone at the table raised their glasses in unison. "Ray Lane."

"Right lads, get drinking. Let's celebrate," Harry shouted just as he caught sight of Jamie and Johnny Quinn and three other unfamiliar faces entering the club.

"South London are in, Harry," one of the lads said.

"Yep. Noted, mate. I'll go and greet our guests," Harry replied.

Before the Quinns could make it to the bar, Harry stood in their path. "Evening, lads. Allow me, what you having?"

Jamie's eyes met Harry's and he slowly broke into a smile. "That's very generous of you, Harry." He rolled off the drinks for himself and his mates as the attentive barman listened.

"What brings you over the water then, Jamie?" Harry asked as he motioned them to an empty booth with a gentle touch on the small of Jamie's back.

Just as Jamie was about to reply, his brother Johnny cut in. "Why? Was you expecting us to ask your permission then, Lane?"

Harry noted the arrogance in the tone of Johnny's voice but chose to ignore it.

"Heard good reports about this place, Harry. We were on our way up West and I fancied a little detour here for a look," Jamie replied with a wholly more amenable attitude.

Both brothers were dressed in suits and ties, although Jamie's attire was much sharper than Johnny's and his attitude was much calmer and business-like. It was well established within their circles that Jamie was the more intelligent of the two and Johnny the violent, non-negotiable one. Jamie, at twenty-nine, was the older of the two by a couple of years. He was slightly taller with a fit, wiry build compared to Johnny's stockier weight.

The Quinns and their firm had South London sown up and Harry had zero interest in South London. He often said it was a foreign country over the water. What he did have an interest in breaking into, in whatever form he saw best, was the West End. That's where the big dollars were. He also knew the Quinns already had interests within Soho and the West End.

Harry sat opposite the Quinns at a large table within one of the lavishly decorated booths, directly in their eyeline. The other three of the Quinns' men were content eyeing up the local women and taking in the music and atmosphere of the club. This suited Harry's mood just fine. He wanted to gauge the brothers' mood and ascertain if there was any sinister underlying reason for their visit or if it was a white flag tour, so small talk with their team of monkeys wasn't on his to-do list.

"I like it, I like it a lot, Harry. Nice atmosphere. You've done a really nice job with this place," said Jamie, nodding approvingly.

"Thanks Jamie. How's the casino and your other interests going?" Harry enquired.

"Really, really becoming a gold mine, Harry. Especially since the government brought the gaming laws in and it's become mainstream." Jamie took a deep draw on his cigarette. As he exhaled a big cloud of smoke into the air, he paused momentarily, obviously deep in thought. Harry's eyes were firmly on him. "We are the biggest casino in South London, but let's face it, punters like a night in the West End at the weekend. That's where I want to plot one up."

"We are looking at one here as well," Johnny cut in, grinning. "That big old unit opposite this gaff. Used to be a furniture store, didn't it?"

Harry glanced at Johnny nonchalantly and quipped, "You make sure you're insured for fire and damage, won't you, Johnny? Just in case." He flashed a sarcastic grin and was pleased when he noticed Johnny's pupils dilate.

"You're only getting any respect round here because you topped old George Parker, Lane," Johnny said, starting to rise from his chair only to be pushed back by his brother.

"Behave, Johnny. We're not here for trouble or to start rumours."

"Such a shame you two are brothers and you've got that rodent Street on your team, 'cause Jamie and I could do business together as we both have brain cells on active duty. But you, Johnny boy, should stick to terrorising little businesses into stocking your one-armed bandits on their premises."

Harry stood up and motioned to the barman with his hand, pushing his thumb into the air to mimic a popping champagne cork. A clearly angry Johnny glared at Harry.

"There's a bottle of fizz on its way to your table, to set you up before you hit the West End. I must get back to my table. I'm celebrating the birth of my son with the chaps tonight."

"What you named it, George? After Parker?" Johnny snarled.

Harry's normally calm demeanour snapped. "Listen, you mouthy prick. Don't come on to my doorstep shouting your trap off about George Parker, or anything else. You've got nothing I want or need, so drink your drinks and go and do whatever it is you do. Each other, probably," Harry added, which caused Jamie to leap from his chair followed by the other three.

"Don't get flash, Harry," Jamie said, his temperament taking on a less friendly tone.

Harry started to laugh. He suddenly had a mental picture of George Coles' character in the St. Trinian's film.

"What's so amusing, Lane?" a now visibly angered Johnny snarled aggressively, just as the champagne arrived.

"Lads, let's cool down. We don't want any trouble here tonight. I'm celebrating, and besides, you're well and truly outnumbered and out of your manor, so it would be rather foolish on your behalf, I think." Harry held their gazes.

"I do hope that isn't a threat, Harry?" Jamie was now face to face with him.

"Not a threat, no. Just a statement of fact." Both the Quinns locked eyes with Harry for the longest time possible. Harry found the sheer childishness of this unnecessary animosity that had suddenly arisen simultaneously annoying and amusing, not that his face betrayed either emotion. These two were used to instilling fear in people. But the truth was, Harry wasn't in the least bit frightened of them and they knew it and didn't like it. They obviously believed the speculation that Harry had murdered George Parker with zero repercussions and no evidence pointing to him, which told them the level he was prepared to go to if need be. With the Government tariff for murder still carrying the death sentence, it made him a man to be respected or at least to be cautious of.

Although Harry wasn't overly bothered by the Quinns, he was very wary of them and their capabilities. He had always been sensible in regards to any possible adversaries and he really didn't want or need any pointless aggravation that didn't involve an earner at the end of it. Violence for violence's sake was more in line with the mind-set of

Johnny Quinn. Harry was always motivated by money, so he reasoned that undue rows or a gang war with the Quinns was to be avoided if possible.

But he would not take any nonsense, either. Particularly on home turf.

Jamie broke the silence and cracked a semi-smile. "We will pass on the champagne, Harry. Places to go, people to see. You know how it is."

"Indeed I do, Jamie," Harry replied as he diverted his eyes to a scowling Johnny. "Enjoy your evening, lads. I may drop in to the casino one night for a little flutter."

Harry watched the Quinns leave the club and admitted to himself he was relieved it hadn't escalated.

As he headed back towards his table, he spotted a young couple sitting embracing on one of the small sofas that lined the outskirts of the hall. He placed the champagne bucket on their table as the lad pulled away from his kiss and nervously looked up at him.

"There you go, son, nice drop of bubbly for you and your girlfriend."

"Wow, thanks, Mr Lane," the pair replied in stereo.

7.

1964

Harry sat opposite Ronny Piper inside Valentines Café. It was their regular eating and meeting venue and the place where many a money-making decision had been made and job had been planned over an Italian coffee and a full English. The contrasting menu this little café offered was something of local legend. Although he suspected the place's popularity among the young lads in the area was enhanced by the presence of the family's daughters Valentine and Maria working behind the counter. They were both Italian stunners with chirpy characters to match. Harry marvelled at the way the family dealt with the breakfast rush and a steady flow of customers, steam and noise and banter filling the kitchen air as they prepared and delivered the meals. Valentine was an expert at balancing so many plates and cups in one go, it never failed to amaze Harry. While most men in there were transfixed by her exotic looks, he was always more amazed by her ability to deliver so many meals and memorize her next orders while effortlessly joining in passing conversation on route.

"So, we good to go Friday night then?" Harry enquired, trying to divert Ronny's attention back from watching Valentine exit the café towards the kitchen. Harry looked at Ronny then round at Valentine and began laughing. "Behave yourself, Ronny."

Ronny finally heard Harry but still couldn't divert his eyes. "Jesus, Harry, look at the arse on her, wiggling under that tight dress as she walks. It's like two kids fighting in a tent. And she fancies you, like most around here, you lucky sod."

Harry smiled. "Well, the attention is flattering but I'm a one-woman man. And a family man now, on top of that."

"How are Chrissy and little Ray? You sure you should be on the job on Friday with her seconds from dropping your second child?"

"I'm a blagger, not a midwife," Harry replied, laughing. "Plus, I need to keep busy. Wife, a second child imminent and that greedy blood-sucking bastard Bradshaw building up his pension fund on our graft."

The two men stood up to leave the café. Harry placed enough notes under the plate to cover both meals and a substantial tip, which was noted by a group of lads sat behind their table, who were staring at the two men in adoration. They were well aware of exactly who Harry and Ronny were. Those notes were perfectly safe from being lifted. It was more than their lives were worth.

Harry looked at the team in the van and announced, "Right, lads, time to get busy. Looks like they're nearly loaded and on the move."

The wage van's contents, route and destination had been meticulously mapped out, although Harry was very aware things don't always go to plan and if his gut feeling was wrong he would abort the operation. Today, he felt good about things, although the sight of Big Tony stuffing a sandwich in his mouth like he hadn't eaten in a year almost put him off. Attempting a large wage snatch was amazingly unsettling. He didn't know how Big Tony could eat at such a time.

"Jesus, Tony, you're a perpetual eating machine. Great timing, as well," he said, wryly.

"Sorry H, I was a bit peckish. Was going to leave it until after, but I couldn't resist it. Been playing on my mind all morning. My old woman cooked a lovely roast dinner yesterday and made me a sarnie for work this morning with the left overs."

The nervous tension inside the van was broken by laughter just as the wage van moved away. Unless there had been a major change in their plans, the van was filled with wages for staff from a whole industrial estate of factories and warehouses, so quite a substantial cash haul.

Harry looked into the empty chambers of his shot gun as he pushed two cartridges down and clicked the barrel shut. He wasn't happy that the team had to now carry guns but they had learnt their lesson a few years back when they hit a van with batons and coshes only to be greeted with an armed guard in the back who had opened fire, putting a bullet into one of his men, causing them to flee the scene without the prize and their tails very much between their legs. Not to mention an extended period of aggravation and expense as their firm paid off the doctor who patched up the wounded.

As the wage van took the left fork in the road, their van went right and the driver put his foot hard to the floor. They needed to make up thirty seconds of time to cut their target off further up the road.

"Right, masks on and brace yourselves for the hit, lads," Harry said calmly.

His heart rate rose and adrenaline soared as their van crudely smashed directly into the oncoming wage van. Their preparation for the deliberate crash made their exit a speedy affair and a totally different reaction to the occupants of the other van who were stunned and shaken up. They were now staring out of the windscreen at shot guns and barked orders to get out.

Harry and Tony led the driver and co-driver to the back of the van while their own van was being manoeuvred to make loading easier.

"You got any surprises in the back for us, old son? You shout to him to open up and throw his piece out or you two are on your way to St. Thomas's Hospital," Harry ordered.

Ronny had finished flattening their tyres and had joined the others. He laughed as he witnessed the three guards doing all the work, unloading their van and transferring what looked like a nice little earner into theirs, at gunpoint and looking utterly bewildered.

They tied the guards up and then taped their mouths, locked the van back up and calmly drove away.

Harry removed his mask and gloves and grinned at the others. "Blimey, lads, that's better than sex, the rush I get from this."

"We need a better way of doing jobs than smash and grab. I'm getting bastard whiplash," Paul, the driver, said, rubbing his bad neck. He pulled the van up opposite Clarkes scrap metal and car breakers yard and waited for the sign to pull in.

Harry smiled at Danny Clarke as the two men shook hands.

"Can I use your phone while the cargo is unloaded, Danny? Chrissy's threatening to fill the air of the Lane household with another screaming mini-Lane."

"No problem, Harry. Up in the office, you know where it is. And wipe the door handle and phone after. I don't want your prints on anything here," Danny replied, laughing.

There was no reply from his house phone so he rang Nightingales.

"Hello, Nightingales," Harry recognised the voice at the other end of the phone as Janet, one of his bar staff.

"Afternoon Janet, it's Harry. Just phoning to find out if there are any messages for me."

Janet replied excitedly, "Hello, Mr Lane. Yes, one message. Your wife went into labour about two hours ago and is over at St Paul's Hospital now."

"Shit!" Harry spurted out. "I'd better get over there sharpish." He threw the receiver down and ran out of the office, just catching sight of the van being lifted by a crane onto Danny Clarke's car crusher.

As Harry rushed down the stairs, he informed the others that Chrissy was about to give birth and he was leaving proceedings in their capable hands and heading straight there.

Harry looked across at his wife holding the new addition to their family and felt totally filled with love for her and the tiny bundle she was tenderly cradling in her arms. He sat next to her on the hospital bed and gently kissed her and smiled.

"He is a cracker, Chrissy. Look at him. Some head of hair as well." The baby stared, un-blinking, up at his parents. Harry laughed. "He looks like he has the right hump. Look at the eyes on him. He looks like Dennis the Menace with that tuft of hair and them dark little mischievous eyes. He has your eyes, Love. He will be a little terror if he takes after his mother."

"You cheeky sod," Chrissy replied, smiling and looking visibly shattered.

A nurse entered and offered to take the baby to let Chrissy rest. Harry thanked her and stretched out on the bed, holding Chrissy's hand.

He suddenly broke the brief silence with, "Denny. Sounds like a good name, Denny Lane. What do you think, love?"

She grinned through her exhaustion. "What, after Dennis the Menace?"

They both burst out laughing.

Harry kissed his wife on the lips then the forehead as he got up from the bed. "I love you, Mrs Lane. We have a family now, my love. I'll protect you all. No one will ever split us apart, ever. You will all have everything you ever wanted."

She smiled up at him as she struggled to keep her eyes open. She felt so content, warm and happy. She had everything she had ever wanted; her Harry and a family. She felt complete again, somehow, after losing both her parents and having to grow up so early using her own streetwise wits. She was proud of what she had achieved in her life. No one would ever come between her and her family, she thought, as she drifted off into a well-deserved sleep.

8.

1966

Harry was chatting happily to a group of revellers in Nightingales when his attention was interrupted by a commotion over by the main entrance. He smiled to the group he was with, doing his best to conceal his annoyance, and excused himself, wishing them an enjoyable evening.

As Harry got closer to the entrance, the cause of the aggravation became evident as he caught sight of two of his doormen struggling to remove a raging Vince Street from the foyer.

As Street caught sight of Harry, his eyes bulged with temper and drug-induced frenzy.

"You slag, Lane! You got it coming!"

Harry's mind raced. Not in any way out of fear of Street, but by the possible embarrassment and bad press this could give both him and Nightingales with this pest screaming his head off right in front of the main entrance. He felt annoyed with himself, as he knew Street had been peddling drugs in the area, which was a liberty in itself, right on his doorstep. Now he was right outside the club shouting his mouth off in full view of far too many customers.

Harry knew he needed to calm the situation the best way he could, and quickly. He needed to appear like the gentleman and pillar of the community he was expected to be in front of his paying customers.

Fully aware that this spectacle now had a growing, unwanted audience, Harry spoke as loud as he could, making sure it was heard by everyone in range. "Come on now, Mr Street. You know you are not welcome at Nightingales after the way you treated my staff last time."

Harry looked at a group of young men and women standing, watching the incensed Street being dragged out into the road towards his Austin 11 that was half on the pavement, half on the road, engine still running. He shook his head. "Sorry you had to witness this nonsense, ladies and gents. Always one who can't handle their drink. Hope it does not spoil your evening."

"You are going to get yours, Lane, you hear me?" Street screamed as the doorman shoved him forcefully towards his car.

Harry tutted and rolled his eyes then stated to the crowd, "Nothing to see here, go straight in. No charge, the night's on me."

This had the desired effect as the prospect of free entry promptly turn everyone's attention away from Street's abusive tirade and into the club.

Harry looked to see if there were any more witnesses around then delivered a crunching punch into Street's kidneys, sending him down on to one knee. He followed it up with a stinging open-handed slap across his face, opening a flow of blood from his lip and nose.

"First and last warning, Street. Get yourself in that car and out of this manor. I see you again, you're dead. I hear you've been anywhere near here again, selling your drugs, you no good snake, I'll gut you."

Harry resisted the temptation to do the job there and then. With so many witnesses to the earlier commotion, it would have been suicide. He inwardly kicked himself for not having dealt with this pest a long time ago, and he knew he was going to have to be dealt with at some stage in the future. If possible, without causing unnecessary aggravation. He would arrange a nice little accident or some way of getting rid of the nuisance that was Vince Street, without any comeback on him from either the old bill or the Quinns.

A fuming, bleeding Street was reluctantly pushed into his car. After fumbling with the gear stick, he shouted from his open window as the car screeched away, "Count the days, Lane, you slag! I'll be seeing you!"

Harry looked at his two doormen and smiled. "Do you think he has got it in for me, lads?"

One of the concerned doormen produced a 45 from his pocket.

"What have you got that on you for? You trying to get us closed down with that prick's help?" a surprised Harry asked.

"It's not mine, boss. I got it off Street in the struggle. Mad bastard was waving it about in the road, screaming your name."

Harry took the gun off his man. "OK, lads, I'll sort this out. And thanks for your reaction. Hopefully it will just be a drunken tale to tell for the few who saw that maniac in action tonight. I could do without that nosey bastard Roswell poking his beak around the place."

Harry sat in his office with a glass of brandy and opened the barrel of Street's gun.

"Fully loaded, the lunatic," he said out loud. "What planet is he on?"

He felt his anger rising as he thought about his wife and two boys and how close he may have come tonight to them losing a husband and a dad. If Street was mad enough to pull that out in full view of the whole club, with a view to murdering him, then he needed to be dealt with sooner rather than later.

Harry sat looking at his two sons sleeping soundly and reflected on the evening's madness. Only a few years ago he would have probably taken Street out there and then, had he been so blatantly disrespectful. But these two were like little chicks in a nest waiting for food to be brought back. And his lovely Chrissy in the other room, his soul mate, she needed him and likewise he needed her. So now more than ever, he had to use intelligence over brawn and not make any rash decisions. His family needed him here and he not only needed to be there for them, he wanted to be there for them, like nothing else in the world. He loved being a husband, a father, a protector and provider. The means by which he provided for them was irrelevant to him, as long as he did it. One day, he would teach his boys the same codes and values by which he lived; the importance of loyalty towards family and friends. He wouldn't let anyone come between his ability to provide for and protect his own. Least of all the likes of Vince Street. Or the Quinns. Or, indeed, the old bill.

Harry walked into his own bedroom, slipped his shoes off and lay on the bed next to his wife with his arms folded behind his head, staring pensively at the ceiling.

"Penny for them," Chrissy said.

Harry turned to her, smiling. "Cost you more than a penny to gain access to my thoughts."

"OK, a penny and a slice off your mum's homemade ginger cake."

"Ah, now you got me." Harry laughed. "I'll tell you anything you want now there is cake on the table."

Harry wrapped his arms around his wife and they snuggled up together.

"You smell of Nightingales," she said.

"Nightingale's what?"

As Harry laughed, she rolled her hands down to his groin and gently squeezed. "You ever even think of that old game, Lane," she whispered, "and these go in that vice in your dad's garden shed."

"Only one woman for me. Always has been, always will be," he returned. And he truly meant it. He loved his wife more than ever and since the boys had arrived, he really saw flirtation as nothing but pound signs and customer care. A means of monetary gain for his home unit.

She released her grip and purred seductively, "Well, just make sure that's the case, mister, and you never know your luck."

He laughed and thought just how much his wife's attitude had changed since having the boys. She rarely showed any interest in the club or business in general. She had softened in her outlook and persona, totally content in her role. As a wife, but more so as a mother. She totally doted on Ray and Denny.

"I looked in on the boys. They were totally sparked out," Harry said as he got up from the bed, loosening his tie and starting to undress.

"I'm not surprised, the way they run around all day, the pair of little sods. I'm shattered myself." Chrissy watched her husband as he placed his suit neatly away in the wardrobe.

"Tell you what, maybe we should swap places for a few nights. You don't see nearly enough of the boys, or mum and dad, for that matter. I'll oversee the club and you stay here with the kids."

Harry looked at his wife and an image of a drunken, drug-fuelled Vince Street entered his mind. He smiled. "Tell you what, you teach the boys mum's ginger cake recipe and continue the marvellous job you are doing here. You could certainly run Nightingales, but there's no way I could run this place or keep up with them two tykes in there."

"OK, it's a deal," she replied and they both laughed.

9.

Jamie Quinn snapped impatiently at a clearly agitated and high Vince Street. "Don't come bouncing into this office uninvited, bending my ear about crack pot schemes, Vince. You are driving me potty."

Johnny Quinn stood silently, watching his brother being far too reasonable with Vince. He was a handy bit of muscle on their firm, with a fearless attitude, but in the last year or so he had slowly become less of an asset and more of a liability.

Vince's eyes were bulging as he paced up and down the office, ranting. "I'm busy all over the place. North London, the West End, putting our name out there!"

"No, Vince! You are all over the place, full stop. A well-known associate of ours making a nuisance of himself selling them silly purple hearts and dexy to kids, and by the looks of you, swallowing half of 'em yourself." Jamie was becoming more and more riled. "You're becoming an embarrassment, Vince. Maybe, as you are so successful, you should walk out that door while you still can and don't come back."

Johnny had heard enough now and could feel the anger building up inside him. "Why don't you shut your trap, Street, and piss off home? When I shout shit, you jump on the shovel."

Although usually Vince would be aware by now that he had been pushing his luck, the Quinns' suspicions had been right and he had been on one of his drink and drug benders. He was out of control, a danger to himself and others, and totally unconcerned by anyone or anything. Including the Quinns.

Jamie opened the drinks cabinet and lined up three tumblers. "I've got some big contracts and investments lined up abroad, Vince. Be very, very lucrative for us all. Yet you want to run around the city making waves." He filled all three glasses with a very generous amount of liquor. "I heard you were causing aggravation over Harry Lane's place the other night, waving a poxy gun about in broad daylight."

"Yeah, and if he hadn't been mob-handed, I'd have done him. Something you pair should have done years back," Street snarled with drug-induced venom.

That was the final straw for Johnny. He reached forward and picked up the big marble paper weight from Jamie's desk.

"Sounds to me like Harry's done you a favour, putting you in your motor and sending you home before you got nicked. Waving guns about in front of a club full of people?" Jamie went to hand Vince the tumbler with a smile. "Seriously, Vinny boy, you need to get over this obsession with Harry Lane and get back in the real world."

Vince swung his arm out in exasperation, knocking the tumbler from Jamie's hand and sending it into the air. Before Jamie could react to this insult, in an explosion of rage, Johnny smashed the paper weight into Street's face as hard as he could. Vince careered backwards, the back of his head connecting with the corner of the radiator with a deadening thud.

Johnny and Jamie stood there for a moment, looking down at the now silent body, staring with wide, dead eyes at the ceiling.

At that moment, two other men from the Quinn firm, Dave Harris and Paul Baker, burst in to the room, alarmed by the commotion. They too stared down at the lifeless body and the large pool of blood that was now slowly creeping across the floor.

"Jesus, Johnny, you've killed him!" Jamie said, exasperated.

"Bollocks to him," Johnny replied nonchalantly as he turned to the two men. "Right, you two, first job today. Get rid of that." He then went to walk out of the office with such disinterest even Jamie was shocked.

Dave looked at Johnny. "What the bleeding hell we meant to do with him?"

Jamie looked at the body oozing blood over his office floor, then across at the doorway where his brother had stopped.

"Wrap him up in that old tarpaulin and sling him in the boot of his car," Johnny stated. "Then drive him over to Harry Lane's club and park it up in the car park. Dave, you drive. Paul, you follow in your motor, then come back together and don't get seen."

Paul and Dave looked at each other in total disbelief. They had drawn the short straw. But equally, they were far too scared to question Johnny and end up joining Vince.

Jamie and Johnny's eyes met.

"You sure about this, brother?" asked Jamie. "It's a bit strong."

"Look, Jamie, it's public knowledge that idiot was over Lane's club two nights ago shouting his mouth off and waving a gun about. I'm not taking the wrap for that piece of shit there. Let Lane deal with it. Might get rid of him as well, if he gets the tug from the old bill."

With that, Johnny turned and headed out the door, not even bothering to turn around again.

"How we going to fit him in the boot of his car?" Paul asked. "Look at the size of him."

"There's a sledge hammer downstairs. Smash his body up with that till he fits in. I don't care, just get rid of it!"

Dave Harris cruised along the road in Street's car, cursing to himself. "Pair of bastards. You can clear up your own mess."

As he hit a bump in the road, he heard the tied-up bundle wrapped in the tarpaulin shift as the suspension gave out a groan. His nerves were shredded and paranoia was at an all-time high as a police car passed by and he turned his head away, knowing full well that Street's car could be recognised by the local constabulary. He nervously fiddled with the wireless and looked in the mirror, watching the police car disappear behind him.

He pulled up about fifty metres from Nightingales and waited for Paul who had gone ahead into the car park in order to give him the signal it was clear.

Paul flashed his headlights and Dave pulled in, parking Street's car up at the back. As he got out, his heart thumped inside his chest as he thought about the risk he had taken, driving all the way from South London, an accessary to murder. Now he was deliberately leaving a car with a body in the boot and framing Harry Lane, who could appear at any moment and catch him in the act. And if he hadn't followed orders and delivered on the job, no doubt he would be next on the Quinns' hit list.

As he locked the car, he eyed the bushes and wasteland beyond. He knew he should throw the keys as far as possible into the thick undergrowth. There was no way he was keeping them in his pocket in case their luck ran out on the way back and they ended up being pulled and searched.

His heart told him that what the Quinns had done, what they had asked him to do, was unacceptable. But he was in it up to his eyeballs now. But surely he could salvage something from this nightmare? There and then, he decided that once he was safely out of the way, he would try to warn Harry.

Making sure Paul was out of his vision, he bent down and stuck the keys inside the exhaust pipe.

As Paul drove them away from the club, Dave turned and looked behind to double check no eyes had spotted them. He felt his whole body go cold and goose bumps appeared over his arms.

He shivered.

Paul turned to him, grinning. "You are as white as a sheet. You OK, son?"

"Just get us out of here," Dave replied. "I'm burning these clothes and gloves when I get in. I don't want any trace of me on that motor."

"Where's the keys?" Paul asked, laughing.

"I threw them right into them bushes. They won't find them. Be like looking for a needle in a haystack."

Paul burst out laughing again. "Ha ha, poor old Harry."

"Don't know why you keep laughing. When Lane finds out, we've got a major gang war on our hands again. And for what? That prat Street and that psychopath Johnny. I don't need this shit."

"Stop worrying, will you, Dave. Lane will be doing years if the old bill open the boot of that motor before he does. And knowing them pair of wicked bastards, the Quinns have probably tipped the old bill off anonymously already."

Dave looked at Paul's grinning face and felt totally empty.

"Just put your foot down and get us out of here, will yah?"

10.

Harry adjusted his tie in the mirror, stood up straight, shrugging his shoulders back so his suit jacket fell nicely into a comfortable place. He looked down and pulled the double-cuffed sleeves out from his jacket on either side, exposing just the right amount of cuff and the beautiful initialled cufflinks. He felt really contented. The way Chrissy happily embraced motherhood had been somewhat of a revelation to him, as had the role of being a father to him. His two boys gave him a great joy and sense of achievement and their antics were a source of fantastic amusement to the family. They were proper little characters in their own unique ways.

Harry and Chrissy had been pleased as punch that little Ray seemed to be enjoying the role of elder brother to Denny and hadn't become jealous of his mother's attention with the arrival of his sibling. The two boys had bonded well and this pleased Harry enormously.

Dave Harris stood nervously in the public phone box as he listened to the ringtone, awaiting a reply. As soon as Paul had dropped him off, he had decided he would try his best to tip Harry off about the car in the back of his club.

"Hello, Nightingales. Harry speaking."

Dave's heart raced as he tried to reply through a dry throat. He'd had just about as much aggravation as he could take in one day. "Hello Harry."

"Who is this?" Harry's voice came back.

"Don't matter who this is, just listen up. Not sure if you have been into your club's carpark, but Vince Street's car is parked up out there with his dead body in the boot."

Before Dave could speak again, Harry interjected, "Right, who is this? And what's your game?"

"Look Harry, do yourself a favour while you still can. Street's motor is in your car park. He is in the boot, dead. The keys are just an inch or two up the exhaust pipe."

With that, he replaced the receiver with a heavy bang and walked away.

"Shit. Bollocks," Harry said to himself as the line went dead. "If this is some kind of a bastard wind up, it's not funny."

He rushed towards the exit and into the carpark at the back of the club. He had parked his car in its usual spot, outside the front, so had not seen the car park or driven that way today.

Harry caught sight of the familiar Austin 11 parked up in an otherwise empty lot at the same time as he spotted Burt Roswell's car come to a halt opposite.

"You have got to be kidding me," Harry mumbled to himself as he gave Roswell a nod of acknowledgement. As Harry walked past Street's car, he noticed a small pool of liquid under the boot that was being added to with a slow but definite drip.

He kept walking without looking at it again, instead keeping his eyes firmly fixed on Roswell who was still sitting in his car, casually looking at Harry as he approached. Harry knew he needed to keep Roswell from getting out of his car. He was bound to want to take a nose at Street's motor. Whatever was dripping from the boot, and he was fairly sure it was blood, would be bound to arouse Roswell's curiosity and lead him to his most successful day on the job. Or quite possibly his worst, as Harry would be forced to add him to the body count.

Harry stood as close to Roswell's car door as he could. Something Roswell couldn't help but note as he looked Harry up and down. He was no doubt tempted to open the door into Harry's legs but decided to wind down the window instead, much to Harry's relief.

"Afternoon, Burt. Out on the prowl again, I see. Bit early for curb crawling isn't it? Wrong area, as well. No brasses round here." Harry decided to be his usual sarcastic self in Roswell's company. Anything else may arouse suspicion, or at least more than usual in Roswell's case.

"I like to keep an eye on my community, Harry, which always

involves regular patrols of this den of nefarious activity you have your name signed to. The acquisition of which was no doubt very debateable."

Harry looked at Roswell and chuckled. As much as he was desperate for Roswell to go, he knew trying to rush the conversation may trigger his inquisitive mindset.

"You know you're always welcome to look at all my documentation in regards to my club, Burt. My accounts are an open book. Just to think of all my taxes going towards your wages so you can harass me."

Roswell decided he had had enough and began winding up the window. As he did, he looked past Harry at the lone car parked up behind them, probably making a mental note of the number plate.

Harry looked round at the car then back at Roswell, smiling. "Probably had too many and decided to take a taxi. You know Nightingales always encourages sensible drinking, Sergeant Roswell."

Roswell pulled away without responding.

"That's it, piss off, you prick," Harry mumbled as the car disappeared.

Harry knelt down, avoiding the puddle, and felt inside the exhaust pipe for the keys. Luckily, they were right near the edge and he retrieved them with ease.

He looked around to check his surroundings then he inserted the key and the boot clicked open. As daylight flooded the boot, he caught sight of the crudely wrapped body in the musty tarpaulin. He had to be sure, though, so he quickly removed a switch blade from his pocket and ripped the rotten material. His curiosity was satisfied quickly enough, as an opening in the material revealed the unmistakable features of a normally animated Vince Street, now very much dead.

He knew he had no time to think or delegate. He had no option but to take the risk and take action himself. Without hesitation, Harry slammed the boot shut, walked briskly but calmly round to the driver's door, got in and started the car up. He thought of his wife and the two boys as he slowly pulled out of the car park. If he was pulled over by Roswell now, he saw no way out. Equally, if he had left the car at the club to bide himself time to think of a game plan, Street may have been reported missing and Roswell would have been back. As handy as bent

Bradshaw was, he couldn't cover everything, and he wouldn't be able to cover this.

Harry pulled up opposite Danny Clarke's yard and awaited the go ahead. He had rung ahead to Danny from a phone box and explained his dire situation. Danny had been none too pleased and told him, in no uncertain terms, that this was a one off, never to be repeated, favour.

Danny directed Harry straight up the car ramps and into the back of a lorry. He jumped from the lorry and stood and watched as Danny locked up the back and the Austin containing Vince Street's body was finally out of sight. Danny shook his head, staring at a now very relieved but still shocked Harry.

"Jesus Christ, Harry, what you trying to do to me? I just hope you wasn't seen coming here."

"So do I, Danny. So do I," Harry said, his face ashen as the reality of the risk he had just taken set in. "Some bastard's put it right on me."

"Any ideas who?"

"Hard to say. He has been making a proper nuisance of himself all over the place lately, so could have pissed anyone off. He was at mine last week shouting his mouth off, high as a kite, waving a gun about."

Danny looked at Harry with a serious look on his face. "You need to find out who it was, and sharpish, because I've not got the facilities for getting shot of cars with bodies in at short notice on a regular basis."

Harry managed a laugh as the two men walked back into the yard.

"You're a total lifesaver, Danny. I can't apologise enough for landing this mess on you. I'll make sure you get hefty compensation, trust me, as soon as possible."

Danny looked up at the sky as it began to rain and said under his breath, "Poxy weather. All it has done is rain all week."

Harry thought of the pool of blood still in the club's car park and the increasing heaviness of the downpour was welcome to him as it would wash away the last trace of Street from his premises.

The two men stood under the cover of a corrugated iron roof as the rain hammered down across the yard, with the activity of the car breakers unaffected.

"I was going to iron that wanker out myself, in my own time, after his performance the other night, but someone beat me to it and left me to tidy up the mess," Harry said, shivering both from the weather and the experience he had just been through.

Danny calmly lit a cigarette and took a long draw on it. As he blew the smoke out into the air, he reminded Harry he needed to set about getting rid of the car and body from his yard. "I suggest you get some feelers out there, Harry. Find out who thinks you and me have gone into the funeral business and thinks it's OK to dump bodies on your doorstep."

Harry went silent for a while, looking pensively into the yard, then commented, "If I could put a face to that voice on the phone it would be handy. Either they're doing me a good turn or think it's amusing watching me run about like a prat with a corpse in the boot."

Danny and Harry shook hands and embraced with a mutual pat on the back.

"I'll call in when the car is safely off the plot for good, Harry."

"Thanks, Danny. You're a legend. I'll stay away from here for a while, then square you up with some dollars."

11.

Burt Roswell congratulated himself as he ended the phone call. He had been right to follow his gut instincts, especially where Harry Lane was concerned. He had jotted down the number plate of the lone car in Nightingales car park that afternoon and after some investigations and with a little help from his contacts in intelligence and the DVLC, that phone call had confirmed the car belonged to a very well-known south London gangster and associate of the Quinn firm.

Vincent Albert Street.

He had also ascertained that Street was a nasty piece of work with a criminal record going back to early childhood. He had an assortment of convictions from petty theft as a youth, through to seasoned robberies, extortion, protection, narcotic dealing and involvement in prostitution.

But the really juicy part that was making Burt's mind rush and his mouth almost salivate was the revelation that Street had been reported missing by his wife a few days ago. And the last known sighting of him had been a heated exchange outside Nightingales club with a certain Harry Lane.

Young Ray Lane squealed with delight as he watched the model train fly round the set, expertly controlled by his grandad Stan. Stan looked down at his grandson and smiled, excited eyes looking back up at him.

"You want a go, Ray?"

"Yes please, grandad!"

Stan squatted slowly down next to him, making groaning sounds as he did. "Don't get old, Ray, it's a real sod."

"It's a sod," Ray repeated, making Stan laugh.

"That it certainly is, Ray Boy, but don't say sod or me and you will get in trouble with your nan. Right, you hold the control box with grandad and let's move these trains out the station."

Ray and Stan held the controller together and as Stan explained how to move the lever to start the motion of the train, Chrissy appeared in the doorway with Denny. Ray's little brother had been down in the kitchen watching his nan knock up some cake mixture, enthusiastically sticking his little hand in the bowl and licking his fingers. Chrissy would drop the boys around to Stan and Molly's any day she had things to do in town. The boys loved being with their grandparents, but Chrissy didn't leave them too long as the pair of rascals were enough of a handful even for her at the best of times. Although Stan and Molly never said a word, the pair must have exhausted them.

"You two lads OK up here?" Chrissy asked, smiling at Stan and Ray.

Stan looked around at Chrissy but Ray didn't acknowledge his mum, his attention completely absorbed in the train flying around the track. "Budding locomotive driver you've got here, Chrissy. He loves it."

"Can I leave Denny up here with you, Stan, while I have a chat with Molly? I'll come get them shortly and take them home."

"'Cause you can, love," Stan said, reaching out his hand. "Come over here with your old grandad, Denny, and help your brother and me get these trains out on time or people will be phoning up the station and complaining." He looked up at Chrissy and gave her a wink and a smile.

Harry smiled at Maria Vital as she placed his coffee on the table. "Thanks, Maria. I'm having the full Vital treatment today. I'll have this then over to the old man for a trim up."

Maria returned his smile then quickly joined the other ever-mobile Vital girls who were attending a never-ending stream of hungry customers.

Harry was sat at his usual table, facing the entrance. The seat was backed against the wall, with a full view of the entire café. Although Harry had never officially laid claim to it, it was generally known and respected by all the locals that this was his particular favourite spot and kept free for him. Not due to any fear as such. Harry was, after all, well-liked and respected in equal measure. Plus, he was careful to keep his world separate from the world of what he and his firm referred to as 'straight people'. Harry's policy had always been to be friendly and keep the local community on side, enhancing his reputation with regular donations to various charities and businesses. Nothing ever went on in his area that he was unaware of or didn't have some kind of input in, so long as there was a pound note to be made.

The fact he had money tied up in little ventures all over the area – that's to say the ones that were on the books legitimately – made his more nefarious activities much easier to conceal, his cash more accountable and provided him with a nice façade among less concerned parties.

Harry's relaxed state was suddenly broken and replaced with a feeling of agitation as he caught sight of who he had labelled the human blue bottle appear at the condensation-misted door.

Sergeant Roswell.

Roswell feigned surprise at seeing Harry, as if he wasn't deliberately stalking his known haunts, but just happened to be passing. "Ah, I'm glad I spotted you, Harry. I'd like to run something past you."

Without answering, Harry leaned across and pulled a chair out for Roswell, not that he would have waited for an invitation. He caught Anna's eye and she left the order she was taking and headed to Harry's table, raising zero protest from the two builders she had been serving. The locals were fully aware of how expert the Vitals were at serving, and this little interruption would not make much difference to their waiting time.

"Can you add whatever Sergeant Roswell is having to my bill please, Anna. Thank you, love."

Roswell was tempted to decline the offer but was sure it would be met with a sarcastic comment from Harry, so he sheepishly asked Anna for a cup of tea.

"Better get him a slice of your mum's cake with that, Anna. He looks a bit weak there, does our local bobby," Harry interjected, much to Roswell's annoyance. Like most of the men in the area, he was taken by the girls' looks and, although married, he was quite shy and became flustered by a beautiful looking lady if he was attracted to them.

Roswell looked at the smiling Anna, trying to look as cool as possible and said, "Just the tea, thank you."

Anna added to his misery and replied, "Don't worry, Sergeant

Roswell, I'll put some biscuits on a saucer for you, on the house." With a wink, she turned and headed for the kitchen, leaving Roswell's complexion reddening with embarrassment.

Roswell turned to Harry, who was struggling with all his might not to burst out laughing. His shyness turned to anger and he looked at Harry for as long as he dared without a word, then finally spoke. "What do you know about the disappearance of Vince Street?" He watched Harry's face, looking for any hint of surprise but although Harry's pulse had gone up and he felt a chill spread over his skin, he was able to compose himself perfectly.

"What's happened, then? He been playing hide and seek with the Quinns? That's about the childish level of them pricks." Harry took a sip of his coffee, keeping his eyes fixed on Roswell.

Roswell looked much more himself now, in charge, relishing grilling Harry.

"Tut tut tut, oh come on, Harry." Roswell leaned forward into Harry's space and continued with almost a whisper. "I have it from a very reliable source that Street was screaming the place down outside your club the other week, waving a shooter about, by all accounts."

Harry laughed, although he didn't like where this conversation was going, or the confident look on Roswell's face. "He was slaughtered drunk, Burt, upsetting the customers. I calmed him down, slipped him a few bob and said he was welcome back another night. I told him to get home and sober up."

Roswell leaned back in his chair. "Where did he go, then, Harry? 'Cause he hasn't been seen since and has been reported missing by his very worried wife."

"I put him in a taxi and paid the driver. I've not seen him since."

"Oh, then that would explain why his Austin was parked in your carpark when I saw you the other day?" Roswell grinned. "I'm sorry, Harry, my apologies, it must have been the taxi driver who abducted Street or he would have been back to collect his car. Then again, when I was on patrol again that evening, the car had gone, so I guess he must have returned. Real mystery, Harry, huh?"

Harry turned and looked out the window, his mind racing. He spotted a group of children at the roadside. "There you go, Burt. Instead of playing at being a detective, why don't you go and see what them kids are doing across the road? More your level."

Roswell was enjoying this now and whether Harry knew Street's whereabouts or not, he knew he was pushing him to the limit. Roswell wiped his mouth with his napkin and stood up slowly. "How much of your crooked money pays Antonio's bills, and for his silence in regards to George Parker?"

Harry felt his temper rise and stood up, knocking the table with enough force to draw looks from other customers. "You're out of order, Roswell." He glanced around the room, then sat back down. "Look, you get this into your thick scull. I know nothing about George Parker, or what happened to him. And Antonio is just my barber and a personal friend."

Roswell leaned down by Harry's ear and for the first time ever, felt like a giant. "Well, all those years ago, the last place George Parker was ever seen alive was entering Antonio's barbers alongside you and that other reptile you associate with. And the last time Vince Street was seen alive, it was in a foul-mouthed exchange of words with you." He stood again, looking down at Harry. "People have a habit of disappearing around you, Lane. I'm onto you, matey."

As he turned to walk away, Roswell felt invincible. He couldn't resist one more twist of the knife before he left. "By the way, Harry, you'll be delighted to know you'll be dealing with me a whole lot more in the future, now your bent ally Bradshaw has been suspended. Looks like you're one of many lowlifes that corrupt snake has been topping his pension up with."

Roswell left the café without staying to savour Harry's expression, feeling very pleased with himself.

As Harry stuck his key in the door of his house, mentally drained, he envisioned the tension-releasing bite of a Glenfiddich sliding down his throat. He caught sight of Chrissy and knew by the look on her face, by the red, swollen, tear-filled eyes and ghostly pallor, that this day's bad vibes were not over yet.

He sat on the sofa, digesting the news.

His dad had suffered a massive heart attack earlier that day, while playing with little Ray and Denny on the train set. He had died, it seemed, instantly. Chrissy began to sob again in Harry's arms.

"I tried everywhere to get a message to you, Harry."

Harry cradled his wife's head. "I know, lovely, I know. You're a total diamond. How are the boys? And mum?"

"The boys are sleeping, and so is mum. I brought her back here. I gave her a pill to help her sleep. Oh Harry, it was awful, just such a shock."

"I know, love," Harry whispered gently as he tenderly stroked her hair. As he felt his wife slowly giving way to exhausted sleep, he stared pensively at the wall.

12.

Antonio Vital expertly worked around Harry's neckline with the razor blade, putting the finishing touches to his monthly trim.

"Still can't get over Stan, Harry. Such a lovely man. Both businesses will be shut down all day as a mark of respect to you and your family."

Harry smiled in the mirror at Antonio. "You don't need to do that, mate. Especially the cafe in the morning. The locals will expect you to be open."

"There is no way I could open, Harry. Just wouldn't feel right. Plus, we would be closed straight after the breakfast rush to attend your father's funeral anyway. No, no, I've decided we will close."

Harry smiled to himself. Even after all these years, Antonio's mix of Italian cockney accent and London sayings delivered in his endearing way still bought a smile to his face.

As Antonio held the mirror behind Harry's head so he could check out the back of his finished haircut, he felt unusually unsettled as he noticed Harry's eyes locked on him with an intense stare.

"Everything OK with the cut, Harry?" he asked.

Harry's stare continued to hold him before he finally spoke. "You had Burt Roswell quizzing you at all in regards to George Parker?"

Antonio was totally taken aback by the question and Harry's serious expression. "No, Harry. He has not brought up George Parker in conversation with me. He never really speaks much at all, just his usual short back and sides and a miserable face."

This made Harry laugh, which in turn made Antonio smile.

"What makes you ask?" Antonio pulled the cloak away and set to work with his little duster brush, removing any stray hairs from his client's neck and clothing.

"Just something he said, and the way he said it, the other day. Gave me the impression he knows something about that day and he is waiting to use it." Harry stood up, straightening his shirt collar.

Antonio handed him some tissue paper to wipe away any hairs he may have missed then met his gaze with a very serious look in his eyes. He took both Harry's hands in his with a gentle but reassuring grip.

"I told you that night, Harry, and I will tell you once more, then it never needs to be said again. What happened that night will stay unspoken and unknown by anybody till my body is laid to rest."

Harry looked into this little man's kind eyes and listened as he continued.

"I'm a family man, Harry, and my family are my world. I love my wife and my children and I would die for them. I know just enough about the life you're involved in to know that it frightens me. But my silence is not through fear of you, but through friendship and loyalty. Listen, Harry, my friend, you was young then, but you need to understand that wasn't the first time Parker had abused me, or taken money from my business, or frightened my wife and children."

Harry listened to Antonio's revelations and as he did, he suddenly had a mental picture of Parker and remembered the brash bully he had also grown to despise. The thought of him terrorising Antonio both angered him and also give him a sense of pleasure and justification that he had been able to end his torment.

Antonio squeezed Harry's hand harder, looking up at him. "I'd dreamed of doing what you done to Parker many times. So, trust me, you done this whole community a favour that day. My word is my word, Harry. Nothing would ever get me to speak of it again. I have blood on my hands from that day, too. I'm directly involved and God will judge me when he feels he needs to. But while I'm here on this earth, so far his judgement is being kept in waiting."

Harry looked around at the huge crowd of people in Nightingales. It surprised even him. He had decided to open the club to everyone and not just the people who had attended Stan's funeral earlier. He had reasoned an open club with plenty of people, music and atmosphere, was just what his mum and Chrissy, and indeed he himself, needed. Not a sombre affair. Ninety per cent of the people in the club would never have even known his dad and were either there out of respect for him or just as an excuse for a party.

As Harry circulated the room, thanking people for attending and accepting their condolences, he became aware of a lone man standing at the bar, eyes fixed on him and a look that was beckoning. Harry broke away from the group he was with and joined the stranger at the bar.

He extended his hand and the man shook it. Both men's grips were friendly yet firm.

"I'm Harry. Nice to see a new face in my club."

"Yes, I know who you are," came the reply.

Harry noted that it wasn't said in any kind of a threatening way. He smiled. "Ah, so you know me, yet I don't know you and I am good when it comes to faces. I even recognise the young tearaways around here when they bring a new mate along."

"Dave Harris," the man replied flatly, then continued, "Firstly, I'm sorry for your loss and I'd like to apologise for coming today of all days, but I decided it had to be done and so here I am."

"So, what brings you here, Mr Harris? Business or pleasure?"

"Well, it's business you need to know. I'm an associate of the Quinns."

Harry felt his mood change immediately and his pulse rise. A feeling of anger came over him almost instantly at the mention of that name.

Before he could respond, a tray of sandwiches were thrust between the two men by a smiling Molly Lane.

"Not for me at the moment, mum. Mr Harris, please help yourself," Harry said, composing himself, checking his appearance in front of his mother and not wanting to show his new acquaintance any obvious signs of agitation.

"Not for me, thank you," Dave replied politely, smiling at Molly.

Molly pointed over at a nearby table, where Big Tony Parish was loading an already buckling paper plate with food. "I'd grab a plateful of food while you can, son, while there is still some left." Molly smiled and walked away, causing both Harry and Dave to laugh, and helping to slightly dissipate the building tension.

"So, what's this all about, Mr Harris?" Harry enquired, looking directly into Dave's eyes.

"Call me Dave, please. And it concerns Vince Street."

Harry felt instantly alert and quickly scanned the room to see if any unwanted guests were circulating unnoticed.

Dave noticed how Harry's whole demeanour had changed. Sensing he could be in danger, he continued, "Please, before I tell you what I'm about to tell you, you should know I'm doing so in an attempt to do what I think is right, as I can't just leave it. But please don't involve me in any repercussions."

Without saying a word, Harry's eyes signalled for Dave to continue.

"The Quinns killed Vince and ordered his body to be dumped at yours." Dave paused and looked at Harry, expecting some reaction. All he got was a stone-cold glare.

What he didn't know was that inwardly, Harry suddenly felt relief at the revelation. He had tormented himself with feelings of paranoia, even thinking it was a police fit-up. Of course it was the Quinns. Who else would be snide enough to take such a liberty? Harry also figured out there and then the owner of the mystery voice.

"So," Harry said, grinning at Dave. "First you ring me to warn me of the body in the car, now you're here giving me the info that it was the Quinns." Harry could tell by Dave's face that he was bemused that Harry recognised his voice, but before he could open his mouth to ask how, Harry carried on. "Trust me, Dave, when you get a phone call from someone giving you the heads-up on a possible long stretch for murder, you never get that voice out of your head." Harry's eyes were piercing into Dave's now. "Glad I can put a face to the voice, and now the puzzle is coming together." Harry looked at Dave's empty glass and said, "Top up?"

Dave nodded. His throat was dry. Would he get to leave Nightingales intact? And if he did, would the Quinns hear of his deceitful visit?

Harry handed Dave his drink and looked at his own, pensively. "So, if you told me all of this out of pure conscience or some kind of guilt, that tells me either you dumped that motor in my car park or you know who did and you're telling me sooner rather than later, or you're here on another twisted errand from that pair of shithouses, which if you are, you're marked, my old son."

"You're right, it was my phone call." Dave took a gulp of his drink then decided to just say it. "I also dumped the car there with another man. I'd rather not say who, but keep this between us and away from that pair's ears."

Harry eyed the now nervous-looking Dave. "So, what you getting out of this, telling me? What's up? You having sleepless nights?"

"Yes, Harry, if you want the honest truth. It was the right thing to do. I don't know you, just of you. But it doesn't matter. What they landed on you is beyond out of order. Those two are out of control. They think they can do what they like, to whoever they like. Look, I'm sorry, but I felt trapped that day with that psychopath. I felt I had no option but to follow orders or end up in the boot with Street. Everybody, inside and outside of our firm, are sick of them two."

Harry was a good judge of character and felt that Dave was genuine. "Right, Dave, I respect you coming here today. Takes a lot of guts. And regardless of you dumping the car, your call saved the situation. Now, how do you fancy helping me out?"

Dave gave Harry a curious look and listened as he spoke.

The conversation ended with a firm hand shake and a smile.

13.

As Harry circulated the room, his mind filled with a mixture of emotions. There was obviously the sadness over his father's passing, although what with all the funeral arrangements and the general busyness of his days, the loss hadn't fully sunk in yet, with waves of grief hitting him in times of quiet reflection. He was also now filled with a feeling of relief, not anger, over the revelations Dave Harris had just broken to him. Harry was also somewhat annoyed he hadn't worked out that it was down to the Quinns before now. Having said that, even if he'd eventually worked it out without Dave's help, he wouldn't have had the proof. Harry knew he should be fuming at the Quinns' disrespect and sheer audacity. But no. If it hadn't been for Dave's speedy tip-off followed by his quick actions, and a hell of a lot of luck, he would be on a murder charge by now.

Harry knew once the rest of his firm heard of this liberty they would be up for revenge and gang war. But Harry had already decided on a different approach. He would play it down in regards to the Quinns and lead them to believe he had no idea they were in the frame for fitting him up, or at least attempting it.

Harry smiled as he caught sight of Eric Bradshaw approaching him. "Eric, good to see you," he said, extending a hand that was enthusiastically met by Eric.

At that very moment, Harry spotted Burt Roswell entering through the main doors. Burt had spotted the pair of them and looked on with an unrestrained look of distain on his face. Obviously, he did not approve of Harry and Eric's open display of affection, a thought that made Harry laugh. He decided to add to Burt's misery by waving at him whilst also signalling a member of staff to offer the policeman a flute of champagne from the complimentary trays circulating the reception room.

"He has got some front, your colleague, I'll give him that. Although I knew he would show his ugly boat in here for a nose at some point."

Eric laughed, more from the effects of the free booze than Harry's comment. "Well, that little partnership is all but over, anyway, Harry."

"Yes, I've been meaning to catch up with you since that snakey little reptile gleefully told me about your suspension. What's the score, Eric?"

Eric pointed to one of the empty booths. "Let's have a chat. Out of the way."

Harry looked across at Burt who was staring at them both and, without speaking, led the way to the empty booth and out of Roswell's direct glare.

As a member of staff delivered two fresh glasses to their table, Harry listened to a very talkative Eric. "I'm basically being given a chance to walk away, Harry, with a very minor indiscretion and also added medical grounds, due to my hearing."

"Yeah, I did notice the hearing aid, but didn't want to say anything in case you were a bit touchy about it."

The blank look on Eric's face told Harry that either it didn't work very well and he hadn't heard him or his mind was elsewhere. Probably the latter, as Eric then continued, "Lots going on at the top, Harry. They've been told to clean things up on the streets, and among us. I'm giving you a heads up to keep yourself as clean as a whistle, because the top are looking to bring you all down. It's starting to look too obvious now, the amount of unsolved crimes and drinks being offered."

Harry listened but couldn't help but let a little laugh go. "Honestly, Eric, I sometimes think the crime in your gang dwarfs the rest of London put together."

Eric looked at Harry with a straight face. "You try living on a copper's wage."

"Roswell manages," Harry replied, laughing.

"Well, with his ambition and straight ways he will go right to the top. Commissioner."

Both men laughed as Harry added, "Yeah, I guess someone needs to actually police."

Eric became serious again. He took a sip of his drink and looked straight into Harry's eyes. "Trust me, Harry, the good days have got to end for us all, at least for the foreseeable future. I've ridden my luck and I'm not getting any younger. I wanted out within the next year, anyway. You see, I made a promise to a certain senior member of the Met who has secrets he can never have revealed, so my suspension will be made to blow over and I can walk away untarnished before anyone picks up on and investigates the rest. Thanks to my knowledge of corruption at the very top, this intervention has been a bit of a life saver."

Harry could feel his trousers being pulled and as he tried to listen to Eric, a little voice said, "Dad, dad, dad." Harry turned his head towards the voice while still holding Eric's gaze and saw little Ray's excited, eager eyes looked up at him. "Dad, dad!"

Harry finally looked down at Ray. "Be quiet a minute, Ray, I'm speaking to Mr Bradshaw. I've always told you never to interrupt when people are speaking."

Ray looked at his dad then pointed up at Eric's hearing aid, protesting. "But look, dad, he isn't even listening to you. He's listening to the radio."

Harry looked at his lovely little boy and resisted the urge to burst out laughing as he looked back at Eric's face and the plastic hearing aid. Harry pulled his wallet from his pocket and took out a coin, placing it into Ray's little hand. "Don't forget, Ray, you are a top member of my team. I'm paying your wages early, but you've got to go and help mum and nanny Molly, OK?"

"Yes dad," Ray replied, looking as proud as punch. His dad had told him he was an important member of his team.

Eric laughed as Ray sped off back into the crowded room. "Tell you what, Harry, I'm glad I'm pulling out of this game. Old Happy Larry Roswell will have his work cut out with him in a few years." He paused for a moment and started to look more relaxed. "If all goes to plan, me and the old woman are moving down to Cornwall, so you won't be seeing much of me again. Nor can I be of any assistance to you."

Harry suddenly felt the importance of the situation. Having men like Bradshaw on the payroll was invaluable in keeping men like him on the right side of prison walls. Harry looked out of the booth and noticed Roswell had somehow managed to position himself in such a way as to just be able to see him but not Eric.

He laughed. "I'm being watched by the human bluebottle as we speak. Just as well you are doing all the talking and he can't see you, as knowing that shithouse he would be lip reading."

Eric stood up, obscuring Roswell's view. "Keep your guard up, Harry. Don't give him any ammunition. He is no mug and he's itching to nail you down."

"Don't I know it," Harry replied, smiling.

"Last favour for you, Harry. My colleagues over the water are building a large case against the Quinns and I have it from reliable sources that there are possible informants prepared to grass on them. Apparently, they are making far too many waves and are involved with high society and lined up for an almighty fall and severe prison terms."

Harry could tell without any exchange of words that Eric knew Harry was involved with the Quinns on some level, but he did not know about the Vince Street situation.

Eric turned and left, exchanging a few unheard words with Burt before walking away into the night. Harry followed in his footsteps and approached Sergeant Roswell.

"Glad you took advantage of the complimentary drinks, Burt. Seems you're lightening up in your old age. Was a time when you always refused my hospitality on visits."

Roswell resisted the urge to say something sarcastic. He considered the occasion and responded politely. "I'm truly sorry for your loss, Harry, and thank you for the drink. I drank as a mark of respect to your father. The fact I never knew much about him, only in passing from time to time, tells me he must have been a hard-working man and a decent member of the community." Roswell's eyes scanned the packed room and couldn't manage to keep the nicety going. "Unlike a large percentage of those in this place, including you."

Harry never bit on this snide remark, but smiled, replying, "If everyone was like my old dad, you wouldn't have a job. Face it, Burt, you need law breakers to keep you busy." Harry was pleased with his nice little counter to Roswell's snide jibe and continued, "Unfortunately, instead of keeping the streets safe for my wife and children and for this community, you're too busy harassing local businessmen like me."

Roswell tipped down the last of his champagne and replaced the empty flute on a passing tray. "I won't intrude on your day any longer, Harry. Once again, sorry for you and your family's loss. As he got up from the bar stool, he moved closer to Harry and almost at a whisper, said. "That's something else you can mourn for. Mourn the loss of Bradshaw, Lane, because you've got me in charge now. I'm up for promotion and the end of your little run is nigh, my old son."

With that, a confident-sounding Roswell turned to walk away.

But Harry wasn't finished with him yet. "Oh, by the way, Burt, I hope my donation to the boxing club helped out."

Roswell turned and glared at Harry. He had been a keen amateur boxer in his youth and his love of the sport had gotten him involved in the local club as a trainer. He was on the committee and he had been elated recently by a massive anonymous donation. But his heart sank now as he found out the identity of the sponsor.

Harry grinned. "I was thinking of myself when I made that generous donation, Burt, what with them two boys of mine. When they are a bit older I'd like them to take up boxing. It will keep them off the streets and out of trouble."

Harry gave Roswell a wink and a victorious smile.

Roswell could only scowl before heading for the exit.

14.

Harry sat waiting patiently for the arrival of Dave Harris. He was parked up in the car park of the Red Lion, a country pub in Hertfordshire, well away from both his and Dave's areas. Harry had stopped off there with Chrissy a few years ago and remembered the place for its scenic location and lovely meal they had enjoyed. He had managed to find a spot that not only gave him a good view of the whole of the car park and the pub's entrance but was also covered by the huge branches of an oak tree, which almost totally obscured his presence from any arrivals.

Harry watched Dave arrive, leave his car and enter the pub. He prided himself and was well-known for his punctuality. But on this occasion, he decided it would be better to arrive ten minutes late so as to see if Dave had been followed or had any company tucked away.

Finally, Harry entered the pub and spotted Dave at the bar. He was already half way down his drink. Dave had positioned himself facing the door and returned a beaming smile and extended hand.

"Good to see you, Dave. I must apologise for my late arrival, old son, got stuck behind one of them poxy farmer's tractors going one mile an hour. Let me shout up a drink and a top up for you."

"Took me a good while to get here and find it myself," Dave replied.

"Well, better to be safe than sorry, particularly for you, Dave. I never underestimate anyone or any situation. Planning and patience are the key."

"Speaking of keys," Dave responded, looking directly at Harry.

Harry grinned back at him and gestured towards a set of seats tucked away across the room. A sign above them aptly named the area 'the snug'.

They sat down with their drinks and Dave nervously removed a box and piece of paper from his pocket, handing them to Harry. As Harry lifted the lid and looked inside, Dave began speaking in a hushed tone.

"That's imprints of all the keys you need, plus the combination to the safe. Don't even ask me how I managed it, but just know it wasn't easy and I nearly landed myself in the same place as Vince Street on more than one occasion."

Harry let out a laugh and raised his glass. "Don't you worry, Dave. That's your job done, mate. Rest is down to me now. All being well, you'll be getting your percentage very soon." Harry's expression took on a more serious tone now. "Your only job now is to cover yourself and make sure any suspicions the Quinns have after I clear that Peter out point elsewhere. You make sure you're either in their company or you're well seen by lots of people nowhere near that casino."

Dave took a large gulp of his drink and looked around the pub at other customers living their normal lives. He knew he was in too deep now to back out. But he also felt his debt to Harry was well and truly covered, which he made a point of emphasizing to Harry now. His only concern was keeping the Quinns in the dark and off his back.

He continued to explain to Harry the exact nights the safe was full of most of the casino's takings before they were moved elsewhere. Always a Sunday night. Dave made a point of letting Harry know that, although he didn't know down to the last coin what the safe would contain, he was pretty sure of his estimate and what he expected his take to be.

This made Harry laugh out loud again. He thought to himself how there was zero loyalty where money was involved. But in Dave's case, it was justified. What that pair of slags had put on both Dave and him needed retribution and Harry had decided to do it in his favourite way. Financial compensation.

"So, how are that pair of wankers, then, Dave?"

Dave shook his head and muttered under his breath, "Total wankers." He then looked up at Harry. "You know something, Harry, it's been discussed amongst our firm how we could put them away."

Harry could sense the exasperation in Dave's body language.

"Let's face it, the firm are their backup and work force, yet most of us can't stand the pair of wankers anymore. Especially after Vince."

Harry listened as Dave continued, his face now betraying real anger.

"We all know Vince could be a pest at the best of times, but he didn't deserve that. Look at the way they just disregarded it and we are expected to clear up the mess." He took a sip of his drink and looked at Harry, almost pleadingly. "Seriously, Harry, they're getting out of hand, especially that bastard Johnny."

Harry suddenly had a flashback to George Parker. "I fully understand where you are coming from, mate."

Dave looked at Harry, waiting for further comment. But he had no intension of expanding on that subject and, once again, put George Parker back into his distant memory.

"Honestly, it would be so easy to put them two out of the game. We have spoken about finding an opportunity, and just how easy it would be."

Harry looked at Dave staring into his glass reflectively and actually felt sorry for him. He broke the silence. "Dave, look at me."

Dave sat upright and looked directly at Harry, almost obediently, such was the tone and command in his voice.

"Right, now you listen to me. Get any silly thoughts of murdering the Quinns out of your head. You know it's madness. You risked getting a pull by the old bill bringing that body over the water to mine. And so did I, getting rid of it. We both could have been on a murder charge then, so shall we have a break from dead bodies?"

Both men thought for a moment about that statement then burst out laughing. As their laughter subsided, Harry's face once again took on a serious appearance.

"You need to know this, Dave. The Quinns' firm are on their way down." Dave gave Harry a serious look. Was he threatening a challenge from either him or another firm? Was a gang war imminent? But as Harry continued, he began to realise the threat was from the biggest gang in London. The police. "I have it from a hundred-per-cent reliable source inside the old bill that the Quinns have not only pissed off our world, but the top people in the old bill too." Harry now returned Dave's serious look. "They're going down, mate. The evidence is being gathered. They want to clean up London."

Dave took a packet of cigarettes from his pocket, offering one to Harry, who declined.

"Odd cigar, me, Dave. When I'm in the mood."

Dave lit one for himself and took a heavy drag, speaking as he exhaled smoke into the air. "Well, that means me as well, then, don't it? Means they're building a case against all the Quinns' associates."

Harry nodded. "Well, of course, Dave. Just be aware and implement whatever you need to, to lower your collateral damage. Tell you what, soon as I've cleared that safe, paid you your whack, I'll be off the scene for a good while. I'm going to concentrate on Nightingales, my wife and kids and invest in other ventures. I suggest you do the same, my old son!" Harry looked across the pub, pensively and said, "I've done my stints of porridge. I've got no intention of doing any more. My Chrissy don't need that, not with the boys. But nor do I, if I can help it."

Dave and Harry stood and shook hands.

"I'll be in touch before we hit the Quinns, so you can cover your end." Harry laughed as he added, "You will know if the job is successful by the reaction of them pair of arseholes."

Dave returned a laugh, although the thought of the Quinns realising their safe had been emptied filled him with dread.

Harry squeezed Dave's hand slightly harder. "Don't forget the information I gave you. Use it wisely."

Dave looked at him and replied sincerely, "Thanks for the heads up. I appreciate it."

Harry smiled warmly. "I'll be in touch when we are ready to go. Be patient, though. Let the dust settle before we give you your percentage."

As Dave went to reply, Harry cut in again. "Don't come near Nightingales or ring me. Don't give them maniacs any reason to suspect you. I'm going nowhere. And nor is your cut." Harry could tell his words had registered and Dave was reassured.

Harry watched as Dave Harris's car disappeared out of sight and picked the menu up off the table. If his memory served him well, the décor had changed, as had the management, since Chrissy and he had visited but he decided to see if the food was still as delicious as he remembered. He was getting hungry and felt some lunch was in order before his drive home.

15.

Harry slowly pulled the van up outside the back of the Quinns' South London casino.

Sat next to him was his right-hand man, Ronny Piper. Although Big Tony would have been handy extra muscle should any passing members of the public or patrons of the casino spot them, he was absent tonight. A description of Tony's size and appearance to any one of the Quinn firm would immediately alert them to the culprits of the robbery. For his part, Tony had watched the casino for many weeks now and, so far, Dave Harris's information in regards to when the place was usually empty, had been correct.

Now it was time to find out if Harris was right about the safe holding the casino's entire week's cash, if his map of the building's layout was accurate and if the keys Harry had had made from Dave's imprints matched the corresponding locks.

Harry's heart rate began to rise as the two men left the van. He felt more nervous now than on any other job he could recall. He knew that if they left any obvious clues pointing to their involvement it would mean certain gang war, possibly arrest, and worse, a potential threat to his family. Of course, he was prepared to kill or die for his family. None the less, the danger was there and he needed to avoid it.

"You ready, Ronny?"

A silent nod was returned and both men simultaneously checked their pockets for their guns. They were both fully prepared to use them if need be.

Although the back door was well out of sight of the main road, there was certainly more than enough light at both ends of the alley to expose the van and their presence should anybody walk by, or worse, walk down the alley. He knew that if a member of the Quinns' staff or a firm member arrived, it was a gun fight either way, so they would have to just get in and out as quickly as possible and take what came.

Harry had decided at the last minute to make the whole job look like a delivery. To that end, he had brought along a couple of fruit machines so that should anybody be nosey enough to enquire, they could explain that they were on a delivery for the casino. Harry had totally removed the guts of the machines so as to render them practically weightless, both for ease of movement and possible storage.

Harry looked at a clearly anxious Ronny as he inserted the key marked on his key chart into the lock on the rear entrance of the casino.

"Nice one, Alan," Harry remarked, in reference to their locksmith, as the lock clicked and the door opened smoothly. The two men removed one gutted fruit machine from the van and manoeuvred it through the main door before unloading two large holdalls from their van. They then removed the second fruit machine and left it by the van.

They found the office door as indicated, luckily within metres of the back entrance. As they entered the main office both men clutched their guns. Harry's natural mistrust of all things Quinn, including, to some extent, Dave Harris, had him half-expecting an ambush.

As yet, there had been no nasty surprises.

Harry had not taken any chances, though, and had had Dave followed some weeks back. Right now, Big Tony Parrish and another associate were parked up in front of his house with instructions to kidnap him should they not receive a message that Harry had been successful and was well out of the danger zone.

Harry knelt in front of a huge safe and worked away at the digits Dave had given him. He looked up at a nervous Ronny.

"Come on, Harry, get that Peter open or let's abort the operation. This gaff is seriously spooking me out."

As the last word left Ronny's mouth, the safe door sprung open to reveal its contents. The safe was almost completely full of notes. Only the top shelf was different. It was loaded with gold bars.

"Jesus wept. How much does this place take in seven days?"

"Who cares? I'm not their poxy bookkeeper," Ronny replied. "Let's just empty the bastard and get out of this place, sharpish!"

The two men set about loading up the holdalls. There was substantially more cash than Dave had let on. And he never mentioned gold bars. The two fruit machines would indeed prove to be handy.

Harry humped the now extremely heavy holdall towards the door.

Just as he went to walk out, a voice called out, "Hello? I say, hello?"

He bent down slowly, lowering the holdall to the floor as quietly as possible. He motioned to Ronny to stop what he was doing and both men removed their revolvers. As Harry slowly opened the door the sight of a little dog pelting past made him react, lifting his gun up just as the voice came again.

"Barney! Come here, you little bleeder!"

As Harry poked his head out the door, he spotted an old man coming through. He replaced his gun, gave Ronny a thumbs up without turning, and walked out, closing the door.

"Oh, hello. I'm so sorry to bother you. I was walking my dog along the alley and he managed to squeeze through your door, the little sod," the slightly breathless old man said. Hearing his master's voice, the dog had now returned and was sniffing and exploring Harry's leg.

Harry resisted the urge to tell it to piss off and kick it. "Ah, that's OK, mate. I thought I heard someone shouting. We are just finishing off fixing up a new fruit machine."

"Yes, I spotted a new machine by your van," said the old man, who had now picked up his little dog under his arm and was telling it off. "I'm so sorry for troubling you and stopping your work, particularly on a Sunday." He waved his finger at the dog. "Such a naughty boy, stopping this man working."

Harry walked out with the old man, still clutching his dog. "Nearly finished now, then home to my warm bed. Unfortunately, Sunday is the only night the casino is shut, so it's the best time for us to work."

The old man smiled then disappeared down the alley, still mumbling and tutting at his dog.

Harry and Ronny loaded the holdalls and the unexpectedly heavily-laden fruit machines into the van as quickly as they could. Both men were eager to get away from the building as quickly as possible, but Harry had one more thing to do. He decided to keep it to himself, for the time being, at least.

He gave the van keys to Ronny. "Start her up. I'm going back in to make sure we are one hundred per cent tidy in there."

"OK, Harry, but hurry up. We are seriously pushing our luck."

As Ronny walked around to the front of the van and out of sight, Harry opened a tool box and pulled out a sealed plastic bag containing the gun he'd taken off Vince Street the night he'd turned up at Nightingales screaming and waving it about.

Harry knew exactly where he was going. He turned in to one of the toilets, lifted the lid of a cistern in one of the many cubicles and tucked the package neatly inside before replacing the lid. On his way out, he took one last look in the Quinns' office. On the side, he spotted a photo of the pair and although he knew he should get the hell out of there, he couldn't resist one last gesture. He picked up a pen and drew moustaches on their faces, along with a pair of glasses on Johnny.

As the van pulled out onto the main road and out of sight of the casino, both men burst out laughing.

"Jesus, Harry, my nerves are shot!"

"Tell me about it! I shit myself when that dog flew past me. I nearly shot its bastard head off."

"How the bleedin' hell did we get away with that?"

"We haven't yet, mate. We are still in shark-infested waters here. Get this van over that pipe and back in North London a bit sharpish. Once we are back in safer territory, I'd better ring the club and leave a message for Big Tony that all is well. Harry looked at his watch. "I'm glad I allowed an extra three hours for his call, what with that unexpected haul, or poor old Harris would be trussed up like a Christmas turkey by now. Let's get rid of this van and get home. We will have a proper look tomorrow and a cut up. I've told Harris not to contact me about his share for a couple of weeks, to let things settle down a bit."

Ronny began laughing. "Tell you what, Harry, I'd love to see that pair of wankers' faces when they see that safe and zero sign of a break in. They'll think there is a gang of ghost blaggers in the area."

Harry turned to Ronny and remarked cautiously, "We could still have a war yet, Ronny, because of the fact there is no sign of a break in. Their whole firm will be under suspicion, including Dave Harris. We need him to hold his bottle, especially if that spiteful bastard Johnny goes to work on him. He would grass us right up."

Harry then burst out laughing as he revealed to Ronny that he had made some additions to the Quinns' office photos and both men laughed in unison as they felt the relief of getting home in one piece.

16.

Chrissy watched her husband walking towards her. Her slight exasperation at yet another phone call, always when they were against time, evaporated when she caught sight of him in his bespoke dark blue suit, a particular favourite of hers. She thought how handsome he looked. Immaculate. As she handed the receiver to him she tried her best to look annoyed, tapped her watch and rolled her eyes, mouthing "Hurry up".

Harry smiled, winked at her as he took the phone and whispered, "Who is it?"

"Dave," she whispered back and headed out of the room.

"Yes, yes, Dave, everything is sorted. But as we discussed previously, let it settle down for a while. It's not even been a week yet."

Harry could hear the panic in Dave Harris's voice. "Them two are going berserk down here, Harry. No one is free from suspicion. I want my cash and out of it before they start killing us all, one by one."

Harry resisted the urge to laugh. The mental picture he had of the Quinns' anger and frustration at the blatant liberty of a robbery on their property was causing him no end of amusement, but he needed to talk some sense into Dave.

"Use your loaf, mate. If you disappear now you will be number one on their list. Hold fire for just another couple of weeks, then I'll be in touch."

As Harry went to continue, Chrissy appeared in the doorway with Ray and Denny, and again, pointed at her watch and mouthed, "Come on." He still had Dave's voice in his ear as he signalled to his wife one minute.

"Two more weeks, Lane, and that's it. I want my cut."

Harry noticed the Lane, not Harry, and the tone in Dave's voice but didn't rise to it. "That's a promise, Dave. I'll be in touch. You've had my word from day one. I've got to go now, mate. I'm off up the West End with my wife, but trust me, you'll be more than happy with your share. Be patient, old son." Harry put the receiver down and promised himself he would try and put the Quinns, Dave and the robbery to the back of his mind and enjoy a rare night out with his wife.

Harry and Chrissy stood in the door of his mum's house as the waiting taxi's engine purred away patiently. Harry looked at his mum, who seemed to have aged suddenly and looked very tired. It shocked him, although he never gave his thoughts away as he spoke to her. Chrissy saw his mum most days and brought the boys in regularly, but he had to admit he had neglected his own visits lately, which suddenly filled him with guilt. The loss of his dad had been particularly hard for her. Although in their banter together it had sometimes sounded as if he was a nuisance, she had loved him deeply, and never really got over the loss of his sudden passing. Luckily, both Chrissy, who Molly loved as if she was her own daughter, and the boys kept her occupied, but he knew that in her quiet times she missed the sight and familiar company of his dad.

"Right, you two, you be good for your nan, you listening?" Harry said, looking at Ray and Denny who were standing either side of their nan. Both boys looked back at their dad, who seemed huge to them, and a mystery, as they saw him so much less than their mum.

Chrissy was, of course, with them practically twenty-four seven, and as she added her words, both their faces set still, the obvious sign that she was their main disciplinarian. "When nan says bed, it's bed. No arguments, you two."

"Yes, mum," came the dual reply.

Harry leaned forward and kissed his mum on the forehead.

"Thanks, mum. I'll be over first thing in the morning to pick them up."

Molly smiled. "No rush, boy. You two just go out and enjoy yourselves. These two are just fine."

Chrissy gave Molly a cuddle. "Thanks, mum." She then looked at the boys with a put-on stern look. "Don't forget, you two, no playing up, because I will know."

*

Harry and Chrissy walked out of the theatre and into the night air. It was a lovely mild evening and the West End was packed with revellers.

"Did you enjoy the show, love?" Harry asked, as he placed his hand gently on her waist.

"Yes, it was amazing. The music and dancers were incredible, Harry. It's funny, you know, although it's only really a few miles away from home, a night up west is so different and such a nice change."

Harry pulled Chrissy closer to him as he felt her body shiver slightly. Although it was mild, there was a gentle breeze and she was only in an evening dress.

"I love the lights and the ambience up here," she added.

He could tell the few glasses of champagne had made her very cheerful and she was in the moment as they strolled arm in arm.

"I'm thinking of looking for a building up here and opening another Nightingales." Chrissy giggled, which in turn made him smile. At that very moment she looked just like when they first started dating all those years ago.

"I love you, Harry," she said and rested her head on his shoulder.

He kissed the top of her head. "Unconditional, Chrissy Lane. Let's go and find a night cap, shall we, love?"

"Yes, let's. But Harry, can we try to at least find somewhere nobody knows you? Everywhere we go you have people coming over who want to chat." Although she protested, she did secretly love how her Harry was so well-known and respected.

Harry leaned forward and topped up Chrissy's flute before replacing the bottle back in the icebox.

"How does mum seem to you, love?" he asked.

"Mum's mum, darling. Why's that?" she replied.

"Don't know. She just looked really tired earlier. Guess it's because I don't see her every day. She is getting old, bless her."

They both sat quietly for a bit then Chrissy spoke. "Mum would never say anything, anyway. She is not one to complain." She started laughing. "She still goes shopping for Mrs Woods and she is younger than mum. We drop the boys at Mrs Woods' and go shopping together. She is a tough old girl, is mum," Chrissy added and they both laughed.

Chrissy's words cheered him up. His mum's appearance earlier had upset him, but now Harry felt totally relaxed and in the moment. He loved his wife's company on these nights out together.

But his heart sank as he looked across the room towards the entrance and caught sight of both Quinn brothers and two of their associates heading towards the bar.

"You've got to be joking," he said under his breath, but loud enough for Chrissy to hear.

"What's that, love?"

"Oh, nothing. Just your famous last words about me knowing people. Jesus, how many bars in London and they walk into this one. We can't get any peace."

Chrissy noticed Harry's change of mood and obvious agitation and looked in the direction of her husband's unblinking stare. She soon spotted the four men at the bar, and two in particular who looked very unhappy.

Harry caught the eye of Jamie Quinn first and suddenly felt uneasy and very vulnerable. He was out with his wife and not carrying a weapon. His mind raced to the recent events at the casino. What were these two here for? And what did they know?

Harry decided to offer a friendly wave across to Jamie as Johnny also spotted him. They had obviously told their two associates to stay put, as they remained at the bar as both Quinn brothers headed towards his table. Harry produced the fakest smile possible and greeted both men as warmly as he could, knowing his wife was watching him.

She was also the most streetwise woman he had ever known and the evil stare Johnny had locked on them both must have told her that these two were definitely not friends.

Harry stood up, followed by Chrissy. "Evening, lads. Nice surprise."

Jamie smiled. "Evening, Harry. And I'm guessing this is Mrs Lane?"

Although they had never been formally introduced, Harry knew full well that they knew who she was.

"Chrissy, this is Jamie and Johnny Quinn. Two business friends of mine."

Chrissy extended her hand to both men. "Lovely to meet you,

gentlemen, and I hope you don't think me rude, but I must go to the ladies. I'll leave you lads to catch up." She turned to Harry. "I just want to ring mum, to check all is OK with her and the boys."

"OK, love," he replied, not taking his eyes off the Quinns.

"Nice to see you spending money in one of our many concerns, Harry."

"One of yours, is it, Jamie? Very nice. We were just finishing off a lovely evening after a show. I like your style, boys, I really do. I give you your due, you're no mugs in regard to business."

Jamie could never tell if Harry was being sarcastic or not, so didn't bite as Johnny spoke.

"Too right we are, Lane. It's good you leave your little area from time to time to get a flavour of how the real kings of clubland run things."

"Funny you should say that, Johnny, because I'm considering a Nightingales in the West End."

Harry knew he was getting under their skin, as usual. He also knew that at the moment they had no idea he had cleared their safe. Jamie was clever, and even if he did know, Harry knew that he'd save it for a clever response. But there was no way Johnny would. He just wasn't clever or subtle enough, which he proved as he said with an evil smirk, "You seen anything of our Vince Street? He seems to have vanished."

Harry stared directly into Johnny's eyes. "I've not seen him since he made a spectacle of himself at my club."

"You sure about that? I heard he was using your club as a car park."

Johnny grinned but this statement brought an annoyed reaction from Jamie. He knew his brother had now basically told Harry who was behind the Vince Street situation.

As Chrissy returned to the table, Harry's reply totally threw Jamie and made him instantly paranoid.

"I had the police at my place asking about him. Told me that he was on the missing file. Obviously they had heard about his little outburst at the club. But honestly, I've not seen or heard anything from him since."

Harry felt Jamie's intense stare on him, looking for any signs of emotion.

"Right, Harry, we will leave you and your lovely wife to enjoy the rest of the evening," Jamie said. "No doubt we will chat again soon."

"Yes, I must get down to your casino for a night out, like I keep promising. I hear it's South London's finest venue and its flourishing."

Harry smiled and winked at Johnny who looked like he was near boiling point.

Harry and Chrissy decided to end the evening with a stroll along the embankment. The Thames and the lights of the City looked lovely.

"Thanks for such a wonderful night," Chrissy said, looking up at him. She then laughed. "You're getting lots of grey hair at the sides, Harry. I can see it under these street lamps."

He looked back at his happy wife and smiled. I should be white all over, the week I've had, he thought to himself.

"Shall we go home, Mrs Lane?" He wrapped his arm around her.

"Yes, let's," she replied, yawning contently as he hailed down a passing black cab.

17.

"So, you're telling me the truth and Lane is lying. Or you're lying and he's telling the truth. Either way, someone is a good liar and I'll find out who today."

Jamie Quinn was now looking directly at Dave Harris and Paul Baker. Usually, when dealing with any issues, Jamie was always the favoured brother to approach. He was definitely the least likely to react. But on this occasion, he was highly agitated. Dave's heart was racing as he tried to keep composed and not look guilty.

The heat was on everyone in the firm in regards to the robbed safe. But it's easy to be honest and truthful when you have no knowledge of an event. And, of course, nobody had but him. He was up to his eyeballs in it. He could feel Johnny's eyes on him now and his mind was racing.

What did these two know? And what was next?

"So, you left Street's car in Lane's car park and left unseen," Jamie asked again.

"Yes, of course. Exactly how you asked and as we explained before," Paul replied.

"Did you check again, to see if he was dead?" Jamie asked with a serious look until Johnny started laughing. Then he realised the stupidity of his question. In an unusual display of defeated confusion, he continued, "Well, what is Vince Street, then? A ghost?" His anger was obvious as he paced the room. "That flash prick Lane said he hasn't seen anything of Vince and even when Johnny practically told him we dumped his car at his place, there was zero reaction. Like he really knew zero about it."

Jamie lit a cigarette and passed it to Johnny, lighting another one for himself without offering one to either Paul or Dave. He took a long drag then, squinting at the two men, he blew the cloud of smoke in their direction and shook his head.

"So, you two dropped Vince's car off with his body in it, yet Lane is giving out like he is unaware of the appearance of an addition to his car park. Then a few days ago, our office safe is relieved of over a month's takings. Not to mention other extremely high value belongings."

Jamie turned his back to them and walked towards the window. He stared out through the blinds. Dave's thoughts had now turned from fear to working out what his percentage of the robbery would be. The Quinns had always banked and dispersed the casino's takings weekly, to his knowledge. Yet he had clearly heard Jamie say a month's worth. He now knew it was important to keep his cool and bluff his way through this. If he did, then he was in for a lot more than he had bargained for.

Dave's reverie was interrupted by Johnny, now standing in front of them with a grin on his face. It was a grin Dave was familiar with and again, his heart rate began to rise in anticipation of a spiteful outburst.

"See, my brother has got very paranoid since the robbery and thinks that Vince is haunting us from the grave and helped himself to our safe." He turned his highly intimidating stare away from them, much to their relief. "Under normal circumstances, I'd think my brother may be losing his marbles, thinking Vince had escaped and was getting his revenge. But Lane's reaction last night, and with no sign of a break in…it does make you think, doesn't it, boys?"

Jamie walked back from the window and both Quinns were facing the men now. "So, we're not stupid men, are we?" Jamie started, as he sat on the edge of his desk. "We know Vince is dead and he never robbed us. So that leaves you lot. An inside job. Or Lane. Those are my number one and number two suspects at the moment."

"This is ridiculous," Paul suddenly burst out. His tone surprised both the Quinns and Dave. "We took a massive risk ourselves, taking that body over the river. And Dave launched the keys. We done our job. I don't know anything after that, honestly, Jamie. We don't know anything. It's got to be Lane's doing."

Dave then turned to Johnny. "It's got to be, Johnny. Who else would have the bottle or expertise to get in here untraced?"

This seemed to cheer Johnny up, as he was itching to start a war with Harry Lane. But it angered Jamie. "Nothing adds up to me. Something just isn't right here."

Jamie was gritting his teeth together. A vein had visibly risen on his temple and Dave could actually see the thumping of his heartbeat.

As the overly agitated Jamie stood up, he noticed the picture frame on his desk was face down. He turned it up the right way without looking at it and muttered, "Bastard cleaners."

As he walked towards the two men, Dave caught sight of the picture. Johnny and Jamie in their best suits with taches and glasses drawn over their faces in marker pen. The intensity of the atmosphere in the room, then the sight of this, suddenly became too much. He couldn't control his nerves anymore and began laughing. Jamie stared at the sniggering Dave, saw where his gaze was directed and turned around to see the defaced picture of him and his brother.

He snapped.

Before he had time to control his actions, Jamie had removed his pistol from his jacket. Without rational thought, he spun around and pulled the trigger, sending a perfect shot straight through Dave Harris's face. The room fell hauntingly silent as the other three men stared in shock at the dead man's body, rapidly turning the office floor claret red.

A visibly merry Harry opened the front door, laughing at something Chrissy had just said to him, to find a very serious looking Ronny Piper stood before them on his doorstep.

"Ronny, my old mate," he said, smiling.

As Ronny went to speak, a giggling Chrissy appeared in the corridor and, slurring slightly, enquired, "Who is it, Harry?"

"It's Ronny, love."

"Do Ron Ron Ron, you do Ron Ron," she sang back, giggling and disappeared.

Ronny shook his head, rolling his eyes. "I need you two, don't I?"

Laughing again, Harry replied, "Me and Chrissy were enjoying a night cap. What brings you here this late, mate? You OK?"

"Well, I thought you might have heard, but obviously not. I've just left the Green Man and been told the Quinns have been nicked."

Harry's look quickly turned serious. "Come in, Ronny. Don't stand on the doorstep. Do you want a drink?"

"I'll have a quick scotch, Harry. I won't stay long. We'll have a proper chat over breakfast at Valentines tomorrow."

As Harry poured Ronny a drink, Chrissy came out of the kitchen and gave Ronny a kiss. "You OK, darling?" she asked, her smiling eyes slightly glazed.

"Yes, great thanks, Chrissy. Sorry to drop by so late, but I spotted your lights on and wanted to run something by Harry while it's still fresh in my mind."

"You're welcome any time, day or night, Ronny, you know that," she replied and headed back into their living room, both men smiling at her.

"So, what's occurred then, Ronny? Have the Old Bill decided to act on the case they have been building?"

As Ronny went to reply, he spotted two silhouettes on the stairs, just visible from the small amount of light being thrown out from the kitchen and living room. He nodded to Harry and whispered, "The boys are listening in."

Harry grinned and the men carried on chatting, pretending not to have noticed Ray and Denny had climbed out of bed when they heard Ronny's voice at the door. They were squatting on the stairs, peering through the railings, whispering and giggling.

The boys often did this when Harry and Chrissy had guests or a party and they were meant to be in bed, and of course Harry always played them and pretended he didn't know. Then he would pounce.

Harry suddenly turned round and ran towards the stairs, making monster noises as the boys scampered up the stairs. He caught them both and tickled them mercilessly as they both screamed and giggled.

"Right, you two reptiles, bed! If I catch you down these stairs again, I'll go and ring Big Tony up and get him to come around and fart on you both."

"Err, yuck! No!" Ray protested, both boys laughing as Harry tucked them in.

As Harry came back down, laughing, Ronny remarked, "Got your work cut out there, H."

"They're great kids, Ronny. Denny will be back again in a few minutes, you watch. That little sod's a nightmare. He tests the water," he said, laughing.

Ronny's expression became serious again as he quickly tried to bring the conversation back to what he had come to say. "The word is, one of the Quinns has shot one of their men dead. A passing beat policeman heard the shot and radioed through for back-up." Ronny drained his scotch and then continued. "Old Bill surrounded the place and they were banged to rights. No time to tidy their mess up and the body was in full view of them when they burst in."

"Jesus, Ronny, are you joking?" a surprised Harry asked and seemed to sober up instantly.

Ronny grinned as he spotted a singular silhouette appear at the stairs again. "Your Denny's back, Harry. I'll see myself out and see what else gives on the news front. I'll see you in the café first thing."

Harry grabbed a screaming and laughing Denny and slung him over his shoulder. "Right, you tyke, that's it," he said as he swung the bedroom door open. "What did I tell you two?"

"But I'm in bed!" Ray protested.

"I don't care," Harry replied as he lay Denny on the bed. "His punishment is yours as well."

Harry stood, looking at his grinning sons as he raised his leg up and farted. Both boys squealed with laughter as Harry waved his arms about to push the smell around the bedroom. He laughed as the boys both shouted, "Yuck!" and pulled themselves under their bed sheets.

He caught a smell of his own odour and had to laugh again as it was rotten.

"Now, sleep, you two! That was a warning shot. Any more noise from you and it's Big Tony treatment, and he will sit his big fat arse on your heads before farting!"

Harry left the room smiling as he heard his sons laughing from under their sheets.

18.

"Right, come on you two, we're off to your nan's," Chrissy declared as she entered the front room. "I've got to get the shopping in for us and your nan as well. She hasn't been well of late."

She heard a squeal and looked around to see her two boys going at each other full pelt with cushions from the sofa. Denny took a full swing and just caught sight of his infuriated mum in the doorway, hands on her hips. It was too late to stop the cushion's flight, though, and it slapped Ray straight across the face.

As Ray went to pull his cushion back to retaliate, he felt a slap across his backside.

A grinning Denny sniggered at him.

"Don't know what you're laughing at, you little sod." A now agitated Chrissy headed towards a wide-eyed Denny. "Are you not satisfied wrecking the pillows on your beds? You're setting about my bleedin' good cushions now!" Denny watched her closely, swerving left and right as she tried to grab him. He expertly set the pace until he spotted his gap and darted under his mum's arm. But she turned just in time to whack his arse with her palm, much to the delight of a laughing Ray.

Of course, Chrissy's anger was never much more than an act towards her boys, and the slaps not much more than a tap. Although she was a streetwise lady who took no nonsense from anyone, she truly doted on them both and although they were cautious not to get on her wrong side too often, they were wise to the fact they could play her and get her back on side quickly.

As the phone began ringing, she looked at them both sternly.

"Right, you two, no more. You play me up again and I'll tell your dad when he gets home, OK?"

With that, she turned and raced to the hallway to pick up the phone.

The boys continued to taunt each other as they heard their mum discussing plans with their nan.

"Molly love, that's great. I'll drop the boys off and you and me can go shopping."

Chrissy replaced the receiver and headed out the front door where the boys were already waiting out on the path.

"Come on, mum," Ray shouted. They loved going round to their nan's, as they knew that they would get fussed over and spoilt.

"That was your nan on the phone. She said she was feeling a little bit better today and wants some fresh air, so she is coming to town with me."

Chrissy heard no response to this and looked down to see Denny just about to pinch Ray's arm.

"You dare do that, you spiteful little sod," she warned. "I'm dropping you two around to Mrs Woods' house while me and your nan are out."

"I don't want to go around Mrs Woods' house, it stinks of piss," Denny whispered to Ray, but too loudly and Chrissy heard him.

Chrissy slapped the back of his head. "Oi, I heard that, you bugger. Don't be nasty about your nan's friend."

"Why can't we come to the shops with you and nan?" Denny complained, scowling.

Ray tugged him by his jumper and pulled him closer, whispering, "Shut up, Denny. Mrs Woods gives us money and sweets, don't forget. Be quiet."

Denny looked up at his older brother and nodded. "OK."

Chrissy was itching to laugh at Denny's comment about old Mrs Woods, but kept up the masquerade of annoyance. "Right, you two, last warning. I don't want to hear any more of your old gallop. Now you be good boys and we can have some lunch at your nan's when we get back from the shops, OK?"

"Yes mum," came the duel reply.

She looked at them both and inwardly felt so proud of them and so content with her current life.

Ronny Piper banged his cigarette packet on the table to loosen the contents up and pulled one out. As he went to put it to his lips, he paused.

"Well, I'd say that's a hundred per cent confirmation, H. Jamie Quinn has murdered Dave Harris."

Harry was looking at Ronny pensively and was slow to reply. "Yeah, of all their gang to kill, it was Dave. That's either done us a right favour, or put us right in the shit if he grassed us up for emptying their Peter before they ironed him out."

Ronny drew heavily on his cigarette as Anna delivered their teas with the usual complimentary biscuits on the side. Anna was the youngest of the two Vital daughters and equally as attractive, although not as aware and flirtatious as Valentine.

Ronny stared at her in lust and Harry laughed.

"Put your tongue away, Ronny, for God's sake. We probably look like old men to them two."

"Turn it in, Harry. You saying you wouldn't?" Ronny grinned.

"Whether I could or not, I wouldn't," Harry replied. "Only one lady for me, mate. Always has been, always will be." He took the little packet of biscuits from the saucer and placed them in his jacket pocket. "You having them biscuits, mate?"

Ronny looked at the biscuits on his saucer and handed them to Harry who added them to the others in his pocket.

"That'll do mum. She loves these ones with her evening cuppa."

"How is Molly?"

Harry looked slightly concerned. "She hasn't been too great at all of late, mate. But she never says anything, bless her." He took a mouthful of his tea. "To be honest, I feel a bit guilty, really. I don't get around as much as I should. Luckily, Chrissy is there pretty much every day. They are out shopping now."

"Good old girl. At least she gets out and about," Ronny remarked, smiling.

Harry lightened up at that statement. "Yeah, I'll drop in tonight on the way home and have a catch up."

Ronny pressed his cigarette butt into the ash tray on the table and blew the last of the smoke into the air. The café was buzzing with the usual pre-work breakfast crowd and the door seemed to be opening and shutting constantly as satisfied customers were replaced by a new, hungry and eager-looking bunch of people.

"What's your thoughts then, H? Do you think we had a touch or not?"

Harry shook his head slowly and answered, "Well, that I don't know, old son. Time will tell. If old Harris has gone to his grave with his knowledge with him, then yes. If he put our names in the frame before he took the bullet, then the Quinns know. Although, no doubt my name will be on their lips anyway."

Harry looked around the café at all the other customers and took in their appearance and general attitude.

"Tell you what, Ronny. Either way, we have pushed our luck long enough. I think it's time we joined this lot, the straight crowd."

Ronny glanced across the room, then back at a serious-looking Harry. "So, what you saying?"

"What I'm saying, Ronny," he said, taking another sip of tea before carrying on. "Old Bradshaw told me the Quinns were going down soon. And now they have been caught bang to rights for Harris, I doubt even they will be out again now, even with their connections."

Ronny nodded in agreement. "That's true. If the Old Bill had decided to shut them down then, paying off bent coppers wasn't going to work. And now Harris. They are totally bollocksed."

Harry laughed, which made Ronny laugh as well.

"What is it, H?"

"Just thinking how much we are riding our luck lately. And that the Quinns have saved us paying Harris's cut." But he then paused and looked at Ronny again, very straight-faced. "Bradshaw warned me to use my loaf from now on, said the top bodies wanted to clean the streets up. And the human bluebottle Roswell is always on to us, the snidey bastard."

Ronny lit up another cigarette and drew heavily on it. As he spoke, he exhaled the smoke away from Harry. "So, time to throw the towel in then, you reckon?"

"Yes I do, Ronny," Harry replied, pushing his finished cup away. "Neither of us are getting any younger. We both have legitimate businesses, wives and kids and plenty of dough tucked away."

Ronny was listening and nodding as Harry continued.

"We are going into a new decade, and my instincts are telling me to get out before my…" He looked directly at his friend. "…our luck runs out."

With that, Ronny stood up, followed by Harry. As they shook hands, Ronny began laughing.

"Right, Harry, I'm off to the council. Put my name down for an allotment and then off to join the Lawn Bowls Club."

Both men laughed.

Harry stood on the door step of his mum's house. He had rung the doorbell twice, but still got no reply. Although he had his own keys, he liked to knock these days, rather than just walk in, especially when it was late and dark outside, in case he made her jump.

Careful not to trample on his mum's flower bed - her pride and joy - he walked across to her front window and looked through the gap in the curtains. He saw that the lights were on and the television was flickering. His mum was in her usual chair, facing the television, but her head was turned away, so he guessed she had nodded off.

He let himself in and as he shut the door behind him, he shouted out, "Mum, mum it's me, Harry."

He walked into the front room, looking at the back of his mum's chair, the television seemingly talking to itself.

"Mum? You awake?"

No response.

Harry sat in silence in his dad's old chair and stared at his mum. Her hands were resting on her lap, one on top of the other. Her head was resting on the back of the chair where he had lifted it and gently closed her eyes. She looked so peaceful, which gave Harry some degree of comfort, knowing that she had passed away peacefully while sitting relaxing in her chair.

He looked away and up at the clock on the mantlepiece and suddenly realised how late it was and how long he had been sitting there in dazed shock.

"Oh, Mum," he said to himself.

He stood up.

"Chrissy, oh Chrissy," he mumbled.

19.

"Plenty more boxes and crates out the back if you need, Harry," Antonio said, smiling.

Harry returned the smile, but Antonio could see the tiredness and sadness in his eyes. It had been two weeks since Molly's funeral and Harry and Chrissy were setting about the task of clearing her house out. It was proving to be very stressful and upsetting for them all.

Harry was just about to close the boot of his car when he heard the familiar and seriously unwanted voice of Burt Roswell, who had just pulled up and was stepping from his own car.

"Morning, lads. Don't close that boot yet, Harry, not until I've inspected the contents, will you?"

Without speaking, Harry slowly shook his head, looking at Antonio, who tutted and headed back towards the café.

"Ask the girls to put me a bacon sarny and a cuppa in, Antonio, there's a good chap," Burt called out to him.

Antonio mumbled something under his breath, shaking his head as he walked into a steam-filled and, as usual, packed Valentines.

Burt looked at the cardboard boxes laid across the seats and the wooden crates in the boot. "Dropping off stolen goods, or off to fill with stolen goods, Lane?"

Harry's anger-filled eyes soon told him that he had touched a nerve. "I'm currently in the process of clearing my mother's house out, Burt. Antonio has been giving me his old fruit and veg boxes, if you want to put that in your notebook," he replied in an exasperated tone.

Burt seemed to get the message that, on this occasion, his banter wasn't appropriate. Molly had been a decent old lady, in fairness, and even Harry Lane deserved to grieve in peace. "I think I can hear my bacon sarny calling, so I'll leave you to get on."

He started to walk away, then stopped.

"Oh, by the way…" He turned and looked at Harry, who now looked straight back at him with such intensity it actually unsettled him. It was a look that told him why people were very respectful of Harry, and also confirmed that he was extremely capable of all the things Burt suspected him of. Proving that, of course, was a different matter. "I thought you might be interested to know that on a search of the Quinns' premises, Vince Street's handgun was found in one of the toilet cisterns."

Burt looked for a reaction, but Harry knew that he was and feigned disinterest. "Them lot hold no interest to me, Burt, particularly in the current climate."

Burt watched him intensely. "Indeed, Harry, indeed. Well, they are going away for a long, long time. The murder of David Harris is at the top of a crime list so long Al Capone would blush."

"Like I said Burt, I need to get on. The Quinns are no concern of mine." With that, Harry closed the boot and headed round to the driver's side, still watched by Burt.

"Well, the gun has been identified as Street's and half the firm have turned Queen's evidence on them. Trouble is, Harry…"

Harry had the driver's door open now, and looked over at a grinning Burt. He showed no sign of it, but felt anxious about what was coming next.

"…as yet, one gun belonging to Street. But still no body. And no car, come to think of it." Burt paused for what seemed an eternity, then added, "But like you say, Harry, nothing to do with you, that lot, eh?"

He gave Harry a knowing look then turned away and continued towards the café.

Harry taped up another box of his parents' possessions and wrote on the top with his marker to indicate the contents. He reflected on how much people could accumulate over the years, and equally just how little his parents really had to show for a lifetime.

As he slid open various drawers, cupboards and wardrobes, and went through various rooms, he found items that had no doubt been long-forgotten and also things that brought memories of his childhood flooding back. There were some things that, as a child, had fascinated him and what had seemed large then, now appeared small. He could hear his mum's voice in his head. "Put that down before you break it!" "Get out of that cupboard, you little sod!" The source of much wonder as a child now seemed tiny. Cupboards he would crawl into, the airing cupboard where the towels were stacked neatly on the shelf and the washing was put to dry on rainy days. There was his play room, as well, with a spare bunk bed and a toy cupboard built on the side by his dad. Hours and hours had been whiled away there, playing games and getting lost in childhood imagination.

He picked up a framed photograph of his parents' wedding day from the sideboard and stared at it. He sighed to himself and took a cloth, wiping the glass, before wrapping it tenderly to protect it in transit. He took the wind-up ceramic figurine of a dancing couple and inspected it. This little ornament had been in the house for as long as he could remember, another source of fascination for him as a boy, much to his mum's annoyance. He looked at the hairline crack down it, where his dad had glued it back together after he had dropped it.

He heard Chrissy shout up the stairs, asking if he wanted a cup of tea. She was clearing things out downstairs. He noticed how her voice echoed as she shouted, the house now almost empty and cold, having lost all of its homely feel. He heard her voice echo up the stairs a second time, but didn't reply.

As her footsteps approached, Harry turned the now rusty key in the back of the dancing couple, then placed it on the sideboard and watched as it moved along the sideboard for a bit, then spun a full circle then reversed back to where it had started before spinning again. *Don't let the sun catch you crying* played from the radio Harry had placed on the sideboard.

Suddenly he was overcome and he choked up and started to cry.

Chrissy stood momentarily in the doorway, looking at her husband on his knees, weeping. She had never seen Harry cry before. He had never shown emotion like this, even in past grief.

She rested her hands gently on his shoulders and kissed the top of his head. He reached his arm out as she sat down next to him on the bare floor. They sat in silence and cuddled each other for a while before he spoke.

"Just me and you now, kid."

"And us," a little voice said and they both turned to see Denny in the doorway, Ray a little way behind him.

Harry smiled and felt himself cheer up at the sight of his sons.

"Come here, boys," he said, stretching his arms out.

Both boys squatted down and Harry pulled them in close, so he had both of them and his wife wrapped in his arms.

"Us four against the world, what do you think, boys?"

Both lads nodded in agreement.

"We are the Lanes. Don't you ever forget that, boys. We stick together." He looked directly at Ray and Denny. "You must always look after each other. Never ever forget that. And most importantly, you look after your mum and protect her against everything."

Chrissy smiled. "Come on, my men, let's go get a well-deserved cuppa."

"You look tired, love," Chrissy said, watching Harry as he taped up another box.

"I'm OK, love. At least we've pretty much broken the back of it," he replied before tearing another piece of tape from the reel with his teeth. "I expect the lads are getting hungry anyway, so we'll call it a day soon."

"They went off over that green to play football. I hope they are not smothered in mud when they get back," Chrissy said under her breath just as a solemn looking Ray came in the room. "Oh, that's handy. Saves me coming to look for you," she said when she spotted him. "Where's your brother? We're going soon."

Ray just mumbled something and looked at the floor.

"What's up with you, Ray?" she asked.

Again, he mumbled. "Nothing."

Harry walked past him to pick up another empty box and rubbed his son's hair. "Cheer up, cocker. What's up, mate?"

Ray looked up at his dad. "The big kids took our ball."

Harry looked at him. "Where are they?"

"Down on the green," an upset Ray answered.

"Right, go down into your grandad's shed. There's an old cricket bat down there. Go back down that green and put it over that kid's head and get your ball back."

Chrissy tutted as she pulled another drawer out. "Don't tell him that, Harry. He will do it!"

Denny was standing just outside the door, listening as his dad replied, taping another box.

"I want him to do it. That bullying prick who has their ball won't do it again then, will he?"

"Let it go this time, Ray," Chrissy said. "I don't need any hassle, darling, not with everything. I'll buy you another ball."

Ray looked up at his dad, sheepishly. Harry tore another piece of tape off the roll with his teeth.

He looked huge as he spoke again. "I want my boys to always deal with bullies and take no shit, the earlier the better."

Chrissy looked at him pleadingly and mouthed, "Not today, please."

She winked, which made him sigh and shake his head. "Alright Ray, go get your brother and then stay here, the both of you. Don't go adrift again," he said, smiling at his son.

Albert Chambers looked up from his push and pull lawn mower as a young lad marched past his garden carrying an old cricket bat that was nearly as big as the boy himself. The stern look on the lad's face made Albert stop what he was doing. He removed a handkerchief from his pocket and wiped the sweat off his brow as he watched Denny Lane disappear round the corner, dragging the bat behind him. Being a big cricket fan, old Albert was very familiar with the sound of willow hitting a ball, but the sound he heard shortly afterwards was totally different.

The dull thud was followed by an agonised scream. Moments later, a much larger and older lad came running by, howling, with tears streaming down his face, followed by Denny Lane, marching back from whence he came, now holding both the cricket bat and a football.

As old Albert went back to mowing his lawn, he thought to himself that this young lad needed to learn the finer points of cricket.

But he had clearly mastered the art of dealing with older bullies.

20.

1972

"Give us some of your sweets!"

Ten-year-old Patrick Corrigan had been happily standing in his own little world, munching away on a packet of Spangles, when the clearly older voice interrupted his reverie.

Patrick felt dread creep over him as he looked up at the two faces towering above him. He recognised them as two fourteen-year-olds from the local area. To Patrick they may as well have been grown men. One of the lads poked Patrick in the chest, sending him into a garden hedge. The force of the shove made his duffel coat open, revealing pockets stuffed full of an assortment of sweets, chocolate bars and crisps.

One of the lads grabbed his collar and twisted it. Laughing, he said, "You're like a walking sweet shop. Let's see what you have for us."

Patrick tried to make a run for it, but the other lad stuck his arm out and blocked him.

Ray and Denny lane walked along the road, both still laughing and well pleased with their earlier efforts. They had thrown bricks and stones through as many windows as they could at the rival school, St Peter's. Denny had thrown one brick so hard it had gone right through the window in the science block and landed in a fish tank on a desk with such perfect force that it had shattered the glass without breaking it. The water within, and its aquatic occupants, were still intact, but any movement was sure to send the tank's contents cascading out across the classroom. The thought of this occurrence happening when the caretaker or a teacher saw the tank was gleefully being pointed out to Ray by a laughing Denny as they turned the corner right into the path of a struggling Patrick and the two older boys.

Although Ray and Denny were only ten and eleven themselves, their dad had already instilled in them a confidence and togetherness that was well respected within their age group in the area. But these two lads were huge in comparison.

Patrick was at the point of tears as the contents of his pockets were raided. He looked up as he heard the voice of little Ray Lane.

"Leave him alone!"

The two older lads spun around to see the Lanes looking at them.

"Ah, this is the full gang then, is it?" one of the lads said, gleefully.

"You get nothing off us, and leave him alone," Ray replied.

"Oh yeah? What you going to do, you pair of little shits? Sort us out?" the other big lad said. His voice was changing pitch from high to low, at the point of breaking.

"No, but my dad will sort you out when he sees you. No one messes with our dad," a now red-faced Denny shouted. Both the older boys laughed, which instantly sent Denny into a rage. 'No one laughs at us,' he said to himself, and clenched his fists.

One of the big lads grabbed a couple of bars of chocolate and a packet of crisps from Patrick and said to his mate, "Come on, let's go."

Both lads walked away from Patrick and, as they did, one grabbed Ray and pushed his face up close to him.

"You little shits watch yourselves when we are about."

As they both laughed, Denny leapt in the air, swinging his little fist with all his might into the side of the lad's jaw. Even with the age gap and their size difference, it was a perfect shot and shook the life out of the lad. He held his cheek, which was now coming out in a clearly visible red mark.

At that moment, he looked up and saw the familiar car belonging to Burt Roswell pulling up on the opposite side of the road. Burt had watched it all unfold as he had driven down the street towards the commotion.

The lad alerted his friend and it didn't take them long to make the decision to cut their losses and run.

Denny, Ray and Patrick did the same, but in the opposite direction. As the three boys ran, Patrick directed them.

"Come on, you two, follow me."

"Where we going?" Ray shouted back.

Patrick led them down an alleyway and into an area full of allotments and sheds. He stopped them at a shed, fished into his back trouser pocket, pulled out a key and opened the door.

"Come in, gentlemen," Patrick said, smiling.

All three walked into the shed which had a sofa up against the wall, an old cabinet and a dartboard on the back of the door. Patrick opened the cabinet and took out three bags of crisps and three cans of Top Deck Shandy, handing one each to Ray and Denny.

"Thanks for helping me out there. I'm Patrick."

"I'm Ray and this is my brother, Denny," Ray replied as Denny surveyed the shed.

"This is brilliant," Denny said. "Is it yours?"

"It's old Mr Roberts' shed. He has two, but never uses this one, so he lets me use it as my hideaway as long as I get his tobacco." Patrick switched on a radio that sat on top of the cabinet. "Make yourselves at home, boys." He pointed at the old sofa. Both Lane brothers laughed. Patrick was funny and used terms like their mum and dad did, which he had obviously picked up himself hanging around adults.

The shed had a musty smell to it and the sofa had foam sprouting from splits in the fabric, but it was super comfortable and the window let in just enough light. The Lanes had built their fair share of camps in the woods, but this was amazing to them.

"I can't believe you smacked that older boy in the mouth. We're dead when they see us next," Patrick said, looking concerned. Both Lanes laughed dismissively. They were totally in the moment, eating their crisps and drinking their shandies.

The boys chatted away, getting acquainted. They learnt that Patrick went to St Peter's school.

Denny laughed out loud. "You may be a bit cold at school on Monday"

"Why?" replied Patrick as he opened a drawer in the cabinet and took out a packet of ten Number 6 cigarettes and a box of Swan Vesta matches, offering the Lanes a cigarette each.

Denny already knew Patrick could be trusted, so proceeded to tell how they had smashed the school's windows earlier. The three boys roared with laughter.

"Where do you get the sweets and cigarettes from?" Ray asked.

"I nick them, of course, and old Mr Roberts' Old Holborn. That's why he lets me use this shed. Stand up, Denny." Patrick instructed Denny to lift the cushion, which he duly did.

Denny couldn't believe his eyes as he caught sight of a handful of top shelf magazines. He giggled as he handed one to Ray. "Nude books, Ray! Look, look!"

Patrick locked up the shed and the boys headed off. "You won't tell anyone about the shed, will you?" he asked, looking pleadingly at the Lanes.

"No, as long as we can come here as well," Denny said.

Patrick agreed readily. He liked the Lanes and had already seen enough, with Denny belting the big lad, to not want to receive the same treatment.

The boys strolled along the road, chatting happily and sealing their new friendship. They were in their own little world. So much so that they didn't notice the seemingly ever-present car of Burt Roswell crawl up beside them.

Burt wound down his window. "Afternoon, men. Don't dream of running away again, or I'll be at your parents' house waiting for you before you arrive."

The boys looked at him as he stopped the car. "Get in the back," he ordered, shaking his head.

"But we ain't done anything wrong," Denny protested.

"Well, you have nothing to worry about then, have you, Rocky Marciano? Now button your lip and get into the car."

The boys sat in the back of Roswell's car. He had to smile to himself as he eyed them in the mirror, all six eyes staring back at him in quiet fury.

"My mum and dad always told us not to get into cars with dodgy men," Ray said.

"Well, you keep listening to your dad, son, and this will not be the last time you are in the back of a police car, of that I have no doubt."

Ray turned to Denny and whispered, "No wonder the old man calls him the human bluebottle."

Roswell heard, but didn't respond.

"What we supposed to have done, then?" Denny asked.

"Yeah," added Patrick, feeling brave and not wanting to be left out.

"Nothing, but I decided I want you off the streets for the rest of the day, and that's the end of it. Now button your lip, or I'll inform your parents you've been smoking."

"No we ain't!" Patrick started.

"The back of my car smells like a tobacconist's shop," Roswell responded.

"So what? When we get in our mum has a cigar and a glass of whisky waiting for us with our dinner," Ray said cockily, which started Patrick giggling. His smile promptly dissipated as his dad's builder's yard came into sight, Corrigan Developments displayed on a huge sign.

"So, I'll drop you off at your dad's then, shall I?" Roswell asked, looking at the boy's expression in his mirror. "No, I thought not."

They continued on a little further then Patrick got out of the car at his house. "See you at base tomorrow, lads." He smiled at the Lanes.

"Go on, hop it, you little sod," Roswell said and pulled away.

As Roswell's car arrived at the Lane house, Harry was struggling up the garden path with a giant Christmas tree. Lowering the tree at the doorstep, he heard Roswell's voice and just spotted his two sons fly past him and straight upstairs. As he turned around, he got a mouthful of needles and a watering eye, which amused the grinning Roswell who now stood in front of him.

"Ho, ho, ho, Harry," he quipped.

Harry couldn't decide what exasperated him more. Roswell's presence, or the knowledge that his sons had darted so quickly up the stairs so that they could take it in turns washing their hands and brushing their teeth before their mother could catch the odour of cigarettes, having been escorted home by the human bluebottle himself.

"Nice to see you're back doing the sort of policing suited to your level, Burt. Children nicking sweets and rescuing old lady's cats from trees."

"Well, just because I'm the sheriff in this area, doesn't mean I can't lend a hand to my deputies from time to time."

"Yeah, alright, you smug bastard. What have they been up to, anyway?" Harry said, brushing bits of Christmas tree off his clothes.

"Well, as far as I know, nothing. Although when they saw me first, they were off like rockets. I caught up with them later."

"So, what's with the door-to-door taxi service, then?"

Roswell explained to Harry the fight he'd witnessed earlier. Harry's mood lightened and he felt pride as he heard they had stopped Declan Corrigan's son getting bullied and had got stuck into two older lads.

As Roswell walked away, he turned back and smiled at Harry. "Drop your lads down the gym. They're old enough now and there's potential there. Especially Denny. If I can calm his temper, that is. Does Santa know you thieved his tree?" He added with a chuckle.

21.

Chrissy smiled to herself as she watched her husband from the front room window heading off down the road flanked either side by her two sons. Both seemed to be growing by the day and, if she did say so herself, they were a very good-looking pair. She was proud of them both, especially how they looked out for each other. She had noticed recently that they were developing very different personalities, but were also very similar in many ways. In her own words, they were her special boys, and not like other families' children. They were both leaders and it had definitely been instilled into their brains that they should respect people. That they understood that they should never bully or be bullied was evident by the reputation they had in the area.

She lingered at the window a little longer, proudly watching all three striding down the road together and out of sight and said to herself as she turned away, "My three boys, the Lanes."

As the Lanes headed towards Antonio's barber shop, Ray couldn't believe his eyes. Coming towards them was the older boy who Denny had whacked, with a man he guessed must be his dad.

Ray dropped back behind his dad, leaned across and tugged his brother's arm. "Look, Denny, it's that big boy you chinned."

Just at that moment, Denny and the older lad's eyes met. The older boy then spotted who the boys were with, and was old enough to be fully aware of exactly who Harry Lane was. He was now filled with dread at the prospect of the incident from the other day being brought up.

Harry smiled at the man in front of him and offered his hand, which was met with a shake.

"Hello, Fred," Harry said.

The man smiled and returned a hello, then turned to his son, who was looking at Harry in fearful anticipation. Before Fred could prompt his son to show some respect, Harry had already offered his hand.

"Hello, son."

"Hello, Mr Lane," came the lad's sheepish reply, which was noted by Ray and Denny. They looked at each other, grinning, then looked up at the lad. He looked at Denny and Ray before settling his gaze on Denny, who's little eyes were searing through him with victorious malice.

Denny was smiling because he now knew that there would be no repercussions from the previous incident. He was now thoroughly enjoying the obvious discomfort their presence was causing this lad, and cherishing how the tables had fully turned from the other day. He was also beginning to realise, more and more each day, just what his dad's name meant in the area, and the respect it would afford him.

Even at such a young age, Denny was starting to enjoy the power fear could bring. Although he saw that others seemed to show them more respect when in his father's company, he didn't yet really understand why. All he knew was he liked it, and he had already decided he intended to maintain this power his family's name seemed to invoke.

As Denny tried to goad the older lad, who was now bowing his head down, trying to avoid eye contact, Ray was listening intently to his dad and Fred's conversation. Like his younger brother, Ray had also realised that, for some reason, the name Lane held fear and respect in equal measure. He was also now realising that the name was also synonymous with business and money. Ray listened to his dad in total admiration, and just like Denny, felt something change in him.

"So, you want three colour televisions and a couple of Christmas trees still, Fred?"

"Yes please, Harry, that will be fantastic. My missus will be over the moon. We'll be the only ones on our street with a colour TV." Fred turned to his son and said, "You make sure you keep your trap shut to your mum about this. It's a surprise."

Ray smiled to himself as he was aware that they always seemed to have things other families didn't, but his mum had told them both they were not allowed to ever show off, and also to share things with the other children.

"Right, drop over to Nightingales later and we can finalise things," Harry said as he stretched his arms out around his sons. "Off to the barbers. Get these two's haircut sorted before Christmas."

This statement annoyed Ray slightly, as he wanted to feel older and in on his dad's business deals. Instead, the fact that he and his brother were being taken to the barbers made him feel childish.

Fred and Harry shook hands and Ray's mood lightened again as he heard the older lad address his dad as Mr Lane again. As they all parted company, Denny's devilish grin was fixed firmly on the red-faced lad to the bitter end.

Antonio smiled at Ray and Denny as he tucked his barber's cloak around Harry's clothes.

"You OK, boys? You wanna drink of anything before I start on your old man's hair?"

The boys both politely declined. They were heading off to Patrick's shed straight after their haircuts and knew there was plenty of stock there, so did not want any of Antonio's. The boys were always on their best behaviour at Antonio's and Maria's, as Harry had always said that the Vitals were to be respected as if they were family. Plus, Denny had a huge crush on both Antonio's daughters, which made him particularly polite towards the Vitals. The liberal supply of top-shelf magazines readily available at the shed were only fuelling his fantasy towards the two girls.

Denny caught sight of the packets of condoms on the shelf next to jars of Brylcream. He nudged Ray and giggled. "I'd like to be able to use them on Valentine and Anna," he whispered.

Ray laughed and replied, "Your nob's too small. They would fall off." They both giggled.

Harry looked at his two boys in the mirror. "What you two reptiles laughing at? Behave, or I'll get Antonio to give you both bald heads, right down to the wood."

"No!" both boys protested as Harry winked at Antonio.

"They are knocking about with Declan Corrigan's boy, Patrick, now," Harry told Antonio.

Denny looked at Ray. "How did he know that?" he asked.

"Don't know," Ray replied.

"The old man's a legend. He knows everyone and everything," Denny said, grinning.

"I bet it was the bluebottle that told him," Ray said and they both grinned.

"I don't think I know this Declan," Antonio commented as he trimmed Harry's eyebrows.

"Yeah, maybe not. He lives a few miles away. Runs a builder's firm." Harry smiled and shook his head slightly. "More dead men on his jobs than there is in Highgate cemetery."

Antonio stopped what he was doing and looked at Harry's reflection. "Dead men? What you mean, dead men?"

Harry laughed at Antonio's worried expression and the boys were now listening with wide eyes. "Don't worry, old son. It's just an old saying. He paused to see the look of relief on Antonio's face, which made him laugh. "Basically, without going into too much detail, when he prices up and puts men out on subcontracted jobs, he always books in a couple of men that aren't there and pockets their wages for himself. Only on the really big jobs for wealthy companies, of course. They don't even notice the missing money."

Ray smiled to himself. He loved listening to his dad's stories. It really excited him and he loved the mystery of it all.

Harry pulled some notes from this pocket, enough for his and the boys' haircuts, and, as always, a very generous tip. This, again, was noted by Ray, who was in awe of his dad. His presence, his clothes, his style, the way people acted around him. He wanted to emulate him.

Denny was already up in the chair, waiting for his haircut and again, eyeing the condoms with thoughts of Anna and Valentine that really were far too naughty for a ten-year-old boy.

"Right, you two, I'm off to see a man about a dog," Harry said. This was a saying he had often used over the years when he was off out and the boys inquired where he was going. They were old enough and wise enough now to know he wasn't seeing a man about a dog and they weren't getting a pet. But they always wondered where their dad was off to and what he was doing.

As Antonio started Denny's haircut, Ray was trying to catch his brother's attention and make him laugh. Denny forced himself not to laugh as he caught sight of Ray in the mirror with his fingers placed either side of his nose in a V sign, moving them up and down his face, grinning.

Harry turned back around before leaving the shop and Ray quickly removed his fingers from his face and tried to look serious.

"Remember what I said. Any lip while I'm gone and Antonio has full instructions to whip your hair right down to the bone. And eyebrows too." He looked across at Antonio and winked as both Ray and Denny giggled.

Harry opened the front door and shouted out for his wife, who poked her head around the door.

"Are the boys in?" he asked.

"No, still out street raking, the little sods," she replied.

"Good," he muttered under his breath as he headed back out to a waiting van. "OK, Barry," he said to a man standing by the back, "let's grab them bikes while the boys are out."

Barry pulled the back of the van open and lifted down the two brand new Raleigh Choppers. Harry handed him a bundle of notes, exchanged a few words, then proceeded to wheel the bikes into the house.

Chrissy looked at the bikes then at her husband who was smiling.

"Great, ain't they, love? These are the brand-new models, just out. I might get one for myself."

She looked at him and rolled her eyes. "It wouldn't surprise me at all if you did. You are like a big kid at times."

He winked at her and smiled. "You wouldn't have me any other way."

This made her laugh. "Go on, you silly old sod, you had better go and hide them before them two get in."

"I'll whack them up in the loft out of the way until Christmas."

"Yes, you do that. And I don't even want to bleeding know where you got them," she added.

He looked at her, then up at the ceiling as he made the sign of the cross, then looked at her again with a pleading, innocent look. They both burst out laughing.

22.

Ray sat on the sofa in the secret shed, watching his brother and Patrick stuffing their faces with the last of their stolen stash of sweets. Both brothers were now firmly involved in Patrick's shoplifting sprees but until now, other than providing old man Roberts with his tobacco to pay rent on their hideout, they had only stolen for themselves.

Watching Denny devouring a Curley Wurley as he flicked through the pages of Razzle magazine and Patrick chomping handfuls of Walkers crisps and a Marathon bar, Ray decided things needed to change. He had watched his dad and listened to his conversations and the bits he had understood told him that making money would be the key to their success.

"Next time we load up on stock, we keep just enough for ourselves and the rest we take into school and sell," Ray suddenly exclaimed without much reaction. Denny was engrossed in his magazine and Patrick in his sweets. Slightly aggravated, he stood up. "You two listening?"

"Yes," Patrick replied and proceeded to hold his crisp packet over his mouth and tip the last of the contents straight down his throat in one go. It was a habit that, when witnessed by his mother, resulted in a clip around the ear, but in the shed the boys did as they pleased.

"What are we going to do with the money when we sell our sweets?" Patrick asked.

Denny looked up from his magazine, grinning. "Me and Ray are going to save ours. You can go and buy some more sweets with yours."

This made Ray laugh. "Let's just see how many are interested when we go back to school after Christmas and we have more stock."

The boys locked the shed up and headed off in their separate directions. It was Christmas Eve and they were all getting excited now. The Lanes loved the atmosphere at their house, as there were always people coming and going. Patrick explained he always had his relatives over for Christmas, so wouldn't be allowed out, but arranged to meet up on Boxing Day. He was too embarrassed to tell Ray and Denny that he had to go to church with his mum and dad, or that he was an altar boy, but he was too scared to ever complain to his parents about his religious duties. He had also decided, in his ten-year-old mind, that his altar boy sacrifice would balance out his sweet stealing in the eyes of God.

Ray and Denny strolled along the High Street, both in contented agreement that Ray's plan to sell what they stole was a great idea. They decided that, to make it work, they needed to steal much more and more regularly to meet the demand the excited boys were convinced they were about to have. They also agreed their faces were probably becoming too familiar in the shops they had been fleecing and would need to search out other places to add to the list.

Woolworths was one of their favourites, as they knew who the store detective was and he was useless, so they had zero fear in there. And as they passed it, Denny laughed when they noticed the hapless guard through the window, trying to chat up one of the young girls at her till.

"Look at Joe Ninety, the four-eyed tosser," Denny jeered and banged on the window, getting the attention of the tall, skinny, be-spectacled store detective who looked out at the two boys making faces at him and laughing.

The detective turned away slowly, reddening and trying to ignore them. The girl at the till had spotted them and was grinning at their antics, much to his annoyance.

It was a particularly cold afternoon, but as the day's natural light gave way to darkness, the fresh, freezing air didn't bother the boys at all. It was Christmas Eve and as the Christmas lights came to life and the decorations illuminated the shop fronts, the two lads darted between people searching for last-minute presents and going about their business. Theirs was an excitement only children truly feel at this time of the year.

Ray looked over at Valentines café and turned to Denny. "Come on, let's go and get a cup of tea and a KitKat before we head home."

"I've got no money on me," Denny replied.

"I have, don't worry. Anyway, we will get them for free once I smile and compliment them all." Ray winked and smiled cockily.

As they approached the café, Denny spotted Anna Vital in conversation with a man about her age in the alleyway at the side. He noticed Anna was looking annoyed.

Ray pushed open the door and entered the familiar surroundings of Valentines, not noticing his brother wasn't behind him. He was already producing a beaming smile and awaiting getting fussed over, Italian style, by the Vital clan.

Now alone, Denny stood at the foot of the alleyway, unnoticed by the arguing pair, watching and listening with an intense stare.

"You've been flirting with me non-stop for weeks, you little tease. Now I find out you're going to Nightingales tonight with that tosspot Dan Green," the man said aggressively.

"Look, Shane, I never said yes to you, and now you are acting like a total prat, I'm glad I didn't," Anna said, as a little voice spoke up.

"Leave her alone, mate. She's my friend."

The voice made Anna and the man turn around and look down to see Denny's little face and dark, serious eyes looking back up at them.

"Ease up, look, Anna. Your bodyguard is here," he said, laughing.

"Hello, Denny." Anna smiled.

"Are you OK, Anna?" Denny asked.

The man laughed out loud. "Look, you little shit, do yourself a favour and piss off."

He was aged about twenty-five and towered over Denny, but this comment both angered and embarrassed him in front of Anna, who had now turned back to the man.

"Leave him alone, you bully. You're such an idiot at times." She turned to Denny. "I'm OK, thanks Denny, darling. Go inside. I'll be in shortly."

"Yeah, go on, little big man. Do as she says and sod off, so us adults can chat before I put my toe up your jacksy."

Ray turned to the door as a red-faced Denny stormed into the café. He entered with such force that nearby customers turned to investigate the commotion. Seeing it was just a kid, they turned back to their meals and conversation.

Denny headed to the counter, eyes narrowed, face stern. He was watched by Ray, who knew this look. Denny passed his brother without a word and went straight to a large tray of cutlery. He pulled out a steak knife, turned and marched back out of the door, followed closely by Ray.

Anna was giggling now as Shane leaned towards her and placed his arm on the wall, by the side of her head.

"Stop it, Shane. I'm going with Dan, and that's the end of it. I don't want you spoiling it tonight, causing bother."

As Shane went to reply he felt a searing pain shoot through his body. Denny had marched up to him in a raging temper and plunged the steak knife straight into his arse cheek with such force the full blade had entered, leaving just the handle exposed.

"Jesus Christ!" Shane yelled at the top of his voice, looking down in shock at Denny, then across at Ray who had just arrived behind his brother.

Shane felt at his buttocks in the dimly lit alleyway and his hand touched the solid handle. He felt the blood stream across his hand, which made him scream in a high-pitched wail.

"He stabbed me! The little bastard has stabbed me! I'm bleeding!" he said in panicked desperation, looking towards Anna who was now looking down at a still unblinking Denny.

Ray grabbed Denny as Shane began sobbing. "Leg it, Denny!"

Denny suddenly snapped from his red mist, looked briefly up at Anna and the crying Shane then the boys darted from the alley.

Shane looked at Anna in desperation. "I need an ambulance. And phone the police!"

Anna took his arm and led him through the side door into the kitchen, away from customers' eyes.

"You and me need to decide what we are going to tell the ambulance people. Decide how this accident happened," she said.

Shane stopped and looked at her in shock and agony. "You saw what happened! That little fucking psychopath stabbed me!"

"Those two are Harry Lane's boys, so like I said, you need to decide how that knife ended up in your arse cheek. Because grassing on them isn't an option, trust me!"

*

Harry wrapped his arms around Chrissy's waist and kissed the back of her neck.

"Cracking night, love. Really busy. We took a few quid. Everyone was in the Christmas mood."

"Including you, judging by the look of you," she replied, smiling. She was quite merry herself, as she had decided to have a drink once the boys were in bed.

"You know how it is over there, love. Especially this time of the year. Everyone wants to have a drink and a chat. You been OK?"

"Yes, got the boys to bed and me and 'Matey' had a bath together before I got a drink for myself."

"Good girl," Harry said. "That's the style, although you and 'Matey' bathing together, it's getting to be a bit of a habit. Is there anything you want to tell me?"

She laughed and kissed him. "Ah, don't be jealous, darling. 'Matey' is a very bubbly guy, but not a patch on you."

They both giggled. "Pour us both a drink, Chrissy, and I'll look in on the lads. If they are both out of the game, I'll grab their bikes out of the loft."

"What, now? Are you sure? You're half pissed. Can you even get up there? Leave it until the morning," she said. But she knew he would get up there anyway.

"No, I'll get them down now and stick them in the bedroom, so the first thing they see when they open their eyes are their brand-new bikes."

She smiled as he walked from the room then clicked open the drinks cabinet.

23.

1974

"Where do you think you are going?"

Chrissy looked over the bannisters at Ray and Denny as they headed through the passage towards the front door with their new bikes. Both lads looked up at their mum without saying a word.

"You two are not going anywhere until I've inspected that pigsty you call a bedroom. It looked like a bomb site this morning."

"We have tidied it, mum," Ray replied, putting on his most innocent face.

Chrissy could melt at such a look, but she always laid the law down and commanded respect from the two boys. They sincerely loved her for it, not that they would admit it. They were well-versed in the rules of the game and fully understood them.

As Chrissy headed upstairs to check they weren't lying to her, the boys waited obediently by the already open front door, ready to escape out into their domain. Chrissy looked into the room and smiled at their efforts as Harry passed her.

"Off to sort some business out, love. I'll be back early," he said, kissing her on the cheek.

Harry walked down the stairs and smiled at the boys waiting patiently for their mum to come back down and give them the green light. "Where are you two reptiles off to, then?" he enquired, smiling.

"See a man about a dog," Denny replied.

Harry laughed and rubbed Denny's hair, scruffing it up. "Cheeky sod. You've got your medicals at the boxing tonight, haven't you?" he asked.

"Yes," Denny returned excitedly. "Then we can box."

"Good. Then, when you are older, you can both turn professional and become world champions, make plenty of money and keep your poor old dad comfortable in his old age."

Chrissy leant over the bannister rail again. "Right, you two. You can go. Behave yourselves." She winked at Harry then watched her two grinning sons as they mounted their bikes on the door step, ready to race off.

Harry shouted after the boys as they cycled away. "Don't forget what I've told you, boys, will you?"

They pulled up and turned to listen to their dad as he approached. "If you get any strange men offering you sweets, you make sure you have it away a bit sharpish or they may not be the only choppers you end up sitting on."

All three burst out laughing then the boys sped off.

Harry sat down opposite Ronny who was drawing heavily on his cigarette. Harry could recognise that look on his face from a mile off.

"I thought we agreed when we turned the Quinns' gaff over we were calling it a day." Harry watched Ronny blow smoke into the air and awaited his response.

"How do you know it's a job, H?"

Harry smiled. "Turn it in, Ronny. I've known you that long and worked with you on so many blags. I know what you are going to say before you even open your mouth."

Ronny grinned as Anna flew past, delivering their teas on her way through to another table with a bacon and egg sandwich on a small plate.

"Thanks, Anna," Harry said, glancing up briefly before his eyes returned and fixed firmly back across the table. "This needs to be good, mate. Why now? You're not skint, and we aren't in our twenties. Playing cops and robbers…it's a young man's game."

Ronny took another long drag and stared down pensively at the ash tray. He moved the ash about with the tip of his cigarette then slowly crushed it.

"My missus wants us to emigrate out to Australia, where her brother lives, for a fresh start. And I want one more hit before I go. I want to top my cash up to the brim, Harry."

Harry held his chin, rubbing it slowly, squinting his eyes in thought for a few seconds.

"This isn't out of the blue, is it mate? She has been on at you for a while about this move." He took a mouthful of tea, then continued. "And you have cased somewhere already and now you want me to cast my eyes over it."

Ronny laughed out loud. "You know me far too well, H. I want you with me. And I promise, one hundred per cent, this is our swan song. Just us. No outside bodies or trades needed."

Harry was looking serious and slowly shook his head. "I don't know, old son. We were pushing it with the Quinns. And it looks like we got away with that by luck in the end."

"That was revenge, H, so not officially a job," Ronny said, grinning. "So, we can't sign off on it."

Harry took another sip of tea and ran his hand across his stubble. He hadn't shaved this morning, which was an unusual occurrence.

"Right, tell me what you've got and I'll decide from there."

"Barclays in the High Street," came Ronny's reply.

"Are you nuts? That's half a mile from my house, if that!"

"I've watched that bank for two months, Harry. The manager shuts the main door, then every Thursday he stays until eight on the dot, leaving through the back door where his little motor is. Same pattern, every Thursday, without fail."

Ronny looked at Harry, looking for any sign of a reply, but he said nothing, just sat deep in thought. So, he continued.

"I've looked into the manager. No wife, no girlfriend, nothing to go home to and no one to expect him home. In love with his job and nothing else."

Still no comment from Harry.

"For God's sake, H, put me out of my misery."

Harry took a deep breath. Almost a sigh. "You're a bastard, Piper, you really are."

Ronny started laughing. "That's a yes, then, I take it, Harry?"

Harry looked directly at him and spoke quietly. "It's a I'll take a look at it for two months myself, then we decide."

"Lane and Piper's last blast. That calls for a celebration," Ronny said, catching Valentine's eye and holding two fingers up, then indicating a T with his index fingers. "Another thing, H. I've a young lad lined up to drive who I need you to meet and OK. Big Tony said he isn't interested anymore. And to be honest, his health isn't great. Plus, the size of him, he'd stand out like a sore thumb this local."

Harry just nodded in response. His mind was already on this new job and working things out. He still had ambitions of opening a Nightingales in the West End and had his connections looking at potential venues. Custom had dropped somewhat at the club, due to the worsening work situation and inflation. So, less money was about for socialising, but there always would be plenty of cash to go around in the West End, so he wanted it to go into his tills at a new venue.

Harry was snapped from his reverie by the sound of Ronny's voice and another tea being delivered.

"How are Chrissy and the boys, H?"

"All good, thanks mate. The boys have got their medicals tonight at the club, then they will have their licences to box."

Ronny laughed. "Last time I saw them they had built a ramp on the green outside yours and were jumping their bikes over a load of kids they had lined up on the floor. Your Denny's back wheel missed some little fellow's nut by about a millimetre."

Harry shook his head and tutted. "I'm hoping the boxing will sort that wild little sod out. He can't keep his mitts to himself, forever whacking someone. When we went to the seaside last summer, he wasn't gone half an hour down the arcade and he had chinned some kid."

Ronny was laughing now as Harry continued.

"Then, the kid's parents turn up, their little lad in tow with claret all over his hooter, shouting the odds about our Denny. So, of course, Chrissy is off then, and about to whack the parents! I tell you, Ronny, my nerves are less shattered out on the rob with you than out with the family."

Both men roared with laughter.

Harry walked through the old wooden door of Spartans Amateur Boxing Club and was greeted by the sounds of punch bags being hit, and the whirling and whipping of skipping ropes as boys aged all the way from ten through to young adults went through their training, individually or put through their paces by the coaches. The musty smell hung thick in the air from years of sweat-soaked bodies crowding this old, wooden hut-like structure.

Harry spotted his boys, both going through their floor circuit; press ups, squat thrusts, burpees. They upped their pace as they caught his eye. Harry smiled at them in acknowledgment then knocked on Roswell's little office door, 'Club Secretary' proudly displayed on a little sign.

Harry was greeted with a smile from Roswell. He was, of course, a policeman to his very core and never off duty, but he did seem to take on a different persona in the boxing environment. He was as devoted to his club and his fighters as he was to the police service.

"So, both medicals went fine then, Burt?" Harry asked, trying with all his might not to laugh at the sight of Burt in his skin-tight Gola tracksuit and old school plimsoles.

"Two fine young men you have there, Harry. And both shaping up nicely, I must say," Roswell commented enthusiastically.

"Good, good," Harry said and pointed to the seat behind the desk. "Take a seat, Burt, I want to run something by you."

Without speaking, Burt sat down as Harry had instructed and watched as Harry walked up and down before stopping and looking out of the glass into the gym, his back to him. It suddenly dawned on him that within a minute, somehow Harry had taken over his office and was dictating things. As he went to complain, Harry turned and spoke.

"I'd like to run a boxing evening at Nightingales in a couple of months and if you can get a match lined up for my boys, I want it to be their debut."

As Burt tried to speak, Harry casually cut in again.

"Oh, and it needs to be a Thursday night, as my Fridays and Saturdays are always my main events."

Still slightly stunned, Burt said, "I'm really not sure it's appropriate for a member of her majesty's police constabulary to be doing business deals with known criminals."

Harry raised his eyebrows nonchalantly. "I'll ignore that slip of the tongue, Burt, as I know you meant local businessman and charity benefactor. Including this very boxing club. Look, Burt, you do a marvellous job here and for the community. And I've seen a great improvement in my boys, so thank you." Harry turned and pointed out to the gym through the glass. "This place needs all the money it can get. There will be zero charge for my venue. All the money from ticket sales is yours. All I want is the bar takings and my lads' first fights to be at Nightingales." He smiled. "Take your police hat off, Burt, and put your business head on. I'll leave you to crack on with things and we'll chat soon."

Harry turned and walked out of the office leaving Burt Roswell, Club Secretary, in speechless amazement.

24.

Ray and Denny arrived at the shed to find a glum-looking Patrick sitting outside, waiting for them. Both boys jumped off their bikes and leaned them up against the shed. Ray noticed a big padlock on the door and a notice saying, 'Council property'. He didn't bother to read the small print, instead he turned and looked down at their dejected friend.

"What's going on, Patrick? What's the lock about?"

"Old Roberts has pegged out and the council have changed the lock and removed everything."

"What you mean, removed everything?" Denny said, walking up to the window. He cupped his hands around his eyes to block out the daylight and peered through the window. The shed was completely empty. Their sofa, the cabinet and drawers, everything. Gone.

"What a fucking cheek!" he shouted. "Look in there, Ray. It's completely empty."

Ray looked into the empty shed then back to Patrick. "Where's all our gear gone, mate?"

"The council slung it all on the back of their shitty wagon. They were just finishing when I got here. Even took my dartboard, the wankers."

Ray realised what the shed had meant to Patrick and how fond he had been of old Roberts. He tried to cheer him up. "Don't worry, mate. You leave it to me and Denny. We will sort us a new place to go." Ray was really only gutted because it was an ideal space to hide their stolen goods. And they had been doing a roaring trade selling them at school.

On top of the pocket money they received from their mum and dad, they had both stuck away a tidy sum. Denny had wanted to waste his money all the time. But Ray, who had clearly taken on board what his father had always said about sticking together as a family and was clearly the more money-driven, had insisted that they pool their resources. He had taken on the role of banker and financial advisor for them both.

"Did you tell them it was your dartboard?" Denny asked.

"Yes, I did, and they told me to hop it and clear off," a frustrated Patrick declared.

"Never mind, mate," Ray said, putting his arm around Patrick's shoulder. "We will be up and running again soon. At least there was no stock in there," he added.

"There was," Patrick replied. "Ten packets of Rothman's. The bastard who put that pissing great paddock on nicked them. I said they were mine. He told me I shouldn't be smoking and to button it. He said the shed was now out of bounds till it was rented out again and if he caught me hanging around, he would put his toe up my arse."

Ray looked at Denny, whose face had taken on that familiar cold-eyed stare. "Well, that's that sorted, then," he stated calmly.

"What's sorted?" Ray asked.

"I'll teach that big-mouth bully prick to upset our mate and steal our fags."

Ray and Patrick both looked at Denny as he continued. Although Denny was Patrick's friend and Denny looked out for him, there were times when he scared the shit out of him.

"If we can't use this shed, then no one else is having it. I'm coming back tonight when it's dark to burn it down."

Ray and Patrick knew full well that Denny was deadly serious and they both thought in this case his actions were justified. The boys agreed a time to meet back at the shed later and a now much more cheerful Patrick cycled off in his direction and the brothers theirs.

Ray and Denny decided to take a short cut back to their house along the canal path. As they sped along, Denny noticed a traffic warden walking along the path, eating a sandwich, obviously taking a slow walk back to the nearby car park. With the shed-burning lined up for the evening, Denny's mindset was hellbent on carnage.

"Ray, Ray!" Denny shouted as his brother applied his brakes and looked back to see what his brother wanted. "Let's throw that traffic warden in the canal. Dad's always saying they are snidey shitbags."

Ray readily agreed and they began cycling towards the warden, who was now perilously close to the edge, blissfully unaware of the boys coming up behind him.

It was a bitterly cold day and the noise of the wind totally blocked out the sound of the boys coming up beside him. Just as the warden became aware of something in his peripheral vision, Ray shouted, "Now!"

Both boys kicked out in unison while moving past at full speed. Their legs made contact as they held onto their bikes, the force sending the warden straight off the path and into the freezing water. They looked over their shoulders at the shocked face of the man flapping in the ice-cold canal and they both roared with laughter before peddling as hard as they could from the scene.

Patrick got off his bike and grabbed the bag that had been hanging across the handle bars, handing it to Denny.

Denny opened it and pulled out a petrol can, looking excitedly back at Patrick. "Nice one, mate. This will speed things up. Where did you get it?"

"In my dad's lockup. He has loads of them. And diesel. All kinds, really."

Denny's dark eyes pieced into Patrick's as a mischievous grin appeared on his face. "You and Ray stay here behind the bushes and keep watch while I go and set fire to the shed, then I'll come back and sit with you."

Ray never questioned this statement. There seemed to be a natural, unspoken agreement between the brothers that destruction, damage and violence were Denny's undertaking and finance and planning were Ray's.

"Go on, Denny, hurry up before someone comes. We will keep watch and whistle if we see anything," Ray said as Denny got up from behind the bushes and headed across the allotments to their former sanctuary.

He opened the top of the fuel can. It was filled to the brim. Slowly, he walked around the shed, tipping petrol out around the base. He then stood back slightly and threw it up the sides. As hard as he tried, he couldn't help splashing petrol over his shoes, hands and clothes. He knew he would probably have to sneak in and ditch his clothes later, in case his mum smelled the petrol.

He noticed an old newspaper on the floor by the shed next door, so grabbed it and laid the pages loosely on the floor and removed a box of matches from his pocket. He was streetwise enough to be careful lighting the paper, as he had spilt quite a lot of petrol on himself. He stood back and watched. The paper seemed to take forever to catch and he actually thought it had gone out when all of a sudden there was a whooshing sound and the small flame connected with the petrol.

Then, as if by magic, the shed was ablaze.

As much as he wanted to stand in front of it, he wasn't that stupid and he ran back to join the others behind the bushes to admire his work. He crouched down and handed the petrol can back to Patrick.

"What am I meant to do with that?"

"Either stick it back in your old man's lockup or throw it somewhere," Denny replied without taking his eyes off the burning shed.

"Why didn't you leave it there to burn with the shed?" Patrick asked.

Ray laughed. "If the old bill or the council blokes find an old burnt petrol can next to the shed, they will know it was deliberate. And seeing as you were the one giving them lip, they'll blame you."

Patrick didn't reply. All three boys peered from the bushes, watching the shed become engulfed in flames, the wood spitting and crackling as the fire made easy work of destroying the structure.

"Them tossers won't be renting that out now, will they?" Denny laughed victoriously, just as Ray spotted a man in the distance heading towards the blaze with his dog.

"Leg it!" he shouted and all three boys jumped on their bikes and rode off into the night.

Harry sat down at his usual table in Valentines, opposite a waiting Ronny. They were about to start their weekly observation of the bank and always had a brew and a chat beforehand.

"You OK, H? You look pissed off," Ronny asked, noting the pensive look on Harry's face and the fact his usual military punctuality was out by a good ten minutes.

"I've just been sorting out some damage limitation over that bleeding pair of mine again. Sorry I'm late, mate."

"What have they been up to this time?"

"Only slung a traffic warden in the bastard canal, that's what!" As Ronny went to reply, Harry cut in. "Oh, and it gets better. He couldn't swim. Luckily, a passer-by saw him going in the water, swallowing most of the canal, and fished him out."

Ronny couldn't help himself and burst out laughing.

"It's not funny, Ronny. Not only did he nearly drown, he has been laid up in bed with shock and probably hypothermia, on top of spewing up nonstop from whatever shit he was gulping out of that water!"

Ronny was now crying so hard with laughter, others were looking at him and smiling, even though they had no idea what was so funny. "Jesus, Harry, you have trained them boys well. Traffic wardens, eh? Next coppers! Good boys."

Harry couldn't help but start laughing himself and continued to tell Ronny what happened. "So, this bloke's back home, shaking, in a terrible state, wrapped up in a blanket by his fire and his old woman phones the old bill. Well, he describes my two to a T, from the hair on their head to the shoes on their feet. Even them poxy Chopper bikes I bought them." Harry took a mouthful of tea and tried to carry on with a straight face, looking at the tears in Ronny's reddened eyes. "Anyway, who spots this young PC's report on his desk? Only that shithouse Roswell. And get this, Ronny. That slippery bastard went round on the quiet and talked this traffic warden into going down the boxing club tonight when all the lads are in and pointing Ray and Denny out."

With that, Ronny's laughter slowly dissipated. "That's one snake. So, how did you hear about it all?"

Luckily, the young copper was chatting about it in Albie Kingsley's butcher shop. Old Albie cottoned on he was describing my boys and he had already heard about the warden as his missus comes in for pet mince for her cat. So, he gave me the head's up earlier and got me this geezer's address."

"Blimey, that was handy, mate. Just in time," Ronny said as he wiped his tears with a napkin. "Did he know you when you went round?"

Harry nodded. "Yeah, he knew me but his old woman didn't. I told him to go through with Roswell's plan but not to identify the lads and to tell his missus we are friends from years ago."

Harry took his wallet out and left some notes under his tea cup. "I gave him some cash as an extra sweetener. He looked traumatised and pale as a ghost."

As the men stood up to leave, Ronny asked, "Are you going to warn the boys, H?"

"No, I am not. I'm going to let the little sods sweat when that warden turns up at the club tonight. Tell you what, I'd love to see Burt's face when he says he doesn't recognise them." Harry opened the café door, smiling. "I'll let that pair know tomorrow that, thanks to their old man, they are not in the shit with the old bill."

25.

Harry circulated Nightingales, playing the perfect host for their first boxing evening. He smiled, shook hands, patted backs, kissed cheeks and made sure he was in full view of as many people as possible, particularly Burt Roswell.

Ronny Piper was doing much the same as Harry, in a less obvious and flamboyant manner, but being seen none-the-less.

The atmosphere was fantastic, filled with excitement and anticipation of the night ahead. It was only a Thursday night, but Harry was delighted to see his bar staff rushed off their feet. He had sold a number of VIP tickets for tables close to the full-size ring he'd had erected, which was the result of a deal he had negotiated through a connection he had in the boxing world.

VIP guests were treated to a three-course meal, the contract for which, of course, had been given to the Vitals who, as per usual, had done a marvellous job. Antonio, Maria, Valentine, Anna, Valentine's fiancé and Anna's new boyfriend, and even their eight-year-old son Angelo, were all on duty, supplying the tables with meals. There was a band on stage, entertaining the crowd and the first bouts were scheduled to start at nine o'clock, once the meals were over and cleared away.

Harry checked his watch, then headed across to Ronny, greeting well-wishers on his way.

"Right, let's do this, Ronny," Harry said and apologised for cutting in on the couple Ronny was chatting to. Ronny excused himself and Harry thanked them for coming. With a smile, he added, "I hope you both have a very enjoyable evening."

He steered Ronny away, then said to him, "Give me five minutes, Ronny and I'll be back out. I just want to show my face in on the boys and Roswell."

"No problem, Harry. Don't get caught up, for Christ's sake. We've got a very narrow window of opportunity here." Ronny looked serious and determined.

Harry smiled at his boys, who were sitting with Chrissy, looking at their kits. Harry had got them both brand new boxing boots and shorts with R.L and D.L embroidered on them in gold. Considering tonight would see their first fights, and most of the other lads could only afford bumper boots or plimsoles, it was probably over the top and a bit premature, but both boys and his wife looked proud and happy. And that was all he cared about.

"I've got to shoot out for about an hour, love. Need to sort something for later this evening. Big Tony will look after you. Anyone asks, I'm in my office."

Chrissy smiled, answering, "OK," but Harry knew she was engrossed in their sons and the electric atmosphere. He was convinced that she would hardly miss him while he was gone.

Harry headed over to Roswell, who was in full boxing mentor mode and absorbed in his responsibilities, most of which were in his own head, of course. Usually a twenty-four-hour policeman, he was definitely less observant when on boxing duty, which suited Harry.

"You OK, Burt? Everything good for you back here?" Harry asked, smiling.

"Yes thanks, Harry. All the fighters we have matched up are here, thankfully, so no last-minute stand-ins," Roswell managed to reply as his attention was being taken by two fighters and another club's trainer.

Harry was delighted that Burt was totally absorbed with the evening and glanced at his watch. He tapped Burt on the shoulder as he went to leave. "I'm about, Burt. You need anything, you come and grab me. And don't forget to eat, old son. All the fighters and trainers have been allocated an evening meal."

Roswell acknowledged this statement but was completely in the moment and straight back, fussing around the room.

Harry looked behind him as he stepped out into the car park of Nightingales, making sure nobody spotted him climb into the waiting van. Ronny was already inside the back of the van, dressed in a boiler suit, sitting on the wheel arch. Harry removed his shoes, then slipped on his own boiler suit, which went right over his entire outfit. He then put on a different pair of shoes, all of which would be incinerated after the job had finished.

Harry looked at their driver, Steve. He was a replacement Ronny had brought in, and of course Harry had vetted. He had a wig on, covered by a baker boy cap and a stick-on moustache.

He started to laugh. "Blimey, look at the get up on that, Ronny."

Ronny smiled as Steve turned around. "Yeah, well it's my face on display in this windscreen, if that's alright with you two." He tutted, but then smiled with them both.

"Right, let's go. I want to be back bang on time and ready to watch my boys fight," Harry stated. With that, the van slowly crawled out of the car park and on to the main road.

"They all set, H? I bet they are hyper excited," Ronny asked, adding, "I hope they both win. It will be fantastic."

"Well, they should win the world heavyweight title tonight, the way my Chrissy has been fussing around them."

Harry pulled his sleeve back again to check his watch as the van pulled up in a dimly lit area and Steve got out. Sticking to the carefully laid out plan, he stuck a sign they had made up on either side of the van: Barclays Bank UK PLC.

As he worked, Harry smiled at Ronny and continued, "You know she has been feeding that pair the best fillet steaks the last few weeks. The lads they are fighting have probably been on Spam and Smash instant potatoes, so they ought to bleedin' win!"

Both men laughed as the van started moving once again.

With both back doors opened wide, the van was backed up tight to the back entrance of the bank. Ronny and Harry were now both in balaclavas and Harry was sitting patiently on the wheel arch, facing the door with his sawn-off resting across his thigh, leather-gloved hand gripping it tightly.

The van was now completely silent, the men inwardly praying this bank manager would stick to the clockwork schedule he had not deviated from for four months now. They knew that even if he was sixty seconds late, it could be too much. The false signs on their van may well convince the passing public all was normal, but not the police.

Ronny and Harry tensed as they heard the sound of the door being opened. The unsuspecting bank manager, deep in his own thoughts and expecting to walk out into the cold, dark night and across to his waiting car, was instead greeted by the sight of the back of the van, two masked men and the barrel of the shot gun pointed straight at him.

Harry spoke calmly, still sitting on the wheel arch. "Obviously you can see why we are here. Do as you are told, make no fuss, and you will be home safe and sound with your goldfish and stamp collection in no time. You understand?"

The terrified man nodded.

"Good man," Harry said as Ronny leapt from the van. "Lead the way, old son."

Harry, now out of the van as well and pointing the gun at the bank manager, said, "You know what to do. Get that safe open. No stupidity, no alarms. I'm far too old and long-in-the-tooth for any unnecessary poncing about and I won't hesitate to leave your cleaner more than the normal tidying up to do in the morning."

Once the safe was open, Harry taped the bank manager's hands and feet up and, for good measure, put a piece of tape across his mouth. "You breathing OK?" he asked. The man nodded. "Good lad. Don't worry, it will be over soon and we will be gone. You'll be OK."

Harry looked into the van to see Steve who was sitting quietly, showing no signs of any disturbances, and got to work with Ronny unloading the safe into their bags.

Just as they cleared the last of the contents, they were suddenly thrown into complete darkness.

"Bollocks! Not now, surely," Ronny said, exasperated.

"Them poxy blackouts. What's the bleeding point of putting in the paper the times when they are going to schedule them if they are going to cut the bastard anyway?" Harry said as Steve called out under his breath and slung a torch into the back of the van from the driver's seat, already switched on.

"Nice one," Ronny said.

"Keep that beam low," Harry whispered. "Let's finish this and get out of here sharpish."

Harry swung the torch round to the bank manager, who jumped as Harry spoke and grabbed his shoulder. "You're OK. You relax now, mate. That old electric will come on soon, no doubt, and you'll be sorted."

The van doors were pulled shut and Steve slowly edged away from the back of the bank. He drove off towards their pull-off area where he removed the Barclays signs.

"Just as well we had that torch, Harry. Poxy power cuts," Ronny said in a relieved voice.

"Well, it might just do us a favour if it's still out when we slip back into the club. Plus, if anyone has been looking for us, we have the best reason for being adrift," Harry pointed out.

He was silent for a while, then said, "Hope to Christ they are out no more than the usual hour, or that's the boxing ruined."

Both Harry and Ronny were out of their boiler suits and back in their evening wear, complete with ties and shoes, as Steve pulled into the Nightingales car park. Once they were certain the coast was clear, the pair left the van.

"Take care, Steve. Ring me ASAP once you are back at the safe house," Harry whispered.

Just as the two men headed gingerly up the corridor, under the dim light of people holding candles and lighters, the lights suddenly came back on, an almighty cheer breaking out in the packed club.

Much relieved, Harry headed straight to the stage to make an announcement. He wanted to get the boxing proceedings going without any further interruptions.

Harry sat hand in hand with Chrissy at the ringside as Denny overpowered a young lad, stopping him in the second round, and Ray boxed skilfully to a points decision. Once both boys were changed, they sat with their parents, proudly showing off their winner's medals. The evening was in full swing now as the bouts worked up through the weight and age categories to the senior bouts.

Harry smiled at Ray and Denny, both buzzing from the evening.

"You two make sure that if you see them two lads you fought, you shake hands with them, like sportsmen."

Chrissy smiled. "Yes, and get them both a lemonade each and make sure they've had plenty to eat."

"Excuse me, Mr Lane?" Harry looked up to see one of his bar staff in front of him. "There's a phone call for you."

Harry ruffled both boys' hair and pretended to make a fuss of being interrupted before heading to the phone behind the bar.

"OK, Steve mate, you go and relax. We will meet up soon."

Harry put the receiver down and took a cigar from his suit pocket. Steve had confirmed that he and the proceeds from the night's job were safely tucked away.

He lit his cigar up as Ronny joined him at the bar and they discussed the night's activities. As they chatted, they both faced the ring area where two big heavyweights were slugging away at each other. It wasn't long before they spotted two men, who stood out like sore thumbs as old bill, heading towards the corner of the ring where an animated Roswell was screaming instructions at one of the fighters.

Finally, they got Roswell's attention and, presumably, relayed the news to him that a robbery had taken place at the local Barclays bank. Harry inhaled deeply on his cigar as Roswell's eyes scanned the room, finally fixing on Harry with a stern look.

Harry smiled and waved, blowing a huge cloud of smoke into the air.

26.

1976

Ray, Denny and Patrick headed towards the tube station. It was ten in the morning and the sun was already blazing down on them. The weather this summer had been stifling and it wasn't even the summer holidays yet. The boys had never experienced weather like it, being consistently hot every day. They had made up their minds the day before that going to school today was not an option. Instead, bunking off for a day in the West End was on the agenda.

"What's the plan then, boys? And what's in your bag, Ray?" Patrick asked as they stood on the crowded platform waiting for the train.

"We can just float about and go with the flow," Ray replied, then added, "But first we need to earn a few quid."

"I'm not thieving no more, Ray. Not after we nearly got caught raiding Robinson's Supermarket and after what Steve King told me about his brother being in Borstal. I'm not having any of that," a concerned Patrick stated.

Denny started laughing. "Well, with a name like Wayne King, he deserves Borstal. And his parents need locking up, as well."

The lads burst out laughing as the train pulled in and the platform emptied. It was the usual morning routine of bodies pushing and shoving each other to get a space on the train, excusing each other to try and maintain the façade of politeness while inwardly cursing anyone who managed to get a seat. Or worse, your shoving efforts not being quite enough and the doors closing, leaving you on the platform waiting for the next train to arrive.

The boys emerged from Oxford Circus station into the dazzling sunlight on Oxford Street.

"Right, men, let's earn some money," Ray said and put his carrier bag on the floor. He knelt down, opened it up and pulled out three plastic charity boxes, one for himself and one each for Denny and Patrick.

"What the bleeding hell are these?" Patrick asked as he inspected his box.

Ray grinned at him. "Good, aren't they? I got hold of them and made up the labels myself. Very professional, I think."

"What we meant to do with them?" a puzzled-looking Denny enquired.

"We are on the busiest street in London, packed with people. We are going to collect for our designated charities and make ourselves a few quid," Ray explained, smiling.

"I bunked off school to have a mooch about and a laugh, not collect for charity," Patrick moaned.

"Shut up, you fairy. We need some cash before we can have a laugh, and I'm taking Sarah Calver to Saturday morning pictures, so I want more money. You got any better ideas?" Ray asked. Patrick didn't reply, so he continued, "Exactly! Trust me, we do two hours, that's all, then see what we have made. If I left the money-making up to you pair, we would still be nicking sweets or taking our empty Corona bottles back to the shops for small change. Not a good look at our age."

Denny looked at the label on his box. "Battersea Dogs Home," he murmured.

"Yes," a grinning Ray replied. "I thought you could collect for all the girls you're always asking out at school."

Patrick giggled, then looked at his label. "Spastic Society?"

Denny laughed. "You are going to collect the most, Patrick. When people look at that label then at you, they will think you're collecting for you and your family."

"Piss off, Denny, you tosser." Patrick grinned and looked at Ray's box, which said, 'Cancer and Polio'. "What's Polio, Ray?" he asked.

"No idea, mate. I heard some geezer at the neighbour's door saying he was collecting for Cancer and Polio and thought it sounded good."

"Maybe it makes your breath smell of mints," a grinning Denny quipped and the boys all laughed before Ray took charge of proceedings again.

"Right, I'll head up Marble Arch way. You stay here, Patrick, and Denny, you head down Tottenham Court Road end."

Ray looked at his watch and back to the other two, who were both awaiting more instructions.

"We'll meet back up in two hours on Carnaby Street. Whoever collects the least amount pays for all our lunches. Fair?"

Both Patrick and Denny nodded in agreement and turned away. Before Ray disappeared, he reminded them both, "Don't forget. Look as innocent and genuine as possible, and always be polite and professional. Any old bill about, leg it. And Denny, don't chin anyone!"

As Ray caught sight of the sign at the end of Carnaby Street in the distance, he stopped and emptied all the money he had in his pockets and pushed it into his collection box to add to the money he had collected from the public. There was no way he was going to incur the cost of their lunches.

All three boys sat on a bench, promptly tore the charity labels off their boxes and threw them away before setting about counting their cash. Patrick was amazed at the amount he had managed to collect in two hours, as was Denny.

"See, I told you we would do OK. And you were moaning earlier," Ray exclaimed.

Denny caught sight of his brother's obviously larger stash of money. It included notes, which he noticed neither him nor Patrick had managed. "How did you raise that amount of money?" he inquired, narrowing his eyes. It had aroused Patrick's suspicions as well.

Ray put on his best innocent face and informed them both that he had walked into Bond Street as well, which was renowned for wealthy inhabitants.

The news that Denny had raised the least out of the three did nothing to ease the suspicions he had of his brother's remarkable charity collection.

"Stop moaning, you two. You're both richer than you were this morning. Now sling them boxes in the bin and let's have a mooch about."

Ray's suggestion was met with approval as all three headed off in the blazing sunshine.

As the boys strolled through Chinatown, they took in the sights, smells and sounds of this tiny little section of London just on the border of Soho. It was full of restaurants with people sitting outside, eating various rice and noodle dishes, signs with Chinese writing adorning various shops selling Chinese foods, herbs and ancient traditional medicines.

Patrick pointed, laughing, at a window with a rotisserie of roasted chickens and ducks hanging up. "Look at the colour of them chickens! They're red!"

"They're not chickens, they're dogs." Denny grinned.

"Ahh, piss off, Denny. They're not dogs. Look at them!"

"I'm telling you, Patrick, they are dogs. When your old lady dishes you up your beef or lamb on Sunday with your spuds and veg, these lot are getting stuck into roast rover."

Ray was now laughing at Patrick's disgusted face. "It's true, mate. They love nothing better than poodle pie and roast rover."

Patrick burst out laughing. "You two are gross!"

All three boys' eyes lit up as they came into Soho and were surrounded by various sex shops. Everywhere they looked they were greeted with signs advertising sauna and massage, strip tease, magazines, book exchanges, live exotic shows.

"Let's go in there," Patrick said and all three walked into a sex shop.

A disinterested assistant glanced up from the book he was reading as the bell on the door sounded. Not noticing the boys' ages, he took no interest as they looked up at the shelves with their backs to him.

Ray took down a magazine that caught his eye and was disappointed to see it was sealed, raising a complaint from Patrick about the magazines all being wrapped in plastic so you couldn't look at them unless you bought them. Both boys then turned and roared with laughter as Denny stood in front of the them with a giant dildo he had taken from the shelf and stuck between his legs.

Their laughter had now raised the attention of the assistant, who was screaming at them to leave his stock alone and get out of his shop.

Denny looked directly at the man and slung the rubber dildo with full force at him. It flew over the top of the startled man, bounced on the wall behind him, and fell, landing perfectly on his lap. As the man looked down in disbelief, the boys roared with laughter before belting through the door and down the street.

Once they were a safe distance away, sure the man had not given chase, they slowed up to catch their breath, their laughter finally subsiding. They turned down an alley where they spotted a sign.

'Peep Shows.'

Patrick pulled aside the multi-coloured strip blind that was hanging across the doorway and looked in. There was a little wooden stall, a small fan rotating, a cup of tea on the floor and an open newspaper.

He turned to the others. "There's no one here. Quick, lets sneak in for a look."

All three crept in and up the stairs onto a dimly lit corridor with various doors with what looked like letter boxes with a coin slot on the side.

Ray stuck the correct amount of money in to one and watched excitedly as the letterbox lifted up and he pressed his face up against the door, peering in. He couldn't believe his eyes as he saw a double bed revolving slowly with a naked couple having sex. Patrick and Denny pushed at him, shouting, "Let me see!" Ray strained his neck to carry on viewing the scene as the other two, eyes wide open, shoved him out of the way. All three were now struggling with each other to look as the letterbox slowly came back down to block out the source of their titillation.

"Put some more coins in, quick, quick!" Patrick hollered.

"Hold on, let's try a different one," Ray whispered and they crossed the corridor, giggling, to another door. As the hatch opened, all three tried to squeeze their faces into the slot for an eyeful. On the other side of the door, a fat, naked, middle-aged woman gyrated in front of them, squeezing her breasts together, her eyes looking directly at the excited lads.

She suddenly stopped what she was doing as she noticed the commotion. "Only one person at a time. Only one!" she shouted. The boys were now roaring with laughter at the sight in front of them. With a maddening rage, she got up and pulled the letterbox down from her side of the door.

"Oi, you lot!" a loud, gruff voice shouted and they turned to see a scruffy looking man in a tattered old string vest and a big white beard coming towards them. "What you doing up here? Get out of here!"

They realised there was no way out but past him and all three, still laughing, darted towards the man. As they got nearer, they realised he was old and out of shape and no real challenge. He was clearly hot, bothered and agitated. He suited the dingy, seedy set up they were in, but as teenagers, they thought the whole thing was hilarious.

"Go on, hop it! Sod off, the lot of you!" he snapped, angrily.

"Alright, alright, calm down, Captain Birdseye," Ray answered.

Denny stopped right in front of the man and stared right at him, which suddenly unsettled him. Denny then broke into a grin.

"Do us a favour, mate. Get some decent birds in this place, will you? That fat old thing in there has more fag burns on her arse cheeks than a pub ash tray."

The man looked down at Denny's dark, staring grin and couldn't bring himself to reply. He just watched as the boy arrogantly swaggered off behind the other two.

27.

Harry stared out of the window of Valentines at the rain hammering down and shook his head. "Poxy weather. Think I'll book a couple of weeks away with Chrissy and the boys. Get some sun on my skin," he said, then turned back to face Ronny. "Talking of sun, how's things going with your move to Australia?"

"All pretty much sorted at last, H. What a bleedin' game that's been, what with one thing and another. But I reckon six months and we will be over there in our new house and the kids settled in their new school."

"Well, as much as I'm going to miss you, my old mate, I think you're doing the right thing."

"Yes, I think so too, Harry. We've got to give it a go and my business is done here. It's not just my old woman. I want a fresh start for myself. And the kids, as well."

Harry nodded in thoughtful agreement. "Going to be very busy myself if this new venture in the West End goes through. It's looking like it's eighty percent good to go for Nightingales Two, at long last."

"That's fantastic, Harry," Ronny replied as he sparked the end of his cigarette up and continued talking, simultaneously drawing in a hit of tobacco. "Hopefully I'll still be in London to celebrate the grand opening. Seems we are both reaping the benefits of our hard-earned work," he said with a wink, breathing out smoke through his wide grin.

Harry returned a smile, which promptly left his face as he diverted his gaze to the cafe entrance. "Hold up, Burt Alert," he murmured. Before Ronny could speak, Burt Roswell had grabbed a chair from another table and pulled it up to the end of theirs, Harry to his left and Ronny to his right.

"Of course you can join us, Mr Roswell. Pull up a chair," Harry remarked sarcastically.

"Trust me, this is a brief visit. The less time being seen in the company of known felons and blatant abusers of her majesty's royal mint distributors, the better."

Ronny blew a cloud of smoke from the corner of his mouth deliberately in the direction of Burt's face and muttered, "The feeling is mutual, trust me."

"I'm glad you're here, Harry, it saves me ringing you. Tomorrow's boxing tournament in Hertfordshire. I won't be able to attend, unfortunately."

Harry knew Burt considered himself as the most important thing to the Spartan Boxing Club and that he was expecting a disappointed reaction to his revelation, so he answered nonchalantly, "OK, mate," then turned to Ronny. "Shame you can't make it, Ronny. It'll be a good night. Minibus of us going down."

Inwardly gutted by Harry's disinterested attitude, Burt cut in, "Well, I've prepared all the lads and I'll try my very best to get across later, as I know they need me."

Harry kept his game going. "Good lad, Burt. Don't worry, though, we'll manage just fine." He returned his attention to Ronny, who had acknowledged Harry's tease and was grinning at a slightly dejected-looking Burt.

Clearly frustrated, Burt suddenly burst out, "Well, if the reason I can't make it goes through, I'll be leaving the Spartan Club and this area for good."

Harry and Ronny both looked at Burt as he continued, now rather smugly.

"Yep, it's the West End for me. And a promotion." He turned first to Ronny and then to Harry. "Trust me, I'll be leaving my substantial file on you two with my successor. And remember, we are called the Metropolitan Police and just because I'm not in the area does not mean I won't be watching you like a hawk." He continued to stare at Harry. "You and I both know there's a number of unsolved crimes in this area, and I will solve them. You can trust me on that."

Harry held his gaze and smiled. "Well, it will be good to have a familiar face to work alongside, Burt. You see, old son, you're not the only one with good news, 'cause all being well, I'm opening a brand-new Nightingales right in the heart of the West End soon."

Burt couldn't hide his utter distain and stood up angrily from his chair, snapping, "No doubt funded by our local Barclays Bank." He glared at the grinning pair and refrained from adding anything else. Instead, he left Valentines without saying another word.

As the minibus pulled up at the venue and the doors opened, Harry shouted out to everyone, "This is it, we're here. Be careful, you lot, we are in the sticks now. You've got to watch these old country bumpkins."

"It's only twenty odd miles from London, Harry," a laughing voice from the back of the bus countered.

"It don't matter," a smiling Harry replied. "We are dealing with men who have sex with farm animals in preference to their wives and jump about Morris dancing, and all kinds." He winked at his sons and added, "Don't say I didn't warn you, you lot."

"Quicker I get my fight over with, the better. I spotted a Wimpy bar on the high street. There's a cheese burger and a knickerbocker glory there with my name on it," Denny stated.

"Yeah, and I clocked the girl behind the counter through the window. I'm having a chat to her," Ray cut in.

"You and girls. If you spent as much time training as you do chasing girls, you'd be a champion," Harry said, wryly.

"Six fights, six wins," Ray replied, smiling cockily.

"Seven and nil." Denny lifted his closed fist to his mouth and kissed it.

Harry watched Ray moving around the ring, up on his toes, bobbing and weaving himself around every blow he threw and received. Ray was game and holding his own, but this other kid was slowly getting the better of him as the fight was nearing its end, and definitely ahead on points.

After a gruelling fight, the referee held the other boy's hand aloft, awarding him the win, and the local crowd roared their appreciation. The place was at full capacity and Harry felt a definite hostility in the air, particularly from a very loud and obviously drunk crowd up by the bar.

Harry looked at his programme. One fight to go, then Denny was up. He would have to sit and fight his other son's battle with him while looking through the ropes.

Ray looked slightly dejected as he climbed down the steps from the ring. Harry grabbed his arm. "Well done, Ray. You boxed well, mate. Go and get showered up, son."

Ray slunk off to the changing rooms and Harry headed up to the bar to get a drink before Denny's fight. Again, he noticed the loud bunch who were taking up a good portion of the bar area and decided it was best to divert to the far side where there was a gap and waited patiently to be served. He continued to survey the room, keeping a close watch on the drunk men and also trying to catch a bit of the next bout.

Drinks in hand, he returned to his spot by the ring just in time to catch Denny's fight.

"Come on, Davey, be first! Use your reach, put that jab together." Harry turned around to see who was shouting encouragement to the young lad who was out-boxing Denny. He recognised him as one of the gang from up at the bar and he had since learnt that they were the local rugby team.

Harry ducked down so he could see the action through the ropes and watched as Denny stalked the taller, more skilful boy. He was picking Denny off with perfectly-timed jabs and Denny's eyes were narrowed, intense with concentration. He launched an attack, but again the other lad rode the blows and countered with a beautiful combination on Denny's face.

"That's it, Davey boy! Be first, boy! Be first!" the animated voice was now starting to piss Harry off. The bell sounded for the end of the second round just as Ray turned up and joined his dad.

Harry wrapped his arm round his son. "Alright, mate?"

"How's Denny doing?" Ray enquired.

"Behind on points, but getting stuck in."

They both looked up at the ring upon the sound of the bell starting the third and final round.

Denny looked across at the other boy, his nose smeared with blood where the corner man had attended to the bleeding. He let out a scream, revealing his gum shield, his dark eyes full of vicious intent and headed towards the opposite corner. The sight of Denny steaming towards him seemed to make the other lad freeze momentarily as a barrage of blows descended on him. He sunk back into the ropes as Denny swung wildly, punching into his body and head, finally catching him with a stunning punch on the top side of his temple.

The referee stepped in and gave a standing eight count. The boy was clearly stunned by Denny's attack and now had a bleeding nose to match Denny's, which the referee addressed before he signalled the two boys back to the centre of the ring and commanded, "Box!"

Denny stalked the now cautious boy who had composed himself and managed to use his skill to jab and survive to the bell. Denny didn't look bothered in the least when the other lad was awarded the decision. He was happy he had turned it from a boxing match into a punch-up.

Harry searched the room for the boys. They had both shot off earlier to grab a meal at the Wimpy bar and he hadn't seen them since. The last bout of the evening was into the last round and there had been a couple of minor scuffles outside the ring. The whole evening had had an uncomfortable atmosphere about it and a definite air of animosity towards the visitors. Harry was unknown in this area and had not been afforded his usual respect. He was keen to get away from the place.

Just as Harry caught sight of Ray up at the bar ordering a coke, a brawl erupted between the rugby players, including the man who was cheering the boy who had fought Denny, and another group of men.

In seconds it exploded, fists and legs flying everywhere and pint glasses smashing into the wall. Screaming women ran for cover as Harry saw Denny appear.

Ray was pushed to the floor in the melee and by the time Harry had darted across the room, both his teenage boys had become embroiled in a mass fight between grown men. Denny had spotted the boy he had fought and headbutted him, instantly making up for his loss in the ring, before punching the boy into the wall. The lad was crying his eyes out as the man who had been cheering at the ringside grabbed both Ray and Denny and pinned them to the floor by the throat.

Harry had seen enough and landed into the man with an explosion of rage, punching him with such force the stunned man released his grip on Ray and Denny's throats. Both boys quickly got back on their feet and watched in amazement as their dad continued raining blows into the man's face. He punched the man repeatedly, screaming, "Try and hurt my boys, will yah? You no good bastard!"

Harry shoved his thumb into the struggling man's eye socket, paying no attention as he kicked and cried out in pain, trying with all his might to escape Harry's vicious onslaught. Someone reached down, trying to pull Harry away. Without any hesitation, both Denny and Ray flew at him in unison, swinging wildly.

Although only teenage boys, their joint efforts were enough to repel the second man from their dad, who continued punching the face of his now unconscious adversary.

The terrified staff had already pulled down the bar shutters to save any more destruction and called the police.

The whole bar area was a mass of utter carnage as men, mostly drunk or high, attacked whatever was in front of them and stunned onlookers either watched in horror or tried in vain to stop the madness.

"You have had the phone call you are entitled to, Mr Lane. We have released your lot, including your hooligan sons. But you, sir, are going nowhere."

Harry, in sheer exasperation and still raging, looked up at the policeman at the doorway of his holding cell. "Hooligans? Are you insane? They're teenage boys who were being strangled by a grown man and caught up in a mass punch up!" he snapped.

"Yes, that would be the man you then proceeded to attack with such venom, you smashed him unconscious and is currently in hospital. Amongst other injuries, it looks like he may lose sight in one eye."

Harry glared at the policeman with distain. "I was protecting my boys. That lot were at it all night, causing bother."

The policeman shook his head, unimpressed. "I have witness accounts saying your son physically attacked the son of this man, whose only possible reaction was to physically pull him off his boy. I also have a dozen statements saying they have never witnessed violence such as that you dealt out to my colleague."

Harry registered the choice of words.

The policeman looked into his raging, piercing blue eyes and added, "You have hospitalised a friend of mine. A colleague. An off-duty serving police officer. You are going nowhere any time soon, Mr Harry Lane of North London."

He turned to walk out then swung round.

"I've checked up on you, mister. Very colourful character, aren't we, sir. There was a bank raid in our town two weeks ago. Be an awful shame if your fingerprints were to suddenly turn up at the scene."

Harry looked back at him in shocked disbelief, without speaking a word.

"You hurt one of ours, we will hurt you, Mr Lane. I shall leave you to dwell on that thought."

The cell door was slammed shut.

28.

1977

Ronny sat in the visitors' room of Woodhall Prison and watched as a stream of prisoners entered the room. They were of various ages, sizes and ethnicities, and they all scoured the room's tables, searching out their friends, family and loved ones. Ronny's eyes met Harry's and both men greeted each other with a warm, welcoming smile. As Harry reached his seat, the two men gave each other a firm handshake and Ronny could see by Harry's expression that he was very pleased to see his friend and ally, but also keen to hear about the goings on outside and get instructions to various people.

"How you doing, Harry? Shit question, I know, under the circumstances, but well, you know what I mean," he said, looking at Harry's pensive face.

Harry smiled at Ronny's obvious embarrassment at his opening line. "Well, apart from the fact I'm stuck in this shithole for the next three years and unable to do anything about it, or run my business concerns, or keep an eye out for Chrissy and the boys…I'm alright." His eyes scanned the room. "I'd hoped my days in these places and amongst these people were long behind me."

Ronny too looked around the room at the other tables. Some men were smiling happily with their relatives, wives and girlfriends. Others were having heated exchanges and frowning, all while being watched like hawks by the numerous prison wardens spaced around the room.

Ronny removed a cigarette from its packet and ignited it with his trusty Dunhill lighter. He took a long hit of tobacco while studying his friend's face. Harry looked frustrated and trapped and Ronny felt desperately sorry for him. Of course, both men had done their share of time behind the door as younger men, but it becomes more painful and pointless with age, particularly with family and business commitments.

"Tell you what, Ronny, I think I'll take up smoking them myself. Being banged up in here is driving me potty. Especially as I can't oversee anything."

Ronny took another long drag on his cigarette before answering. "I've been thinking, Harry. If you need me here, I can send the wife and kids over to Australia and join them later."

Harry responded with a wide-eyed and excited, "No way!" He shook his head. "I wouldn't hear of it, Ronny, my old mate. But thanks for the gesture. It's bad enough I'm in here and Chrissy and the lads are suffering, without any more people being affected. No, no, you get off and start a new life."

Ronny nodded, flicking his ash into the ashtray. "Well, this will be my last visit then, mate. We are flying out next week."

Harry felt a wave of sadness go through him. Not because he wasn't pleased for his friend; he was ecstatic for him and thought it was a great move. But they had been through so much together and he was feeling particularly low today and not his usual self.

"How're the lads, Ronny? Have you seen them?" he enquired. He saw Ronny was smiling and winking at another inmate's wife, which suddenly lifted his mood. "Ray and Denny, have you seen them?" he asked again.

Ronny took one last draw on his cigarette and extinguished it. He began laughing. "Oh, I see them, mate. They are legends in the area, within their age group and others, all because they went toe-to-toe with grown men alongside their old man. They were both surrounded by girls when I spotted them, no doubt embellishing tales of their battle."

Harry laughed. "Well, it's understandable the girls like them. They take after their old man, the handsome bastard."

Ronny looked around the room again as a smiling Harry watched him. "Lots of men in here gone a very long time without sex, Harry." He was grinning now. "You being handsome on the outside is an advantage. But in here!" He feigned a worried expression and sucked in a breath through pursed lips, before shaking his head and tutting. "By the time you've finished your time and get out of here, your arsehole will look like a blood orange."

Both men roared with laughter, which didn't seem to impress the warden watching them. Harry caught sight of his miserable, stern face and suddenly felt another wave of anxious emptiness in the pit of his stomach. "Ah, Jesus, Ronny, what a bastard nightmare this is. All over a poxy punch up. All we've been up to in the past and I'm back behind the door for that."

Ronny was genuinely amazed himself at how events had turned. Things had been going so well for Harry. "What's occurring with the West End and Nightingales?" he asked.

Harry answered instantly. Suddenly, he was not in prison, under rules, but back in decisive control mode and suddenly felt his energy return at the enquiry. "All bets are off, mate. West End project is off, obviously, and I got Patrick Hambleton in and instructed him to put Nightingales on the market for a quick sale." Harry noted the look of shock on Ronny's face at the news. He quickly added, "he has had an offer already from some property developer. I've told him to take it."

"Blimey, Harry, this is sudden," Ronny said as he lit another cigarette.

Harry now looked totally in charge of proceedings. As always, he was convinced his judgement was right. "No good me lying in my cell listening to my poxy Roberts Rambler all day, driving myself nuts over the club and things I can't control, is there?"

Ronny knew that, if Harry couldn't be there as boss, he would never allow a manager to oversee things and he could understand, from his own spells in prison, how it would torment a man to frustration. He blew a cloud of smoke into the air and enquired, "Got a good price, H?"

"Not fantastic, mate, but considerably more than I paid for it," a smiling Harry responded. "Patrick advised me to take it and let's face it, when it comes to money, he is no mug. He said if I waited, I could find myself with a building I couldn't sell, as there is a serious downturn in the economy."

Ronny filled the air with Sir Walter Raleigh's finest and pondered on Harry's words. He knew that, in the current situation, it was the correct move. "More money and less stress for Chrissy, as well, if the sale goes through."

"Exactly." Harry nodded in agreement. "I told Patrick to pay the staff six months wages and wrap up my books. You know what an expert he is on that front." Both men grinned.

Harry suddenly had a memory come back to him. He couldn't believe he had forgotten it, considering its significance. He leaned in close to Ronny and, under his breath, given that he knew his every move was being monitored by the warden, said, "I saw Johnny Quinn on the landing last week. He's gone now, though. Been transferred out."

Ronny listened intently, without saying a word.

"Get this, Ronny. He was full of pleasantries. Even seemed genuinely pleased to see me. It was quite bizarre."

Ronny laughed. "Probably drugging the mad bastard's tea."

"Well, not that he will be seeing the light of day any time soon. Judging by his demeanour, he has no idea we turned their gaff over." Harry leaned back in his chair and gave the warden an unfriendly, lingering stare, which seemed to faze the man, and he turned away. Harry then turned back to Ronny. "Has that wanker Roswell packed his desk up and left the area, yet?"

"I think it's due, yes, but I need to tell you…Ray and Denny have been asking questions about you because that prick planted a seed in their heads."

Harry suddenly felt his anger and frustration rise again at the sheer helplessness of the position he was in. "What's he said, the arsehole?"

Ronny could see Harry was becoming agitated. "Well, he hinted that, considering your track record, you got off lightly."

Harry sat quietly for a few seconds, then spoke quietly, more to himself than to his friend. "Considering I thought them bastards were going to fit me up with a blag I was nothing to do with, I probably have." Before he could say anything else, the bell sounded to signal the end of the visiting session and the wardens started circulating the room, prompting people to start saying their goodbyes.

Harry spoke more loudly and directly at Ronny, using the commotion as cover as both of them stood up from their chairs. "Do me a favour, mate."

"Anything, H, you know that."

Harry smiled and spoke with an assured authority, knowing that his decision was the right one. "I want you to sit the boys down and tell them everything about us. George Parker, the robberies, the scams, the deals, the Quinns, Vince Street, the lot."

Harry noted the genuine surprise on Ronny's face and continued, as a passing warden told them to finish up.

"It's the only way, mate. I'm stuck in here for three years. Time I get out, they will be practically grown men. The size they're getting and the way they carry on, they're not far from men now."

Ronny smiled. "Well. I hate to say it, H, but even at their age, they are commanding respect. And it's not going to be easy for your influence in the area not to rub off on them."

"Exactly. Well, I know they both idolise me and god knows what they'll think of me after your revelations. I've got to take that chance, though, 'cause Snidey Roswell's words to them is an indication that others will be setting tongues wagging and spreading misinformation, surmising things we have done. And I don't want them either quizzing their mother about things or ending up in here for lashing out at someone. Nope, it's a done deal. They need telling."

The men shook hands and Ronny said, "Consider it done, H."

Harry felt comforted. He knew Ronny was the only person he could truly trust to deliver these secrets. He was anxious about the effects this new information would have on his boys, but equally felt his incarceration meant it was necessary, and second-hand information would be far more destructive in the long run. Had his life not taken this unexpected turn, he may never have told them the full story of his life choices. Or at least not this way. But Ronny was leaving for Australia, so it was going to have to be done ASAP.

Burt Roswell pulled his Hillman Hunter on to the dual carriageway on his journey to the West End. Caught up in his own thoughts about both his new position and the area he was leaving behind, his attention was suddenly focused on the bridge rapidly heading into view. He looked up at the bold lettering painted right across the bridge.

FREE HARRY LANE!
HARRY LANE IS INNOCENT!

"Unbelievable! These people treat him like a hero! He's nothing but a thief and a murderer!" Burt said to himself as he passed under the bridge. He looked in his mirror to see the same message sprawled across the opposite side of the bridge for all to see.

"I'll have you, Harry Lane, if it's the last thing I do. In prison for a scuffle at a boxing tournament when you have blood on your hands and a business built on the proceeds of crime. You mark my words, Lane, I'll nail you," he muttered as he finally took his eyes away from his rear-view mirror and fixed his gaze on the road ahead.

29.

Ronny smiled as the door of Valentines sprang open and the two Lane brothers strode confidently through the entrance like they owned the place. He had popped round to see Chrissy the previous evening, as he did every week, to make sure all was well with her. He had caught the boys while their mother was brewing up a pot of tea and told them he wanted to see them at the café for a meeting. This had intrigued and excited both boys in equal measure. They liked the feeling of importance that meeting their dad's friend instilled in them. At last, they felt like they were being taken seriously in the eyes of adults.

Ronny was sat in his usual seat and still couldn't get used to the empty space opposite. But the appearance of Ray and Denny cheered him up. Particularly Ray, who seemed to look more and more like their dad by the day. Both of them were growing in size, no doubt enhanced by their boxing training. He glanced at his watch as the Lanes joined him at the table.

"I'm very impressed, boys. Punctual, just like your father."

The obvious pride in both their expressions was noted by Ronny, who was hoping the information he was about to relay to them would not sully their adulation of their dad.

Both lads had already decided they were having Maria's famous full English breakfast. Ronny was just having a sausage sandwich and his usual cuppa. He scanned the café, noting the patrons and, at the counter, the familiar faces of the Vitals undergoing their usual business.

Denny was grinning to himself as he knew it had been noted by the other customers, including a scowling Shane Wilson, that the boys were in their dad's spot and talking to Ronny Piper. He was still only a teenager, but Denny already felt it was their rightful place and they were unlikely to be challenged by the men in the café, and definitely not poor old Shane who, after experiencing a steak knife in his arse cheek, had no intensions of upsetting an older and more powerful version of Denny.

Ronny snapped out of his reverie.

"Tell you what, lads, I really am excited about Australia, but I'm going to miss this old place. One hell of a history for me here, particularly with your dad." He held both boys' gazes. "Once you two have eaten that breakfast, I've got a lot to tell you. Your dad feels you're old enough to know and he has asked me to tell you everything."

The boys hadn't even noticed their breakfast being delivered, both transfixed on Ronny and waiting on every word. Ronny looked up and thanked Anna and they then looked at their plates, thanked Anna politely in unison, then looked straight back at Ronny, who pointed at their plates.

"Eat your grub first, then we've got a lot to cover," he said then, laughing at the mountain of food on their plates, added, "that's if you haven't exploded first."

Denny mopped up the last of his breakfast with a slice of bread and butter. Ray, having finished a while ago, was waving out the window at a passing girl who smiled and mouthed back, "See you later." Ronny laughed at the pair and, noticing both had cleared their plates, flicked his cigarette packet open and removed what he considered to be a well-needed cigarette.

Both boys sat in silence as Ronny slowly worked his way through their considerable back story. The crimes, the scams, the robberies and the money laundering, as well as the legitimate businesses. Any fears of the brothers being disappointed in their father or their admiration being lost were alleviated as Ronny saw they were both totally absorbed and fascinated by what he had to tell them.

Ray had always been full of pride at their family's ability to obtain money, and it was now evident to him that it wasn't just their dad's ownership of Nightingales that had provided their family with all the latest household commodities that most of their neighbours and friends did not have.

Ronny had to admit he'd been somewhat unsettled by Denny's enthusiasm for the demise of George Parker and also his obvious rage at the liberty taken by the Quinn firm trying to put Vince Street's murder on their dad's doorstep.

Ray grinned at Ronny. "I love how basic the long firm was. A perfect exploitation of the companies' happiness to offer credit and get people into debt."

Ronny was taken aback, not only by Ray's use of words, but also by how rapidly his brain understood the scams and what they entailed.

"Well, considering most of the firms in London were at it, I'm surprised the companies never cottoned on," Ronny said before drawing in a large hit of tobacco.

Without hesitating, Ray replied, "'Cause, as a city, the amount of people scamming them was such a tiny percentage against the honest businesses that always paid back their credit. They would always take that risk to shift their products."

Ronny paused and stared at Ray. He had to remind himself it wasn't Harry in front of him. "Don't forget, neither your dad nor me ever took risks unless we were one hundred percent prepared and would fold a job and walk away without a second thought if something felt off."

Both the Lanes smiled and Denny looked up at Maria at the counter. "No wonder dad always told us old Antonio was to be treated like family."

Ronny's expression took on a stern, concerned tone. "You two must never, ever let that knowledge about your dad and Antonio leave us three." He held their gazes separately for a few seconds, then reiterated, "Your dad told me to tell you everything. You're Lanes, and don't you forget it."

Ray and Denny both turned and looked at each other. Ronny looked on in fascination as no words were exchanged, but he knew his words had sunk deep. He also knew that his final phone call to Harry before he left the UK would provide him with a sense of relief that the brothers had both taken the news well.

Ronny ordered three more cups of tea just as young Angelo came into the dining room from the kitchen. Shane's voice could be heard above the noise of the café.

"Hold up, look. Here he is, the milkman's son."

Angelo was sixteen years younger than the youngest daughter, Anna, and it was a joke amongst the locals, taken in good spirit by the Vitals, that old Antonio was too old to have produced Angelo with that age gap, the milkman having nipped in and done the deed. Under normal circumstances, nothing would have been said, but after hearing what had happened all those years ago in the barber's shop, and the connection with his dad, Denny took umbrage.

Without a word, he slid his chair back and stood up. He paused momentarily, then said, "Excuse me," and headed across the room.

He stood at the head of Shane's table. Shane looked up at Denny's emotionless stare and suddenly felt dread. There were two other men at the table, both looking at Denny as well, not entirely sure what to make of him.

"Seems you don't learn your lesson, do you? Picking on kids again?" Denny said calmly as young Angelo, only a year or two younger than Denny, looked on in awe.

"It's just banter, Denny. We all do it," Shane replied nervously as Ronny watched on in fascination at the genuine fear this teenager was provoking.

"Well, not anymore, you don't. It ends today. How do you think Angelo feels, hearing that every day?" Denny asked and looked at a stunned and somewhat embarrassed Angelo, then back at Shane who was gutted he was being spoken to like this, but equally too scared to respond. "I don't like bullies, Shane, and you're a bully. Remember when I stuck that knife in your arse? Next time I'll put it through your eye socket."

Denny looked briefly across at Angelo, then headed back to his table.

Witnessing this display, and contemplating Ray's obvious aptitude with money matters, Ronny was realising that, after all these years of risking arrest to build up money for his family, any hope Harry had had of his son's taking a different path were probably fruitless. It was evident to anyone in the know that this pair were cut from the Harry Lane cloth and they were not going to settle down for a straight life.

Ronny got up and asked for a pen and paper from Anna behind the counter. When he returned, he proceeded to write down names, addresses and numbers of various people, under the watchful gaze of the Lane brothers.

"Thanks for everything you've done for the old man and mum, Ronny," Ray said.

"And us two, as well," Denny added.

Ronny glanced up from his writing. "It's all about you two now. You've got to look after your mum now. You're the men of the house now Harry isn't there."

He placed the paper in front of them both, rather than handing it to either one in particular.

"Just remember what I said to you earlier. Everything your dad did, and all the risks he took, were to make a better life for you, so you don't have to do the same things." He smiled before shaking his head. "But my instincts tell me you will, anyway."

Denny grinned devilishly and Ray finally leaned across and picked up the paper, examining it.

"I won't be here, but that's a few names of extremely helpful contacts, should the need arise." Ronny stood up, followed by Ray and Denny in unison. He gave them both a firm handshake as Denny suddenly burst out laughing.

"I still can't believe you and the old man robbed that bank the same night we boxed. You two are legends."

Ronny smiled and winked at them. "Well, you just make sure no one hears about it, particularly your mum."

Ray and Denny had entered Valentines for the meeting with Ronny Piper as teenagers. They left as grown men.

Chrissy looked out of the bus window as it passed the closed Nightingales, its doors and windows boarded up, the "for sale" sign still hanging loosely and the grass area overgrown, unattended and lifeless. She felt an intense wave of sadness pass over her and her mind was awash with memories of the times she had spent there, of how glamourous and important she had felt back then.

Ray and Denny both acknowledged their mother's sad expression and were acutely aware of the cause.

"You OK, mum?" Denny asked.

She turned her gaze away from the rapidly deteriorating building and towards her boys. "I'm alright, love. But you know what, in future when we go to the train station to visit your dad, I'm taking a different route." She stared blankly in front of her and mumbled, "I never want to see that building again. Not like that."

"Don't worry, mum. Me and Denny will get that place back again one day. Trust me," Ray exclaimed.

"Yeah, we will, and that's a promise," Denny pitched in and the two brothers nodded at each other in agreement.

Chrissy looked at her two handsome sons and immediately felt her mood improve. She smiled warmly. "I have no doubt you two will achieve that. And I will not pass by that place again until that day."

She faced forward again and her mind drifted off to happier times.

30.

1980

Harry smiled at Chrissy as he sat down and kissed her tenderly. As usual, she was dressed immaculately. Her hair had been cut and expertly dyed and he felt proud as he noticed the admiring looks she was receiving from fellow inmates and their partners alike. She carried herself with poise and always had a knack of making an event of her entrance to any location, even a prison.

Harry knew she was playing an act, not just for others, but also for him, doing her best to lift his mood. Her efforts certainly had the desired effect. He loved her just as much now in middle age as he did when they were teenagers.

It had never ceased to amaze him how she had been loyal to him over the years, sticking by him and acknowledging that his life choices brought both good and bad to them. In his eyes, their special bond would never be broken. But he knew his current incarceration had been particularly tough on her, so the fact she managed to still show up for visits like royalty made Harry feel grateful and guilty in equal measure.

Chrissy had decided to take a part time job at the Green Man public house a year ago. She had grown more and more tired of her days without her husband's presence. Her duties as a mother had also become less and less a focal point as Ray and Denny were almost always out and concealing their activities more and more from their mother. Harry had had the word that they were beginning to make themselves busy. He had been pleased Chrissy had taken up the job. She knew the ins and outs of the pub game from her youth, and although she had hidden it well, so as not to worry him, he knew her mood had taken a downturn while he was away.

But that had improved immensely since she had taken the job, so this gave him one less thing that he couldn't control to worry about.

Chrissy had always been streetwise and tough, with a no-nonsense approach, which had calmed a lot upon the arrival of the boys. She had always put their needs first and largely put her own on a back seat in favour of motherhood. Even visits to Nightingales had been rare. But now the brothers were grown up, and she was back in the public eye, she had regained her old attitude somewhat, much to the shock of the odd lippy, drunk customer, who she was able to quickly put in their place. She had proved to be a very popular addition to the Green Man and, unbeknown to her, the landlord, Terry Waller, had decided he wanted to sell the pub after many years. Harry got the word to him via Patrick Hambleton that he wanted it.

Terry had agreed a price and Harry had signed the paperwork, so barring the odd few final arrangements, the Green Man was now Harry's and Chrissy's. Everyone involved had been told that it was to remain a secret, particularly to his wife, until he was released. Harry was nearing the end of his sentence and he was not only full of excitement over this new venture, but the prospect of being back in business and in control of his destiny once again filled him with an energy and an enthusiasm he hadn't felt since before his arrest.

But despite her immaculate look as he arrived, he could tell that something wasn't quite right with his wife. "What's up, love? I know, before you say anything, it's bad news on the way."

Chrissy's eyes suddenly filled with tears, more at the thought of her husband's reaction to the news she was about to tell him than the loss itself. "It's big Tony. He's dead," she stated, saying no more. She just watched and waited for Harry's response.

Harry didn't say anything for a few seconds as he absorbed the information, then finally asked, "What happened, love?"

"Massive heart attack. He died instantly, by all accounts."

Harry shook his head. "Poor old Tony. Where was he?"

"In Valentines. Apparently, he let out a groan, clutching his chest, and went face down into his plate of spaghetti bolognese, dead on the spot."

Harry stared at his wife's serious, sad face, then thought of the scene in the café. It was probably a nervous reaction, but he burst out laughing, which at first shocked his wife. "Well, at least he died doing what he loved, stuffing his face."

Chrissy felt relieved and started to laugh as well. "Well, if the heart attack didn't kill him, the face full of piping hot spaghetti would have done." They both chuckled.

"How're the lads performing, love? I heard the boxing club shut last month through lack of funding. Say one thing for that old tosser Roswell, he held that gym together when he was there."

"They are doing OK, Harry. You know what they're like."

Harry's face creased into a smile at the thought of his sons, a constant source of worry and amusement over the years.

Chrissy looked at her husband and immediately thought how handsome and distinguished he looked. He had gone very grey since he had been incarcerated, but she thought how much it really suited him.

"Well, boxing has taken a back seat recently. It's more about girls with them two now. Particularly Ray. And that sod Denny hardly needs a boxing ring to find a reason to fight, does he?" she asked, tutting.

Harry laughed, then looked around him at the bleakness of prison life.

"Oh, and they seem to have discovered the delights of alcohol of late," she added. "The way they staggered in the door the other night, both grinning at me, the pair of idiots. I told them, any old gallop and they're out the door."

Harry laughed. "You're turning into my old mum, love."

Chrissy smiled then sighed at the thought of Stan and Molly, then her thoughts turned to the sixties and the glamour of Nightingales then, the memory of that time invoking a longing to be young again. Without saying a word, Harry understood exactly where his wife's pensive daydreams had taken her, and he felt exactly the same emotions she was feeling. After all, he had felt it too, every single night for nearly three years.

Ray and Denny walked through the door of Miles Snooker Hall and surveyed the room. There was an assortment of snooker tables and full-size American pool tables. Directly in front of them was a long bar area; to the right, a line of dart boards with mats on the floor indicating the correct foot markings to play; to the left, a long row of windows that were letting in the bright sunlight through a set of partially-opened blinds, highlighting the fine particles of dust above a snooker table.

"We are shut," a gruff voice came from behind them.

They turned to see a man slowly heading towards them from an office door. He approached slowly, without speaking, giving them a good looking-over without making it obvious. He was a very stocky man. In fact, he probably weighed more than both Ray and Denny put together, and they were by no means small themselves anymore. He was early sixties, with a head of thick, curly, greyish hair, dressed in a shirt, the top two buttons undone, hanging over a pair of cream trousers, on top of a pair of ox blood brown boots.

As he drew level with them, he eyed them both up and down, nonchalantly, as if he had seen a million fresh faces in this building and was world weary with it all. He had registered that there was something about the look of the boys, particularly Ray, but couldn't quite put his finger on it in that split second.

He carried on walking past them, towards the bar, speaking as he ambled with disinterest. "I'll get you some membership forms. You're obviously not members, as I'd know your faces. And you would know that we don't open until midday."

"We don't want to join. We want to speak to Darren Miles about some business," Denny said.

Without turning, the man said, "And what business with Mr Miles would you two young men be wanting then?"

Ray followed the man towards the bar. "We are friends of Ronny Piper and he gave us your details, should we need assistance, before he went to Australia."

The man spun around and eyed the two of them again with an emotionless expression. "And who might you two be, then?"

"I'm Denny and this is Ray," Denny replied.

The man slowly broke into a grin. "Denny and Ray who? Or are you like Elvis, you only go by your first names?"

"Ray and Denny Lane," Ray exclaimed.

As the man took in their appearance, his face lit up with a beaming smile. "I knew there was something familiar about you. Jesus, you don't half look like your old man when he was young." He extended his hand, shaking first Ray's, then Denny's. "Darren Miles. So, what can I do for you, then?"

Ray had already removed a piece of paper from his pocket, listing the items they wanted, and handed it to him with a dark-eyed Denny looking on, grinning.

Darren eyed the paper, then the two boys with a slight shake of his head.

"Can you help us, then?" Denny asked.

"Yes, I can. I'll get back ASAP with a price and your means of collection," Darren replied, then added, "Your old man know you're here?"

"No. And there's no need for him to know. It's our business. That alright with you?" Ray answered, somewhat arrogantly.

Darren noted the confidence as a smiling Denny spoke.

"We want to give the old man a decent party when he comes out."

"Well, you make sure you two don't replace him on a set of bunk beds in there. And the same rules apply with you two as with everyone. Once you collect your goods, it's down to you. You never purchased anything of this nature from me."

"We know the rules, Mr Miles," Ray reassured him with another handshake and Darren shook his head again, allowing himself a wry smile.

As he turned away, he mumbled, "One generation retires and along comes a new lot!"

Denny pulled on a cigarette in unison with a stressed-out-looking Patrick as they stood by the entrance of a building site together with Ray.

"Why can't you two get a normal job like me, instead of robbing?" Patrick asked.

"Cause it's less hours and better money," Ray replied.

"Yeah, till you get caught and end up in nick, like your dad." Patrick immediately apologised as he looked at Denny.

Denny took a final drag and flicked his cigarette at the fence, causing sparks of burning embers to disperse. "Look, we need you for this little job, so stop being a fairy. Have we ever let you down?" Denny asked.

"No, but I'm doing OK working for my dad's firm. I don't need risks. Them days are over for me."

"Just this one time, mate," Ray cut in. "We only trust you. Promise we will never ask again. I know you've got a job and you're sorted."

"Yeah, a job and a company car with it," a laughing Denny said and pointed at the dumper full of sand with the engine still running. Patrick had leapt from it when the Lanes had arrived, which had made Denny laugh.

"You're such a prick, Denny," said Patrick, contemptuously.

"Look, we have both been in that bus depot and we have it from a good source in the know that there is a good ten grand or more up for grabs. That Ford Capri you've been saving up for can be yours in one hit if you help us," Denny confirmed.

"So, they've seen both your faces, now you're going to rob them?" Patrick asked.

"We needed to see the outlay and if there was money for the taking. I walked in and asked for a job application for bus drivers and Ray did the same a couple of weeks later."

Patrick laughed. "You two don't give a shite, do you?"

"Yes, we do. That's why we plan things. We have a motorbike for a quick getaway. We just need you waiting in your van for us," said Ray, smiling at a contemplative Patrick.

"Yeah, my fucking van with Corrigan Developments and our phone number right across it in full view!"

Denny gave him a playful grab on the cheek. "Look, stop worrying. We want you to meet us on Sawbridge Lane. It's five minutes from Barrett's builder's merchants, so you have just been there for supplies if anyone asks. Nothing out of place there, is there?"

Patrick looked around at the site in the distance, where his dad was barking orders with an exasperated urgency. "Driving me mad today, the old man. I seriously need a pint."

"Well, trust me, son, you'll have enough for that Capri you want and plenty of pints after this," Ray assured him.

31.

Patrick stood at the counter of Barrett's builder's merchants, waiting for his till receipt and chatting to the man behind the counter. All the staff were familiar with Patrick, who glanced somewhat nervously at the clock on the wall. It was a brick design with the name Barrett's written on it with a trowel and a spirit level for clock hands. Patrick thanked the man and folded his receipt, noting the correct time and date were on it, before he placed it in his pocket and pushed his trolley with his materials out of the store, nodding and greeting other customers politely as he passed them.

Ray pulled their motorcycle to a stop right outside the cashing up office of their local bus depot. He looked through the visor of his helmet at the giant wash plant as an engineer was edging a double decker bus through it, soap suds and water spraying over it as the giant roller brushes worked their way across the top. Other buses were either leaving the depot or arriving back and various drivers went about their business, not even noticing the two men now off the parked up motorcycle.

Ray lifted off two very large saddle bags and followed Denny in through the office door. Both had their visors up far enough to allow them to give verbal instructions, but low enough to obscure their faces so that identification would be impossible.

The man looked up through the paying-in window as Denny stood back slightly and pulled a sawn-off shot gun from his coat pocket and pointed it at him. Within a second, the man had gone from a contented dream-like state as he worked away at his job in autopilot, whistling away to a tune on the radio, to petrified shock as he stared down the barrel of the gun.

"Unlock that door, mate, and quick!" Denny shouted.

The man scurried across the room and duly did as he was told as Denny looked in through the window at the table loaded with cash. There was another man and a woman at the table, counting the money, who had now been stirred from their concentration as the door was unlocked and Ray burst in.

Denny quickly followed Ray through the door and herded the three startled staff into a corner at gunpoint.

Ray promptly removed his wire cutters and cut through the phone line to allow them extra time for their exit.

Next, he placed the saddle bags on the desk and instructed the three hapless staff members to help him load the cash into them as fast as they could.

Before any of them could contemplate becoming a hero, they were reminded of their situation by Denny who shouted, "Hurry up!" as his dark eyes stared at them intensely along the sawn-off barrel. They obediently grabbed handfuls of notes and cash bags and loaded them in.

Meanwhile, unnoticed by Denny, two drivers had entered the room to cash up their day's takings. As one of them looked through the cash window, still laughing about something his colleague was telling him, he suddenly caught sight of the scene in the cash room.

His presence at the window caused the cash office manager to look up from his loading, which suddenly alerted Denny. Before the driver's brain had registered what to do, Denny was back out of the office and pointing the gun at them.

"In you come, boys, in the office, now!"

Both men did as they were told, in utter shock at their sudden predicament. "Put your cash boxes straight in them bags and go and stand by the back wall," Ray demanded and started zipping the bags up and closing the straps down on them, the last of the table's contents now cleared.

"Keys! Keys! Give me the keys to this door!" Ray shouted at the manager, who was now shaking uncontrollably. He fumbled desperately in his pockets and the keys fell, hitting the floor.

The adrenaline fuelled Denny twitched, causing him to lift the gun in the air and his finger to press on the trigger.

The bang of the gun going off was deafening in the small office. The shot had exploded into the ceiling at the back of the office, causing dust and pieces of ceiling tile to fall, along with a fluorescent light and its fixtures.

Ray looked at Denny in disbelief as the three staff now cowered down by the table, holding their ears. Denny was equally surprised, as he had been pretty sure the safety catch was on.

The two drivers by the back wall were frozen to the spot, their hair and uniforms now covered in dust and fragments of shattered fibreglass, the light fitting swinging in front of them.

"Let's get out of here!" Denny screamed as a somewhat stunned Ray looked around the room through the clouds of dust.

They ran, Ray locking the door of the office behind them and tucking the key in his pocket. Denny had already concealed his shotgun and was struggling to attach the saddle bags to the motorbike.

The unexpected sound of the shotgun blast had echoed right through the depot yard and people were coming to investigate as Ray and Denny mounted the loaded bike and started it up. Two men came running from the office, having been informed of the robbery in progress through the cash office window, and raced towards them. Much to Denny's relief, just as one of the men reached out to grab at his coat, Ray pulled the bike away and towards the exit, swerving around an incoming bus, Denny's arms wrapped round his brother's waist, head down into his back.

Patrick was parked up at Sawbridge Lane, as instructed. He was at the back of the van and had the doors open, a wheel barrow and some bags of sand laid out around him. He wanted to make it look, to anyone passing, that he was either doing some kind of roadworks or rearranging his van because his materials had started moving in transit. Just sitting in the van, parked up, could look suspicious and stick in the memory of anyone passing.

At last, having stood nervously on the country lane for what seemed like hours, he was relieved to hear, then see the Lanes' motorbike heading towards him. He was even more relieved to notice that no one was following them and there was no sound of sirens.

He checked to see if any traffic was coming the other way, then signalled Ray to pull up to the van. Without an exchange of words, the saddle bags were removed quickly and put in the back of the van, then all three hoisted the motorbike in before both Lanes climbed in behind it. Patrick watched as a car passed, pulling his van door back. It gave the impression of a polite acknowledgement of the passing driver, but also obscured any vision of the Lanes or the bike if they looked in their rear-view mirror.

Patrick loaded the sand bags and the wheel barrow into the back and slammed the door on the Lanes, who then eagerly removed their helmets.

As Patrick started the van and pulled away, Denny turned to his brother. "Jesus, Ray, look at my hands! I'm shaking like a shitting dog!"

Ray looked at his brother, his heart pounding, adrenaline flooding through him. "What the fuck did you pull that trigger for, yah nutter?" he asked.

"I thought the safety was on. It wasn't deliberate, I tell you."

Ray saw the grin on his brother's face. He honesty wasn't sure if he was telling the truth. "Well, thank fuck it went into the ceiling and not into anyone in the room."

As Patrick pulled up to the junction, he couldn't believe his eyes, as racing towards him on the left were three police cars with sirens blaring.

"Shut up, you two," he said as his mouth instantly started to dry up. "It's the old bill."

He watched as the cars flew by, then slowly crept out of the junction onto the main road, looking in his mirror to see the tails of the screeching police cars and the back of Ray and Denny's heads peering out the little square windows in the back doors.

"Wonder where they're going." Denny laughed, mischievously.

Patrick shook his head. "Jesus, sometimes I wish I'd never met you two all those years ago and you had left me to get a good kicking."

The Lanes looked at each other and burst out laughing, which, as usual, then set Patrick off and suddenly all three were roaring with nervous laughter.

Harry looked at Ray and Denny across the waiting room table.

"I wish the last three years had gone as quickly as the time from you two being born to now. Look at you, both strapping men˙in front of me."

Harry had asked Patrick Hambleton to bring them both to see him on their own, without their mother's knowledge. Patrick had remained in the car.

"So, you've been busy at the local bus depot on a motorbike, I hear," Harry said and smiled at his sons' astonished expressions. "I haven't got time to listen to, nor will I except any bullshit, lads, so don't start. I know where you bought the shotguns. A bus garage and two betting shops in a fortnight. Even I was never that busy."

Ray spoke first. "We turned over the bus depot. No betting shops." He then turned to a grinning Denny.

"Sorry Ray, I was annoyed with myself for letting off that shot, so wanted to test myself out again." Denny could see the anger and upset in Ray's face. He was furious that his brother had done a solo job without a word to him. "I really am sorry, Ray. I'll explain later. And it's more money for us all."

Before Ray could answer, Harry spoke and their attention was instantly on their father. "Do you think I took all those risks, being in and out of these shitholes when I was younger, to set us up so that you two can carry on the same?" Harry looked at them both and knew what they were probably thinking, but were too scared and respectful to ever criticize him or call him a hypocrite. He had gotten reports back to him that the seeds had been sown years ago, anyway.

"Sorry, dad. We want to buy the boxing club and get Patrick's firm involved to build on the land behind it. You know, add a new gym and run it as a business together, me and Denny."

Denny nodded his agreement, then added, "Do you remember when we were kids and nan died? Dad, you cuddled me, Ray and mum together and said, 'We are the Lanes and we stick together.' Well, that's what we are doing. Everything me and Ray do and everything we get is ours. Me, Ray, you and mum."

"Yeah, and when you get out, dad, we will really get going," Ray added with authority in his voice. It both surprised Harry and filled him with pride. He knew there and then that very soon he would only be an advisor to these two and they would be their own men.

Harry cleared his throat and looked intently at them both. "Right, lads, you're your own men now and I won't interfere with your business ventures. But to cover your backs and make sure the money you robbed can't be traced, Patrick will fill out the paperwork to make it look like I've released the money from my sale of Nightingales to set you up in business with the boxing club. How you run it is down to you."

"That's brilliant, dad. Thanks," Ray said with a beaming smile.

Harry stood up and the boys followed his lead. "I'll tell your mum I'm setting you up in business, or she may be a bit suspicious how you two raised that amount of cash. And remember, you need to keep it a secret that I've bought the pub for us. It's a surprise for your mum." All three burst out laughing and shook hands then embraced. "Looks like the Lanes are back in business," Harry said proudly.

Burt Roswell tutted as he looked at the paper and mumbled to himself. A detective sat typing a report next to him and caught his boss' agitated ramblings.

"That has Lane written all over it," he groaned.

"You what, Sir?" the detective asked, not looking away from his typing.

"Ah, nothing. Just reading something about my old patch. Cash robbery at the bus depot, with a shot put into the ceiling and two local betting shops turned over as well. It all has the Lane mark on it, I bleeding well know."

"I thought you said Harry Lane was in prison, Sir."

"He is, but his two sons aren't."

The detective was grinning now, as it was common knowledge in the building his boss was obsessed with Harry Lane and his old area.

"You mean, Harry is like Mr Bridger in the Italian Job and controlling the robberies from inside, Sir?"

The sarcasm in the detective's remark wasn't lost on Burt as he walked away. "I'd put nothing past that man, absolutely nothing."

The detective was still smiling as he watched his boss walking away, muttering. He shook his head and continued with his typing.

32.

Ray and Denny walked through the doors of Miles Snooker Hall, both immaculately dressed in bespoke suits, handmade shirts, ties and beautifully polished shoes. They certainly stood out by the way they dressed and carried themselves, even if they admitted it themselves. They were, of course, trying to emulate their father somewhat, but ever since they had bought the boxing club as a legitimate business, they had discussed how they wanted to look the part and give people the right impression.

On many occasions when they were growing up, Harry had pointed out to them the importance of treating people with respect, unless crossed, and to get members of the community on side. They would encounter enough enemies on their journey through life, especially with their background.

He also emphasized the importance of seeing everybody as a possible earner or business opportunity.

They had rung Darren Miles this time, rather than just turning up on the chance the hall was open. He'd said he would be present, although it was pretty empty except for two middle-aged men playing snooker and a couple of younger lads on a pool table.

It was only twelve thirty on a weekday afternoon and as they both approached the bar, a girl who had been crouching down loading bottles onto the shelves, stood up and turned around, straight into Ray's eyeline. Both looked at each other with a wordless, lingering look.

'You're gorgeous,' Ray thought to himself. From the look on her face, she was thinking just how handsome he was, too. He smiled, which made her automatically return a smile back. "Two light and bitters, please," he requested kindly.

"Are you members?" the girl asked, clearly hoping that he would say yes, although she had never seen him before.

"No, we're not. Me and my brother are here to discuss some business with Mr Miles." Ray noted the obvious intrigue on her face. She was clearly taken by their smart attire and they were obviously making an impression. "I'm Ray, by the way. And this is my brother, Denny." He extended his hand, giving the girl, who was now blushing slightly, no option but to shake it and offer her name.

"I'm Georgie," she said and Ray held her gaze for the perfect length of time to set the seed of a thought in her brain. He could tell she wanted him and the feeling was mutual. But, of course, he would flirt and play it cool for the time being.

Denny was grinning. "Georgie. That's an unfortunate name, isn't it?"

Georgie looked briefly at Denny's dark eyes then back to Ray, slightly bemused.

"Shut up, Denny. Don't be an idiot." Ray handed Denny a pint glass, half filled with bitter, and a bottle of light ale. "Take no notice of him, Georgie. He was the after birth, but we look after him now and take him out with us."

Georgie giggled.

"Your name is beautiful, as are you," Ray said and winked at her, making her blush again.

Denny was studying his pint as he slowly poured the light ale in, the bitter foaming as the liquid rose up the glass. Without looking up, he raised an eyebrow. "Your surname ain't Parker, by any chance, is it Georgie?" he teased.

"No. Why?"

"Turn it in, Denny," Ray said, closing his fist and feigning that Denny was in for a punch if he didn't stop the banter. Both brothers laughed. "Georgie's surname will be Lane if she plays her cards right. What you reckon, Georgie?" Ray asked, winking at her again. "Mind you, you need to behave yourself if you want me to take you out. Or you'll have to join the ever-growing queue."

Georgie giggled and shook her head. "You're full of it, you are," she said and turned away to the optics, pretending to be busy, a huge grin on her face.

"Ah, young Ray and Denny. The Lane boys."

The brothers turned to see Darren Miles striding towards them, a friendly smile on his face, and a hand outstretched to greet them. "Georgie, can you nip into the store room and bring that delivery in while I chat to the boys? I'll come and help you out once I've finished this little bit of business."

"Yes, Mr Miles," she replied and walked out from behind the bar. As she walked past the boys, she gave Ray a coy, knowing smile.

Darren tutted and shook his head. His eyes creased into a warm smile. "I heard you, chatting up my staff."

"Be rude not to, wouldn't it, Darren?" a pleased-looking Ray replied.

"Just like your old man, you are. The girls loved your dad. Flirt for England, he could." Darren laughed. "He would flirt with women, men, priests, nuns, dogs, cats, anything, as long as he thought he could get a few quid out of them. Tell you what, lads, your old dad had his choice of women back then. Made it so bleedin' obvious it was embarrassing to watch as they threw themselves at him." His face suddenly took on a serious look. "Not when your mum was about, though. She would have torn their bleedin' eyes out."

Ray and Denny burst out laughing.

"Good old mum," Denny said.

"Tell you what, though," Darren continued, thoughtfully, "and I'm not just saying this, all that attention from the ladies, and your old man never strayed once. Was only ever your mum for him. That relationship is an old-fashioned love story, I tell yah."

"Talking of our old man, any danger we could purchase things off you in future without you grassing us up to him? We were summoned to the nick on the strength of that." Denny's serious face suddenly broke into a smile. "Done us a favour, anyway, Darren, as the old man fixed us up with Patrick Hambleton sorting out the purchase of the gym."

"Sorry lads, wasn't grassing. Just me and Harry go back a long way. And when his two boys come to me to buy weapons and ammunition, I have to respect him and let him know. You understand, lads."

Denny laughed. "Well, it never stopped you selling them to us, did it?"

Darren took a big, over-exaggerated sigh. "You know what, men? I've eaten in some of the finest restaurants in the world." He held their gaze for dramatic effect. "You know what the most expensive meal I've eaten is?" Ray and Denny shook their heads. "My wife's pussy. In the fifties, and that bastard meal has been costing me ever since." He turned and walked back to the bar. "So, if you or anyone else comes to me with cash for anything, I'm taking it, regardless of your dad or anyone else. When my missus' purse starts running low, I need to top it up. It's just not worth the misery."

Ray and Denny looked at each other, then back at the world-weary Darren and roared with laughter.

Darren paused briefly, watching the boys laughing, then reached into his pocket and removed a neatly folded piece of paper, handing it to Ray.

"This is the price for what you two asked for on the phone the other day."

Ray eyed the paper then glanced at Darren. "That's a bit strong, ain't it, Darren?"

"Best I can do you. Jesus, what you want? You come into my snooker hall asking me to sell you pool tables. While they're on your tables, they're not on mine.

Ray laughed. He loved Darren's banter. "It's only two tables for people to unwind on after training."

"Yeah, and top up with cash as well." Darren smiled, then took on a pensive look. "Right, tell you what. Two pool tables and I'll throw in a Space Invaders machine, how's that?"

Denny grinned. "Two tables, one Space Invaders and an Asteroid machine. I like playing asteroids."

"Jesus wept. You two want my blood. You're actually robbing me without pointing them poxy guns at me."

"So, you're saying it's a deal, then?" Ray chuckled and shook a reluctant, but impressed Darren's hand.

"Well, if you can make it, Georgie, I'd love that. It's the opening day of mine and Denny's gym. Plus, our parents are taking charge of the Green Man."

Georgie was ecstatic. Ray had invited her to their opening night and she knew she would be there, one hundred percent, but she wanted to keep it cool. "I'll try to make it, but I can't promise, as I'm always very busy," she answered.

Darren was listening in as he stacked the shelves with crisps and smiled at the masquerade being played out.

Chrissy cuddled Harry and laughed at Ray and Denny as the photographer for the local paper took various pictures of them in front of the boxing club. He had taken pictures of the refurbished boxing area inside, too. Patrick and his dad's firm had built a whole new extension at the back, housing weight training equipment and a host of new additions. It wasn't just a boxing club now, but the best gym in the area.

"Look at them, Harry, they are in their element, lording it up," Chrissy said.

Harry smiled. "Must admit, love, the place looks fantastic. I'm proud of the boys, they have done well."

Chrissy watched Ray chatting away to Georgie. "She seems a nice girl, Harry, what do you reckon?"

Harry laughed. "Well, he has the looks and style of the old man, so she must be a cracker."

Chrissy rolled her eyes and tutted. "I see you're back to your big-headed self, now you're out of prison." She smiled and rested her head on his shoulder. "God, it's good to have you home, Harry." She squeezed his hand tightly and he kissed her on the top of her head.

He spoke quietly. "It certainly is, love."

The photographer shouted out to the crowd, thoroughly engrossed in his duties. "Right, may I have everybody in this picture, please. All the staff, trainers and boxers. Littlest at the front, squatting, please." He then called to Harry and Chrissy. "Can we have mum and dad in this picture as well, please, up front with Ray and Denny?"

"Here we go, love, we are on duty," Harry said, gently encouraging his wife to follow the photographer's enthusiastic instructions.

"That's it, Mrs Lane, just there will do fine. Few more snaps and we will adjourn to the Green Man for further pictures."

"I thought that was it? We've got that little prat coming back to the pub with us as well? What's he want to take pictures there for?" she whispered just in Harry's earshot.

"Not your cuppa, him then, love?"

She smiled back. "Are you winding me up, Harry? Look at him. He's a right ponce."

They both laughed. "He probably just wants a few pictures at the pub to show the celebration," Harry lied.

The Green Man was packed with locals and friends from the many circles the Lanes mixed in. Trays of sandwiches and a mixed assortment of savouries were laid out on tables, covered in cling film, with flutes of champagne for everybody.

Chrissy squeezed Harry's arm. "Blimey, I didn't know you were going this overboard. Terry never said anything last night when I finished my shift. He just said there'd be a few drinks."

Harry smiled back at his wife just as the photographer stood next to them, clutching his camera.

"Can I grab some pictures of the new landlord and landlady, please? I'm running a bit behind schedule. Got a wedding, you see," he said, looking rather flustered.

Harry grinned at his wife. "He is talking to us, Chrissy."

She looked at him, confused, and was just about to speak when the photographer spoke hurriedly.

"Outside. Let's take a nice picture outside. Yes, yes, that's best, I think."

She allowed herself to be lead outside, still not registering what was happening. Harry pointed up at the sign above the door.

Mrs. Christine Lane, licensed to sell
intoxicating liquor for consumption on these
premises

She was speechless for a few seconds, then announced, "But I don't get it."

Harry laughed and wrapped his arm around her shoulder. "It's ours, love. We own this place now. All sorted while I was in nick."

She smiled and kissed him. "You're one crafty, sneaky sod, Harry Lane."

"Well, of course I am," he replied and winked as the now panicking photographer pleaded with them.

"I really must get some pictures and dash."

Chrissy looked at the man and back to Harry and burst out laughing. "Quick, Harry, go grab Ray and Denny. I want them in our pictures."

Burt Roswell slung the newspaper down on his desk in exasperated disgust. It was the local rag from his former area, open at a big, two-page spread.

"Bastard unbelievable!" he shouted.

"You OK, Sir?" a WPC, who had just entered the room, asked.

"They have only bought my old boxing club and the local pub," an agitated Burt said to the bemused lady.

"Who, Sir?"

"The Lanes. The Lanes, of course. The damn, scheming Lanes."

He picked the paper up again and jabbed at the article, repeating his words. "My boxing club! And they've changed the bleeding name."

He showed her the paper and she took a good look. It meant nothing to her, but she could see her boss' frustration. He looked like he may either explode or break down in tears.

DOUBLE CELEBRATION FOR
LOCAL FAMILY
*Two young businessmen open new boxing club
and gym for their community as their parents take
ownership of the Green Man public house*

She scanned the first few lines and looked at their pictures. "Very handsome men, Sir."

She jumped as a red-faced Burt snatched the paper from her hands and slung it across the office, scattering sheets of paper everywhere.

33.

1982

Denny approached a table of young lads, all of similar ages to him and Ray, and reached inside his suit, pulling out an envelope. The group looked up at him as he nonchalantly threw the envelope on the table.

"There's your money back from the incident the other week, less mine and Ray's commission. Next time, have a go back instead of being mugged off."

One of the lads tore open the envelope and looked at the notes inside just as Ray arrived, also dressed immaculately. He stood next to his brother, greeting the table's occupants and smiling at them.

"Alright boys, me and Denny are heading up the West End for a drink. You lot fancy it?" Ray asked.

There were a few muffled responses of 'not tonight'. They seemed more interested in the envelope and how it had been obtained.

The previous week, the lads had left the pub, gone back to one of their flats and decided to phone an escort agency for some spur of the moment entertainment. The girls had left and within thirty minutes, two heavies had returned, claiming the girls had left their handbags there, full of money. Which of course they hadn't. They were then marched unceremoniously to a cash point and forced to draw out the amount that was meant to be in the missing bags, which they knew nothing about, but were far too scared to argue about. So, they paid them, plus the money that had already been handed to the scheming girls, who had obviously gone and told their minders they were an easy target. The dejected lads had explained their situation to Denny, who had taken the escort agency card and said he would look into it.

"Nice one, Denny. You're a total star, thanks so much," one of the lads said.

"Don't mention it," Denny replied. "You should have had a go yourselves, though."

"You're joking! Them geezers were huge. We had no choice," the lad said, shaking his head, then muttered, "Bully bastards."

Denny grinned. "Well, they seemed to shrink once me and Ray spoke to them."

The lads looked at Denny in total awe. "What did you say to 'em?"

Denny looked at his captivated audience and his dark eyes were unblinkered, his face suddenly cold. "I said, if they wanted to run a bunch of brasses in our manor, they better do it without taking liberties with our mates or I'd burn their office to the ground. I then told that ugly junky-looking pimp boss of theirs, I'd cut him up into tiny pieces and post bits of his body in jiffy bags all around the country."

The lads looked up at Denny in utter amazement. He suddenly broke into a smile and clapped his hands together. "Right, are you sad, solemn wankers coming up west, or what?" The cheerful grin had returned. The lads never knew how to take Denny, or to fully believe what he said, but would certainly never question him. He had got them their money back, less their cut, so they had to be grateful.

"I can't do it tonight, lads. I was slaughtered when I got in last night," one at the table stated. "My old woman will kill me if I come home like that again tonight."

Another cut in, "Fact you pissed in the wardrobe didn't help," and they all laughed, Denny and Ray included.

"How about the rest of you? You coming? You may even pull some birds instead of getting conned by brasses," Ray said wryly.

"We never even shagged them. If we had had a bunk up it wouldn't have been so bad," one of them moaned. "All we did was get them to peel their kit off and do a double act on the floor for us while we sat drinking."

"Right, come on, Ray. Let's leave these miserable wankers to wallow in self-pity." Denny pulled his handkerchief from his pocket and mocked wiping tears from his eyes, which made them all laugh.

Ray and Denny were well-liked and respected by everyone in the pub. They never bullied anyone, but it was fully understood that bad behaviour wouldn't be tolerated in their parents' establishment. The atmosphere amongst all the pub's regulars was fantastic, with a real community spirit.

Denny neatly folded and replaced his handkerchief.

"Don't say you wasn't offered, lads." Ray smiled.

"Definitely next time," a voice offered.

"Well, when you sad bastards are sitting in your flats all alone snorting speed from the plastic tits of a blow-up doll, me and Ray will be doing Columbia's finest from the real thing," Denny said and laughed, as did the lads.

As they watched Ray and Denny leave, one shouted out, "Oi, Denny, did you fuck that bird you left with the other night?"

Denny didn't reply. Both men continued walking towards the door before Ray turned and hollered, "We are Lanes. We don't fuck women; we make love to them. And trust me, they always come back wanting more."

With that, they were gone.

"They are unreal, them two. You've got to love 'em," one of the lads said.

"Yeah, glad they're mates, and on our side," another chipped in.

"Can't believe they got our cash back off that bloke." They all raised their glasses. "Ray and Denny," they roared and continued laughing.

Ray laughed to himself as he headed back to a table occupied by a group of both men and women. He watched Denny through now very merry eyes as he moved around the dance floor with a girl who was laughing at whatever he was shouting into her ear.

The pair had landed in the West End with no real plan for a spur of the moment night out, which always seemed to be the best ones. They had gone from bar to bar and found themselves in this disco, now somewhat the worst for wear, but both in great spirits and enjoying themselves. As per usual the brothers seemed to attract attention and both men and women alike were drawn to their natural aura. Ray, like his father, had the knack of charming and convincing people of anything, while Denny's dry humour and obvious lack of fear, the hint of volent intentions in his eyes, seemed to attract and unsettle people in equal measure. Both men were fiercely loyal, making exceptional friends and protecting people they liked and trusted. Again, like their father, they were superb at adapting to most people and situations. All eyes were on them as they held court.

As Denny returned to the table with his dancing partner, Ray looked across at him, smiled and winked. Denny acknowledged his brother with a grin, then leaned in to the woman.

Her name was Danielle. Tall, slim, with long, black hair, she was quite attractive, Ray thought as his drunk, hazy mind drifted to thoughts of his Georgie. She was the total opposite to Danielle. Georgie was very petite, blond, and had gorgeous green eyes. Very attractive, with a determined but very kind nature. She had been studying hair and beauty when Ray had first met her and working part-time at Miles Snooker Hall, but now worked at a salon. As Ray's mind wandered in mellow, drunk contemplation, he decided he was going to ask Georgie to marry him and buy her her own beauty salon. He smiled away to himself and silently congratulated himself for what he considered, after six hours of drinking, a brilliant idea.

"I'm going to marry Georgie," he said to a man to his left and then repeated it to a lady on his right, who both returned his smile but had no idea what he had actually said as the music was so loud.

Denny tried to understand Danielle as she shouted in his ear, spraying spit over it. His eyes, though, were transfixed on the dance floor where an inebriated man, dancing with his partner with a lit cigarette in his mouth, slowly nodded off on her shoulder for a few seconds. They were both still in motion, in pace with a slow, romantic, number. Denny watched in fascination as the man's cigarette began burning a hole in her dress, then he roared with laughter as the burning ember finally made contact with her skin and she exploded in shocked rage, slapping her dance partner across the face.

Meanwhile, Ray tried to understand the man opposite him who was screaming something about a house party and did they want to go. He read his lips as saying 'south' but couldn't catch the rest, just nodded and mouthed 'yes'.

The next thing they knew, the brothers were heading across the Thames in a taxi, Ray's glazed eyes taking in the spectacle of the London skyline at night, his head drunkenly wobbling with every bump in the road.

Ray's eyes opened slowly and he gingerly looked up at a grinning Denny, who was clearly still drunk. As he hauled himself forward to sit up, he felt a weight on his shoulder disappear and glanced around to see a woman slide off him and onto the sofa cushion, letting out a soft moan as she slumped, but not waking.

"Come on, Ray, let's get out of here before they all wake up," Denny said as Ray looked at the state of the room; cans and empty bottles, ash trays full of dogends and spliffs, people lying scattered across the floor, asleep or floating about in a haze, whimpering and hungover.

"Go and have a cowboy wash and straighten up, then let's get on our toes," a livelier and more alert Denny instructed his brother.

Ray fumbled his way to the bathroom and looked down at the man in the bath, asleep, shirt still on, but no trousers, just underpants and socks. He then caught sight of his own bloodshot eyes in the mirror above the sink. He ran the tap, cupping his hands and scooping water over his face, pushing his wet hands through his hair to tidy it up. He removed the tie which was hanging loosely around his neck, rolled it up neatly and placed it in the inside pocket of his suit.

He looked at the man snoring in the bath and mumbled to himself, "Let's get out of here."

"Where the bleeding hell are we, Denny?" Ray asked as the brothers walked along the road, trying to get some bearings.

"Somewhere in South London, poxy hole," Denny moaned. "Nothing anywhere, by the looks of it. No shops, tubes, trains, nothing. And I need a shit again. Been twice already and now I'm in trouble again."

Ray looked at his brother's distressed face and laughed. "That's all that drink going through you, son."

Denny now looked pale. "I'm touching cloth, Ray. If I don't find somewhere soon, I'm dropping my kecks here and going."

As they approached a sports field, Ray spotted a public toilet. "There you go, Denny boy, you're saved," he said, laughing at his brother, who was now walking like he was squeezing a coin between his arse cheeks.

Approaching the toilets, they saw that there was an attendant cleaning around the area and an out of order sign on the door to the gents. Denny rushed towards the door of the disabled toilets as the old attendant shouted out, "Excuse me, sir, they are disabled only."

Denny carried on running and shouted back, "I will be disabled if I don't go. I'll have a bad case of chocolate legs."

Ray looked at the man and shook his head. "We don't want that, do we, mate?"

Denny closed the cubicle door, but before he could even sit on the pan, his arse exploded, firing brown liquid everywhere. Disgusted with the scene, and with sweat on his brow, the worst hangover he'd ever known started taking over him. He tidied the area the best he could, but decided he couldn't stand anymore, washed his hands and left.

He tucked his shirt in and tidied himself up, then walked over to the attendant and handed him a note.

"There you go, mate, get yourself a pint tonight. You done me a favour, letting me use the disabled toilet."

The man looked at the note and said a quiet thank you. Denny held the man's shoulder gently and leaned in. "I tell you what, my old mate, I don't know who used that toilet before me but judging by the skid marks on the back of that pan, they must have an arsehole in the small of their back. Honestly, it's unmerciful."

The man didn't reply, just looked at Denny's fake sympathetic expression.

"I'm just marking your card, mate, that's all. I'd hate you to think that in there is down to me!"

As their taxi brought them closer to home, Ray pointed to the still-derelict Nightingales.

"We need to get a team together and go to work. I want us to open that place up again before it's knocked down for good."

Denny looked out the window and nodded without speaking.

"I'm going to ask Georgie to marry me, as well, so I need to load up on cash," Ray continued, pensively.

Denny stuck a glass under the optic and poured a measure of whisky as his mum walked into the bar in her dressing gown.

"Oi, what you doing on that at eight in the morning? And where's

Ray?"

"Morning, mum," Denny said grinning, and kissed her on the forehead as Ray appeared.

Denny handed him the drink.

"Not you as well," she said as Ray took a mouthful.

"Morning, mum." He smiled. "Strictly medicinal, these are. We've had a heavy night. But I'm also going to ask Georgie to marry me, so it's a celebration as well."

Chrissy looked at her two sons and smiled. "Well, go get a shower, the pair of you. You stink." She tutted and added wryly, "She sees the state of you, there is a very good chance her answer will be no!"

As she walked away, a grinning Denny shouted, "Is that a full English I can hear you doing in that kitchen, mum?"

34.

Denny stood inside the closed entrance of Pikes betting shop. He had locked it and turned the sign to closed. Even though it was due to shut in ten minutes anyway, it was Grand National day and there were still quite a few nervous punters in the shop. Ray and Denny knew that choosing National Day, even right before closing time, they ran the risk of the shop being busy, with more customers than usual. But the prospect of the shop's tills and safe having a much larger prize in them was too much of a temptation. The shop was decked with Grand National regalia; posters, balloons and lots of empty bottles of cheap Prosecco and empty plastic cups on the tables. It was obvious that free drinks had been provided on arrival, all part of the day's promotion.

Denny pointed his sawn-off towards the counter, with occasional sweeps either side at the motionless punters, some still clutching betting slips or the shop's tiny pens. They had been shocked into stunned silence by the brothers' swift entrance. They had bellowed instructions at both the customers and staff, telling them to relax and do as they were told so no one would get hurt.

Ray pointed a revolver at the two staff members and told them to start loading two very large sports bags with the contents of the safe and tills while he set about cutting the phone wires.

When he was done, Ray took one of the sports bags, now bulging with notes and bags of coins, zipped it up and slung it across the room to Denny, who trapped it with his foot while still pointing the sawn-off at the room. Ray had, by now, tucked his pistol under his belt, but it was still visible. He set about zipping up the other bag, picking it up and backing up towards the front door where Denny was slowly concealing his own gun inside his jacket.

Denny unlocked the door, and the men left the shop. As they turned, Denny shouted, "Thanks for your patience, everybody. I hope you all had winners today. And same to the staff, you were very hospitable." He then reached up and burst one of the balloons that was dangling by the door.

Then he was gone, much to the relief of the occupants of the turf accountants.

Brian Green sat patiently with the engine of his Ford Granada purring. He was wearing a cap, sunglasses and false mustache in order to disguise his features. Brian was known across London as a superb driver who would work freelance for any firm if the price was right. This was his third job with the Lanes in seven days, and the last on their list.

Ray and Denny opened the back door and slung in their sports bags. In the split second just before Ray threw himself into the car behind his brother, he spotted a young policeman who was strolling with his hands behind his back in a carefree manner on the opposite side of the street. The policeman seemed to momentarily freeze as he saw the balaclava-clad man tuck himself into the car and slam the door, then, in disbelief at what he was witnessing, he finally fumbled for his radio as the car moved out into the traffic. As it sped past him, he saw Denny's eyes staring directly back at him through his balaclava.

The car was totally silent now. All three men were fully aware the PC had radioed details through and they could expect company any minute. Not only was Brian a fantastically skilled driver, he also had an understanding of London's streets on a par with a black cab driver's Knowledge.

Brian swerved skillfully in and out of the traffic whilst simultaneously eyeing the two police cars in pursuit in his mirrors. He knew he was more than a match for these two, but he needed to lose them as fast as possible before back-up arrived.

He headed off the main drag and into a built-up area of houses and flats with the searing sound of sirens still close by.

"I'm going to lead them into a quiet bit, lads, then I reckon you need to put them out of action to bide us some time," Brian shouted and took a sharp left, then another right straight after. They found themselves in a set of garages with a field behind it, so their only escape now was to swing round and back the way they had come. Brian spun the car round, pulled up to a stop between the garages and waited, listening as the sirens drew nearer.

"Right, boys, sort them two out."

Without a word, Ray and Denny climbed out of the Granada and removed their weapons. The two police cars skidded into the garage area and came to an abrupt halt at the sight of the brothers brandishing their weapons. Before they could react, Denny had blasted the tire of the first car then darted to the second car and did the same.

Ray and Denny were now pointing their guns at the windows, screaming at the policemen to get out. Denny instructed the two from the first car and a third from the second to stand by the fence at the back of the garages, overlooking the field, while Ray removed the keys from the two cars and tore the radios from their connections.

As soon as the brothers had climbed back in, Brian's Granada flew out of the garages and right into the housing estate, leaving a long set of tire burn marks on the road. Some children playing football on a nearby green watched in astonishment as the car screeched off.

As Brian expertly negotiated his gears, taking each twist and turn of the narrow lane they were flying down with skill and precision, they suddenly caught sight of a van ahead of them, which had slowed and pulled into a layby to let them past. Brian slowed the car down and, as they neared it, they realized it was a post van.

"Pull over, that will do us," Denny said.

Denny climbed out and pointed his shotgun at the windscreen of the van. He instructed the driver, a man of about thirty years of age, to get out as Brian brought the car around to the back of the vehicle.

"Open the back up, mate, and get in." The postman looked into Denny's dark eyes, through the balaclava, and climbed in. Two sports bags were slung in behind him, then he watched as Ray, Denny and Brian pushed the Granada over a grass verge and out of sight. All three climbed in the back, pulling the doors almost shut, but leaving just enough light to seep in so they could see.

"What's your name, mate?" Ray asked the terrified postman.

"Jamie," the man's croaky voice replied.

"Alright, Jamie, you've got nothing to worry about, my mate. We just need to borrow your van. Once we get a chance, we will drop you off, OK?"

Jamie nodded without speaking.

"Good man. Now take your jacket, shirt and tie off," Ray instructed in a calming voice.

Jamie did as he was told then started unbuckling his belt.

"Don't worry, Jamie, we don't want to bum you. You can leave your trousers on," Denny said.

"We just want the top half, so our driver can put them on or it may stand out, him driving without a uniform," Ray explained, reassuringly.

Brian slowly edged the van away, dressed in Jamie's shirt, tie and Royal Mail jacket. He had removed his cap and shades.

Ray picked up some masking tape that was on the van floor. "I'm just going to cover your eyes, so we can remove these poxy balaclavas, OK, mate?"

Jamie nodded.

"You are not going to get hurt," he said as he taped Jamie's eyes.

"Where do you drink, Jamie?" Denny asked as he removed his face covering.

"The Old Albion," Jamie replied then flinched as he felt Denny right next to him.

"And where do you live?"

Jamie sat silent as Denny picked up a parcel delivery card and a pen from the van floor.

"I know where you drink and what you look like, so tell me where you live."

This prompted Jamie to tell them his address, which Denny jotted down.

"You've been a star today, Jamie. So just tell the truth when you are questioned, then keep an eye on your letterbox in about a month. There will be a nice few quid in an envelope for your trouble, mate. Keep your trap shut about the envelope. That's your compensation," Denny said, patting him on the back.

"Right, mate, we are dropping you out here. You got enough for a tube home?" Ray asked.

"Yes," Jamie said as Brian said it was clear to let him out.

As Brian pulled the van away, he looked at Jamie in his wing mirror, standing on the roadside in vest and trousers, bewildered, slowly trying to pull the tape off his eyes and squinting as the light hit his pupils.

"Poor fucker." He laughed and switched on the radio. As the van headed along the road to their safe house, Brian sang along to *El Camino Real* by Lee Dresser as it blared out and the now relieved and relaxed Lanes joined in with the chorus, laughing as they sang and taking a look inside the sports bags.

"El Camino Real, take me home, back to Monterey, 'cause I didn't have much luck, down in LA. El Camino Real, take me home, back to Monterey, 'cause I didn't have much luck in LA, Well I didn't have much luck down in LA, no, no, no, no, you know I didn't have much luck down in LA."

A grinning WPC turned and winked at her colleague and mouthed "Lane". He smiled and rolled his eyes before they both turned their attention to their boss, Burt Roswell, who was looking at the paper.

"Two banks and one betting shop in seven days. What's that incompetent shower doing? It's obvious it's the Lane brothers," Burt said and looked at his officers.

The WPC spoke without looking away from her typing. "Can't all be the Lanes' work every time, Sir."

"You mark my words, it's them," he said, exasperated. "Now watch another legitimate business miraculously materialize and the locals give them even more money and treat them like sodding heroes," he added and walked out of the room.

"Pint of lager please, mum," Denny said and looked around the pub at the late afternoon crowd, not noticing the lady sitting down, staring intently at him.

"Hello love, you OK? Where's Ray?" Chrissy asked as she flicked the lager tap off and handed the perfectly poured pint to her son.

Denny lifted it to his mouth, took a large gulp, then replied, "He's just sorting some bits out over at the gym with the staff. He'll be about fifteen minutes."

"It's just there's a young lady sitting over there waiting for you. Been here over an hour. Said it was important and she would wait." Chrissy motioned with her eyes to where the young lady was sat and, without speaking, Denny looked round as his mum continued.

"Danielle, she said her name was."

Denny looked back around at his mum's knowing smile and then back to Danielle, who gave him a nervous smile and a wave. He left the bar and approached her.

Chrissy kept an eye as her son sat down and spoke with Danielle. She could only wish she could hear the conversation over the goings on in the bar, especially as she saw it was getting serious.

"It's one hundred per cent positive, and it's yours," Danielle said angrily.

Denny eyed the bar and gave a fake smile back to his mum, who then turned to serve someone.

"Right, until I know for sure it's mine, if she asks, you tell my mum we've been seeing each other for a while," Denny said, looking deep into her eyes.

Danielle felt the urge to mock this request, but his unblinking stare unsettled her.

Before she could think of a response, he laughed suddenly. "I'm quite pleased with myself, really," he stated.

"Why? Because I'm pregnant?" She smiled.

"No, 'cause you're actually attractive. I fancy you. The amount I drank that night, I can't remember a thing! You could have been a nightmare."

He then stood up as he spotted Ray enter the pub, a huge grin on his face.

"Here's Ray. You remember my brother Ray, don't you?"

She just nodded back. She couldn't believe how blasé he was being about the whole situation. As she went to speak, he cut in.

"I'll get you another orange. You can't have anything else in case that baby is down to me. You eaten?"

She looked at him in disbelief. "No, but I need to get my bus soon, back to South London," she answered rather weakly.

"Bus bollocks, we'll have some grub, then I'll pay for a cab home for you."

"Fuck's sake, Denny, is it yours?" Ray asked and looked across from the bar at Danielle.

"She reckons it is, but until she has a test, I'm not trusting her,"

Denny replied then grinned. "I may be a catch, but the way she flicked her knickers off the end of her big toe so quickly that night, tells me I ain't her first."

Ray looked at Denny and shook his head. "What if the baby is yours?" he asked.

"Well, if it is, it's down to me. I'll take her on board. Blood test first, though. I'm very attached to my wallet and its contents. I'm not forking out for some other prick's kid." His smile disappeared as he glanced across at Danielle, then back to his brother. "If she is carrying a Lane, Ray, then that's a whole different ball game. No one brings that baby up but us!"

35.

1985

"Happy Birthday, Mum," Denny said, handing Chrissy a parcel and a huge bouquet of flowers. He kissed her on the cheek, then Ray leaned in, repeating the same action.

"Thanks lads," she said with a beaming smile, cuddling both her sons, then leaning back to inspect them both.

"You all sorted, boys?" Harry asked and winked.

Chrissy looked at her husband and back at her grinning sons. "What are you suspicious sods up to? I know them looks. And you, Lane, you old rogue, you…"

"We've got a little surprise for you, mum. But you've got to go on a little journey in my car," Ray stated.

"Yeah, and I'm afraid that we need to blindfold you so you can't see till we arrive there," Denny added.

Chrissy looked at Harry with a fake stern look. "I thought you said we were going to just relax at the pub tonight. I've had a lovely day, so that would suit me."

Harry had taken Chrissy to a show in the West End the previous evening and they had stayed in a beautiful hotel overlooking the Thames. They had awoken to a champagne breakfast, followed by a shopping spree and a lunch at Simpsons on the Strand. They had staff covering the day at the pub, so she was under the illusion that she and her husband were going to finish the proceedings with a few slow drinks on home ground, but she now found herself being led blindfolded into Ray's car.

Chrissy felt the car gliding through the streets, trying to work out their destination from the various turns.

"Where the bleeding hell are you lot taking me? All these surprises and nights out, I'm not a young girl anymore. I need my relaxation," she said.

"Blimey, champagne breakfast in bed, en suite foam baths, she relaxes any more she will go into a coma," Harry quipped.

"Cheeky sod," she returned and gave him a playful slap. She pulled her hand back and tried to pull at her blindfold, but Harry spotted her and grabbed her hand.

"No peeking, you."

The car came to a stop and Chrissy heard all the doors being opened, then felt Harry taking hold of her hand and guiding her from the vehicle and onto the pavement. There were a few moments of silence then she felt the blindfold being removed and allowed her eyes to adjust to the light. As things came into focus, she looked at a huge sign above her, lit up in bold, purple neon lights.

NIGHTINGALES

She looked at the building, beautifully refurbished, the grass area surrounding it cut and trimmed to perfection, and felt elation at the sight. She suddenly remembered the dishevelled state the exterior had been in the last time she had looked at it, all those years ago. She had kept her promise to never pass the building again while it looked like that.

She turned to Harry. "You bought your business back, love?"

He shook his head and smiled. "No, no, my club-running days are over. Got my work cut out with you and that pub. That's enough for me, now." He motioned towards Ray and Denny. "This is all down to them two. Meet the proud new owners of Nightingales Night Club, your sons."

She looked at her smiling sons with both surprise and pride, as Denny spoke. "Remember when me and Ray were teenagers on the bus, off to see dad, and you said you never wanted to see the old place like that again?"

She nodded. "And you two said you would buy it back in years to come, so I could step through them doors again."

"Exactly," Ray cut in. "And we've done it. Although the process took longer than we had anticipated." He stepped towards the door. "Come on, mum, let's show you what we've done with the old place."

She interlocked her arm with Harry's and tugged at him as they both walked into the club, following their sons' lead.

"You and your secrets, Harry sodding Lane. Suppose you knew all along these two had purchased this place back?"

He said nothing, just gave her a cheeky smile and wink, which she returned.

As they opened the main doors into the hall, there was a brief silence, then she was greeted with a loud roar of "Happy Birthday!" and a cheer as she scanned the hall, seeing all the familiar faces; all the locals from the pub, other friends, and of course a super spread of Vital food.

"So much for a quiet birthday taper-down drink tonight, then, Harry?" she remarked as a flute of champagne was handed to her by a young girl, obviously one of Ray and Denny's new recruits.

The girl smiled and said, "Happy birthday, Mrs Lane," then moved off to serve the other guests.

"Bless her, Harry, she only looks about sixteen. Don't look old enough to be serving alcohol."

"That's 'cause you're getting old, love. She's probably about twenty-five," he said.

Just as she was about to pull him up on his comment, she spotted the reporter from the local paper who had taken the pictures for Ray and Denny's gym and the pub. "There's that annoying little ponce reporter again."

Harry laughed at his wife's words and looked across at the reporter who was trying to do his best David Bailey impression. "Come on, love, let's have a good look about, see what you think of the new look."

Chrissy felt like she was going back in time as they headed across the maple dance floor. She eyed every contour of the new Nightingales. It looked beautiful and, although obviously sections had been upgraded and modernised, there was a lovely balance of old and new and certainly enough of the former design, including the stunning vaulted, coffered ceiling and the shinning dance floor to invoke a flood of memories.

"Here, Harry, let's sit at our old favourite booth and people-watch for a while," she said and the pair went and sat down, both eyeing the room happily.

Ray was playing the perfect host as he circulated the room,

followed by the ever-present photographer, snapping away.

"He is just like you used to be, Harry. Look at him, thinks he is a bleeding celebrity and loves the attention. Both a pair of big-headed sods, aren't you?"

Harry looked at Ray holding court, then at his wife and smiled. "Doing well, though, love. I'm proud of them both."

"Yes, so am I, Harry," she returned then tutted, shaking her head. "Must think I was born yesterday, you lot." He looked at her as she was watching Denny heading back to a table where his wife sat with other friends.

"What's that then, love?" he asked.

"Stan and Molly may have been naïve enough to think you were just a successful businessman, but I'm not. Those two have been up to as much no good as you were back then."

Harry tried to look as innocent as possible, but he knew Chrissy was a totally different ball game to his parents. As he went to speak, she cut him off.

"I don't want to know. They're their own men and I'm not even going to contemplate what they have been up to. All I know is, this wasn't bought and refurbished just on the profits from that gym." She looked directly into his blue eyes. "If they end up in nick, they've got their own wives to visit them. But if you're involved in anything with that pair and you end up in there, you can go stuff yourself, 'cause I'm not going through that again."

Harry looked at her for a while and then, as usual, they both burst out laughing.

"Been through a lot, girl, ain't we?" he said and wrapped his arm around her.

She rested her head on his chest and sighed. "We certainly have, Harry. But never as bad as when you were away last time and this place was derelict. God, I felt low then."

"I know, love, I know," he replied softly and kissed her. "They are no mugs, them two. They'll make a go of this place now, and they've got the gym. Plus, they have men on the doors of other pubs and clubs, doing security for them." He laughed and she lifted her head to look up at him.

"What you laughing at?" she asked, grinning at him.

"I was remembering when Ray first asked Georgie to marry him and her parents said to him, 'And how will you provide for our daughter?'" He laughed again. "Now she owns Georgie's Hair and Beauty Salon, paid for through all these other interests the boys have."

Chrissy sat upright again and finished the last of her champagne. "God, time flies, love. Only seems like yesterday when you were running this place like you were the king of the area and I was breaking the news to mum and dad that I was pregnant. Now they're running the place and they're both married, with Danielle pregnant with number two and Georgie expecting her first."

Chrissy looked across at Ray and Georgie and then over at the table where Denny and Danielle were sat. "I worry about that pair, Harry."

Harry followed his wife's eyeline towards Denny and Danielle. "They'll be OK, love. I know they have their ups and downs, but it works itself out."

Chrissy spoke reflectively, still looking out at her two sons and their wives. "Ray and Georgie, now that's love, like you and me were. Look at her, she is as happy as a sandboy with her life with Ray and running her salon. But that other two, that's convenience, and volatile at the best of times."

"Where is this coming from, love?" Harry enquired, seeing the pensive look on his wife's face.

After a brief pause, she said, "Oh, do me a favour, love, that's the best example of a shotgun wedding I've ever witnessed."

He gave her a surprised look and smiled, suddenly remembering how streetwise she was. Something about her words and the atmosphere made him feel like he was back in the sixties with her again.

"The day Danielle turned up at the pub to tell him she was pregnant - because I know for a fact that's why she was there - the poor cow looked like she was shitting herself. And him there, looking more surprised he had a visitor than anyone. In fact, I'd say he had no idea who she was at first." She began laughing. "And that lying sod told me they had been seeing each other for over six months. And she went along with the story. And that brother of his, straight-faced backing the story up."

"Maybe they were seeing each other, love. You know how secretive

Denny can be, and how unpredictable he is," Harry offered.

"Oh, turn it in," she replied with a very sarcastic tone, rolling her eyes. She stood up. "Come on, grandad Lane, let's go and be sociable and celebrate."

Harry smiled and stood up. "Come on then, grandma Chrissy."

She held his hand as they headed back across the dance floor towards the others. "That was a shotgun wedding, Mr. And this nightclub was funded by shotguns. Don't you lot go thinking you can kid this old bird."

Harry smiled to himself and squeezed her hand.

36.

1988

Ray shook his head as a grinning Denny got into the passenger side of his brand-new Jaguar XJS.

"Don't know what you're grinning about, you nutter. I could hear you and Danielle from out here."

"No, you could hear her shouting, not me. I was laughing and dodging plates," Denny replied as he shut the door.

"Yeah, I heard them smashing, as well. Sounded like a bleedin' Greek restaurant," Ray said as he pulled away. "What's wrong with you pair?"

Denny placed a cigarette in his mouth then pressed the button to open a gap in his door window. He ignited the cigarette, taking a long, slow draw. "She keeps accusing me of being out shagging when I'm working."

Ray laughed. "Well, she is right, isn't she? You're always at it. Just as well I'm a loyal family man and on the ball with our finances, because with your hedonistic lifestyle, we would be out of business or banged up behind the door."

Denny took a final drag of his Benson's and threw the butt out of the window. "Where's the old man? Already over the club?" he asked.

"Yeah, 'course he is. Loves organising the boxing do's, don't he? Right in his element." Both men smiled.

The boxing evenings at Nightingales had become a regular feature soon after the boys had reopened the old place. It had been Harry's idea and the boys had asked their dad to oversee most of the proceedings. These days, all things Lane-related were a team effort and the three men consulted each other on any ideas they had. Although now, Harry had taken more of a back seat with most things and was happier with a quieter life, running the pub with Chrissy, but of course Harry's connections were vast and it would be foolish for Ray and Denny not to involve him.

Harry was at the forefront of the boxing evenings and the Lanes' finances had even been put into promoting and managing two professional fighters. Both lads had worked their way up through the ranks, training at the Lanes' gym and having exceptional amateur careers. When Harry had spotted some well-known faces from the pro ranks nosing around his boys, he had decided he would manage their professional careers himself from their base and with their own investments.

Ray smiled as he caught sight of Harry moving around Nightingales, chatting away to various people. He had a flashback to his father going through the same procedure so many times, in this very building, when he was a child and remembered how it had fascinated him as a youngster. The noises, the people, the atmosphere, the old faces from the past, many of whom had moved or sadly passed away. The ones that remained from those days, although older, still retained their character, always teasing Ray that although he and Denny had made a good go of the new look Nightingales, the golden era was, at least in their own opinions, in the sixties under Harry's reign.

As always, the venue was packed for this quarterly boxing show. In the past, they had hosted professional events and had a couple televised, another cheeky little venture Ray had secured with the help of Harry's connections that had proved very lucrative. Tonight was an amateur event, but it had proven to be very popular nonetheless and brought boxing clubs from all across London and the South East. There were lads as young as eleven taking part, as well as grown men at senior level.

As was now tradition, the Vitals provided the evening meals for the seated customers and there were various singers to provide entertainment during the intervals. Harry always tried to get a couple of celebrities in, normally an ex-top-ranking British professional fighter, to hand out the trophies and medals, pose for photos and sign autographs.

All this was playing out in front of the long-suffering Burt Roswell, who had brought a team of boxers over from the West London club he was now involved with. He eyed his nemesis Harry Lane and his two sons as they posed for photos with an ex-British middleweight for the local press, all dressed in tuxedos and holding their clenched fists up, smiling broadly. Burt quietly seethed at the sight, loathing the celebrity status this family afforded themselves locally.

He had never forgiven them for taking over his beloved Spartan Boxing Club and changing the name.

Denny drew on his cigarette and surveyed the crowded room, then looked up at the ring as the time-keeper rang the bell to end the fight. He watched intently as the judges handed their score cards in, then turned to Patrick Corrigan, who was sat next to him.

"Our boy all day long, there. Good kid, he is. Loves a war, he does."

Patrick smiled. "Bit like you when you was a kid, eh, Denny?"

Both men laughed, then Denny held Patrick's gaze and Patrick recognised the look. "No. Whatever it is, no!" Patrick said defiantly.

A wicked smile spread across Denny's face. "You've not heard what I was going to propose yet, have you?"

"No, and I don't want to. But ever since I was ten years old, I've known that I'm going to hear it anyway," Patrick said, feigning weariness.

Denny pulled on his cigarette and squinted his eyes in thought, then slowly exhaled the smoke. "Got this mate who is in the smuggling game, see. Well, he has a big shipment of cannabis coming in soon and asked if I want in."

Patrick shook his head. "You're not getting involved in drugs now, Denny, are you?"

"Not really drugs, is it, mate? Only a bit of Moroccan. You know me and Ray, we like to have more than one horse in the race and our shot guns and robbery days are over. We are totally off the pavement now, not worth the risk."

"You do what you like, Denny, but like I always say, I'm a family man with a very successful building company. I want no more to do with your madness."

Denny wrapped his arm round Patrick's waist and leaned in closer. "I was just thinking transport, that's all, from the coast when the packages arrive."

Patrick looked at Denny's dark grin.

"Them big old cement lorries you use. I was thinking we could aim the blocks of gear in the barrels, fill them right up, nice little fleet of Corrigan Developments cement lorries heading up the motorway loaded to the hilt with blocks of puff. Easy little earner for you."

Patrick looked at him in utter amazement. "If Ray had said that, I'd think it was a joke. But you, ya mad bastard, you mean it. Two words for you, Denny, and the second one is 'off'." Both men laughed. "Anyway, I'm off on holiday next week. Taking the old woman and the kids to Spain."

Denny nodded to a group of men across the room and indicated that he would be over shortly. "I've got a rake of travellers cheques you can have half price, if you want them for your holiday," Denny said.

Patrick shook his head again. "I thought you said you were off the pavement? That's you who's been blagging all them travel agents, ain't it?"

"Is it, bollocks! I'm hardly going to risk bird poncing about robbing poxy travel agents, am I? Maybe ten years ago, I would have, but not now. No, I'm just helping a mate shift them."

Patrick nodded thoughtfully. "OK, I'll have a look at them tomorrow. Will save me a few quid."

Denny laughed. "You're an expert at saving money. You're still driving that old Capri, I see. I spotted you going through town the other day in it."

Patrick chuckled. "I have to give it a run out every few months for old time's sake. My old woman hates it but I can't face getting rid of it."

Denny signalled to one of his staff that he wanted a refill for him and Patrick, then laughed. "We had some mad old nights out in that old motor when you first got it. Murder for drink driving as well, weren't we?"

Patrick tutted. "We certainly were. Well naughty, really, thinking back."

The barman handed Denny and Patrick their drinks from a tray and disappeared.

"That little sod of a son of mine has pulled the window winder off the passenger side as well. Snapped it clean off." He paused momentarily, then burst out laughing. "Do you remember when you chinned Barry Rowlett when we were driving back from Camden?"

Denny laughed with him. "Yeah, vaguely, now you mention it."

Patrick took a mouthful of his drink then fired it back in the glass, as it went down the wrong way.

"What?" Denny asked, smiling as Patrick laughed and spluttered.

"He drove you mad for about an hour, winding you up, pissed out of his head. I was watching you. I knew it was coming." Patrick wiped tears away from his streaming eyes with his handkerchief. "You never said a word, just pressed the cigarette lighter in, waited, then when it popped out, you stuck the red-hot lighter on his arm." Patrick roared with laughter, setting Denny off again. "The shock on his face looking at you wide-eyed and mouth open, then you chinned him and he was asleep in the back for the rest of the journey."

Denny took a mouthful of his drink and laughed again. "Poor old Bazza. Do you remember when he tried to imitate me and Ray and blagged the post office? He'd sawn his shotgun down so short he had his hand over the end of it, put a shot in to the ceiling and blew his own finger tips off!"

Both men roared with laughter.

"He moved down to Devon with that nutty bird from The Swan, if I remember right," Patrick said.

"Nice enough bloke, Barry, but fuck me, what a liability," Denny returned, wistfully.

Burt Roswell stood next to Ray at the bar. When his drink arrived, he thanked the barman and turned to Ray, shaking his head slightly and sighing thoughtfully. "You could have been good boxers, you and Denny. But particularly you, Ray. You had the skill."

"Ah well, I suppose if I looked like you, Mr Roswell, I may have continued, but a kid as handsome as me needed to look after his looks."

Roswell rolled his eyes. "Just like your old man. Full of yourself," Burt replied as a smiling Harry walked towards them.

"Hello Burt, long time no see. You look well. Does anaemia run in the family?"

Ray laughed at his dad's comment and excused himself. "I'll leave you two old foes to it!"

Harry extended his hand which Burt ignored. He was bored of the arrogant posturing and sarcastic comments from the Lanes. "Nice to see you got a team of lads down at one of our tournaments again."

"Well, you will be seeing a bit more of me again soon, if my transfer goes through. I'll be finishing my career back in my old stomping ground." He paused and held Harry's gaze. "Unfinished business here with you, Mr."

Harry laughed. "You got no business to finish with me. No-one will ever bring my family down. We are here for good, so get used to it. And give up this incessant obsession with trying to pin things on me, Burt. Relax and enjoy life!"

The two men stood staring at each other in a brief stalemate. Then, Harry broke the silence with a smile. "Well, that is fantastic news, Burt. You're coming back to the area. Be good to have you back on the manor. Maybe you could get involved with our boxing club again?"

Burt noticed the emphasize on 'our', which made him flush. "Yes, I heard you're involving yourself with professional boxing now," he snapped.

"Yes, both good lads, and going places."

Burt scowled at Harry. "Well, you have laundered your ill-gotten gains through most industries. Why not the boxing game as well?"

"Come on, Burt, don't be like that. You know I have genuine appreciation of your knowledge of the noble art. It would be a total asset having you back in the area and on Team Lane."

Harry was smiling to himself. He was happy that after all these years, he could still wind Burt up so easily. He decided to keep going while he was on a roll.

"The offer's there. Soon as you are back, nip over the gym and get involved. I respect anyone who steps through those ropes, even the ring girls." He winked at Burt and added, "My community can always use good, old-school bobbies like you, mate."

Burt looked at Harry's beaming smile and used every ounce of his inner strength not to bite back. "Well, we shall see, Harry. But tonight, my priority is my club and my fighters."

"Yes, indeed, Burt. And so it should be. You're right, as per usual. I must get back to my boxers."

Burt watched as Harry walked away. "I'll have you, Harry Bastard Lane. You see if I bloody well don't," he said under his breath in seething exasperation.

37.

1989

Detective Susannah Hendshall sat opposite Burt Roswell as he briefed her on her next undercover operation. She watched every move he made and noted his body language. Her memory for faces and descriptive details of places and people had become legendary among her peers as she had worked her way up rapidly from a WPC to a detective. This, together with the fact she had attained a degree in music and drama before deciding on a career walking the beat rather than treading the boards, had been duly noted by her senior officers. They had recommended undercover work as a natural progression for her.

In her heart, Susannah had always remained smitten with the acting world. Although she would never attend a glamourous red carpet function or realise her childhood dream of taking a bow before her adoring fans on the stage of a West End show, she had found policing to be equally rewarding in many ways. She reasoned that her decision to make policing her career, and undertake undercover work, gave her a chance to take on a completely different persona and, in a way, indulge her desire to act, whilst solving crimes and doing some good at the same time.

"I know your career so far has been exceptional. Your previous two undercover assignments were very successful," Roswell said. As he reached into his briefcase to remove a folder, she looked behind him at the many certificates and pictures on the wall; a mix of police commendations, boxing memorabilia and photos from various police and sporting events and charity functions. "How would you like to make it a hattrick of successes and help me nail this lot?" He handed her a folder with 'LANE' written in bold red marker on the front. "My nemesis," he added, tapping the top of the folder to make a firm point.

She watched him as he turned and paced the room. He was immaculately dressed in a suit, shirt and cravat and polished oxford brogues. His smart appearance and general demeanour instantly reminded her of her late father, who had passed away some years back, not long after she had left college. It had, in fact, been her father who had encouraged her, on many occasions, to consider the force as a more stable career than the world of show business. After a couple of years of mostly failed castings and growing tired of the existence of a starving artist, living off casual employment and financial help from family, she succumbed to the call of Hendon.

Although facially nothing like her father, Roswell's slim build and dress-sense bore remarkable similarities, as did his mannerism. He was smart but somehow old-fashioned, as if time had moved on and left his kind behind long ago.

"I joined the force at eighteen and I'm now…" He paused and gave her a little smile. "Well, let's just say I'm marching on a bit."

She returned his smile.

"This lot have been playing cat and mouse with me all my career, one way or another." He looked reflectively into the empty space above her head and sighed before continuing. "I've decided to take early retirement, but before I go off to tend to my roses, I'm hoping, with your help, we can finally gather enough information to put an end to this family's activities, and give me some solace in my retirement."

"May I?" Susannah said, raising the file from her lap.

"Yes, please do, Miss Hendshall. Take a browse. And I shall fill you in on some further details on this delightful family, together, of course, with your new identity."

She looked down at the profile page of the family as Roswell looked on, noting her reaction. He smiled and spoke. "What were you expecting? A family of grotesque monsters to pop up from the page?"

Slightly embarrassed, she replied, "Were you reading my mind?"

"Well, they're good-looking men, I have to concede. Even from a man's perspective, I can see that. Much as I don't like to indulge that old bugger Lane with a compliment." She looked up at him as he added, "Quite the old charmer, as well. And shrewd as anything. But let's not ever forget I have at least two unsolved murders related to him, not to mention years of robberies and everything unsavoury you care to imagine, connected to the Lanes."

She looked down at the profile pictures. Harry Lane, father. Christine Lane, mother. She paused at Ray Lane and took in his handsome features. "Yes, I see what you mean, Sir. Very attractive people."

He sat on the edge of the desk and looked down at her. "Don't let either young Ray's looks or his smooth ways fool you. Lots of women made the same mistake with Ted Bundy and look how well that turned out."

Although she noted the obvious sarcasm in Roswell's voice, it didn't sound so out of context as her eyes fixed onto the next face. Denny Lane. His face, although again very handsome, had an altogether different aura to it. The picture somehow made her feel uneasy. Unlike the deep blue, attractive eyes of Harry and Ray, Denny's had a darkness to them. An inner madness seemed to radiate from his cold stare that held her gaze, even from a picture on a page, making her feel strangely uncomfortable and shiver slightly. Looking at the rest of the family's profile pictures would give you no initial clues as to their chosen line of business. But Denny's mugshot screamed at you from the page. His eyes seemed to be fixed on your every move with intimidating malice.

"Please don't take this the wrong way, Detective Hendshall, and accept it as a compliment. You are a very attractive lady and I can't deny, along with your many other obvious talents, your looks had a large part in my decision to install you undercover amongst the Lane family, or at least try to."

She blushed slightly, but the reminders of her father in his appearance and demeanour seemed to comfort her. Deep down, she wanted to chuckle at his obvious discomfort at what he had said, but equally, she felt a little sorry for him as, like her father would have been, he would be mortified if his words had caused offence or be seen as misogynistic.

"Thank you for the lovely compliment, Sir. And I fully understand. We may have moved on in regards to equality in the work place, but let's face it, we women can still wrap you men around our little fingers with a little bit of flirting." She deliberately held Roswell's gaze just long enough for him to visibly blush. She smiled, enjoying her tease.

He turned away to avoid her gaze and hide his embarrassment and pretended to rearrange some stationery on his desk. "You see, Ray Lane is known to be popular with the ladies, as his father was before him. It's all part of their charming act, you see."

Susannah thought she could detect a hint of envy in his voice. "Yes, well, I'm sure I can deal with his phony compliments and give as good as I can get, Sir." She smiled.

He looked at her thoughtfully for a few seconds, then returned the smile. "Yes, quiet." He paused again. "Well, you are bound to catch his eye and he won't be able to resist introducing himself. So, I'm hoping this may be your trump card to getting in the door, without compromising either yourself or the investigation."

She smiled at him again. She could see that he was struggling. "Of course, Sir. It's one option among many."

Looking slightly embarrassed, he continued. "Of course, I'm certainly not telling you how to go about your job, Detective. I am confident you will find your own, and the safest way in, and your safety is paramount to us." He held her shoulder lightly and, with a gentle, soothing voice, said, "It's down to you now. We are only here for your safety and back-up at your discretion."

She smiled to herself. She could see the desperation in his eyes, and the hope he had that she could obtain anything to nail this family. She thought to herself that it was more likely she was being used to get as much on the Lanes as she could regardless of her safety. Roswell was clearly desperate to put Harry Lane away. It must have kept him awake for years. Despite her reservations, she smiled at him and played the part of being just as eager as he was to see justice done.

"I will take all this information away and make myself at home in my new apartment. I'll familiarise myself with the area first," she said and stood up. "Right, Sir, time to start building my new life. I'll make contact with you once I'm convinced I'm on the inside."

They shook hands and Roswell showed her out of his office with a gentle, encouraging hand across her back. He stood at the open door and watched her walk down the corridor.

"Good luck, detective Hendshall, and thank you once again," he called after her.

"Thank you, Sir. I'll be in touch," she replied without looking back. "That's that bullshit over with, now let's get into character and work at my own pace," she mumbled to herself as she disappeared from her superior officer's view.

She was on her own now, working under her own rules and in her own domain. This was the kind of police work she loved. The only part she didn't like about going undercover and taking on a new persona, was that she had to have minimal contact with her best friend, her beloved mother.

Susannah finished the call to her mum, who was the only person outside the force who knew she was an undercover officer. Although she never divulged any details of the case, or who she was involved with, she would always let her know when she was about to embark on a new case, and that any visits would be limited. Her mother fully understood the nature of her daughter's work, but that didn't make the separation any easier, especially as her mother was living alone since her husband's untimely passing. She had insisted that her daughter checked in at least twice a week by phone, to reassure her that all was well.

Susannah looked down at her new passport, driving licence and all the other essential documents, then she laid down on her new bed in her newly rented one-bed apartment.

Clare Reynolds, age twenty-seven.

She smiled and said out loud, "Right then, Miss Reynolds. Who are you? And who are you going to become? And how are we going to get enough information to put that little lot away?"

She eyed the folder and laughed at Burt Roswell's bold red lettering.

LANE.

38.

1990

Clare Reynolds sat nursing her second cup of coffee and glanced up towards the counter at the rather bored-looking owner of the café she was sitting in. She was observing the Green Man public house and reasoned that a third coffee would not only be an unnecessary caffeine overload but also might raise suspicions that she was using this empty establishment as nothing more than a resting place. He had already asked her if she would like anything else off the menu. Twice. She had declined, twice, and his expression had told her that he wasn't impressed by people who expected him to pay his rent serving coffees and teas alone.

Besides, she had seen Ray enter the pub ten minutes earlier, so decided it was time to finally introduce Clare Reynolds to the Lanes.

She paused at the entrance to the pub, straightened her top, cleared her throat with a gentle cough, then took a slow, deliberate, calming breath and confirmed to herself quietly, under her breath, "Right, let's do this, Clare Reynolds," as she turned the door handle and entered the pub.

Her eyes fixed instantly on the side profile of Ray Lane, who was sitting up at the bar on a stool, speaking to his mother who was stood behind the bar with a broad smile on her face, listening to whatever her son was saying.

As she approached, Ray and his mum paused their conversation and turned to look at the woman striding purposefully towards them. She walked straight up to the bar without looking at Ray, although she could feel his eyes on her as she looked directly at Chrissy Lane, who greeted her with a warm smile.

"Yes love, what can I get you?" Chrissy asked.

Clare paused momentarily, taking in the appearance of the woman in front of her. Chrissy was dressed immaculately and she was still very attractive. She exuded a confidence and glamour that wouldn't have looked out of place on the set of Dallas or Dynasty, but she spoke with an obvious London accent and a friendly tone.

"Actually, I've popped in on the off chance you may be in need of bar staff. I've just moved into the area, you see, and I'm looking for work."

Before Chrissy could respond, Ray spoke. "You done bar work before, then?"

She turned to face a smiling Ray, who promptly offered his hand.

"Ray Lane. And that, behind the bar, is one half of the biology that produced this handsome fella, Chrissy Lane, my mum."

Somewhat taken aback by Ray's overconfidence, she turned back to a grinning Chrissy, who rolled her eyes to the ceiling. "That's it, love, you've been captured. I won't get a word in edgeways now he's started."

Clare looked at them both in turn, then laughed as she shook Ray's hand. "I'm Clare," she announced.

Ray held her hand gently and held her gaze. As she looked into his eyes, she was overcome by an emotion she had never felt before. Yes, he was a handsome man, but she already knew that from his mugshots and her previous observations of him. What she was feeling wasn't basic attraction, it was something else, something she had never felt before and could not explain. Although it unsettled her somewhat, it also made her feel warm inside, and comforted her in a strange way. Aware that she had gone into a dreamlike state and had been holding his hand for far too long, she snatched her hand away, somewhat embarrassed, which made him laugh.

Ray chatted away to Clare, getting acquainted. Chrissy had quietly slipped away and busied herself around the bar. When the telephone rang, Chrissy left them alone at the bar to answer it. No sooner had she left, two men came in and walked up to the bar. Chrissy eyed Ray as she spoke on the phone and mouthed with a hand gesture that she wanted him to serve the two men.

Ray turned to Clare. "Here you go. Here's your chance to impress mum. Go serve them two."

Clare looked at the two men, then back at Ray. "But what about your mum?"

Ray just gestured to her. "Go on, they're waiting."

She didn't answer, just turned, lifted the bar hatch, walked behind the bar and asked the men what they wanted.

Chrissy watched this all play out as she continued her conversation and then eyed Ray, who smiled back at her as she shook her head, fixing him with a knowing grin.

When she had finished on the phone, Chrissy walked back into the bar. Clare looked at her apologetically, but Chrissy's response was a nod and a smile. "Carry on, darling. I want to speak to my son." She lifted the bar hatch up and walked round to where Ray was sat. She stood next to him, shaking her head. "You men and an attractive woman!"

Ray looked at her innocently. "What?" he asked.

"What, my arse. If that had been a bloke walked in, and not a woman as attractive as her, would they get an interview and trial as quickly as that?"

Ray smiled at his mum. "Well, see what she's like for an hour, mum. You said you wanted to borrow a couple of my staff from the club on Saturday for the old man's birthday, so this may have worked out handy for us."

Chrissy laughed and looked across at Clare, who was serving two other locals in their late twenties who seemed more than happy with the Green Man's new addition.

"Right, let's throw her in at the deep end, then and give her a shot at your dad's party. That's if he even makes it. He went out to get his hair cut four hours ago. Not seen him since."

Ray laughed. "He still seeing that man about a dog, is he?"

"Bleedin' hope not. That used to usually end up with the old bill after us or a house full of shit we didn't need," she said and they both laughed.

Clare surveyed the bar, taking in all the customers and then looked over at Ray and Chrissy. It was a weekday, early afternoon, so one staff member behind the bar was more than adequate. She heard the bar hatch open and glanced around to see a smiling Chrissy heading towards her.

"OK, Clare, I'll take over. You relax."

Clare looked at her, hoping she had made a good impression. A job here would be a perfect way to gauge the Lanes' characters, as well as the locals. And of course, people were always more vocal and liberal when they were lubricated with alcohol, something she had experienced many times before when working in pubs and bars. If she could get a job, she may be able to get some juicy gossip and insights into the family.

"How do you fancy working Saturday night?" Chrissy asked.

"Wow, yes please, that would be fantastic," Clare replied excitedly. She had to admit to herself it was a bit of an over-the-top reaction, but Chrissy didn't seem to notice.

"You walked in at the right time. It's my Harry's sixtieth birthday on Saturday, so an extra person would be handy. Just a trial, though. No guarantees after that, OK?"

"Yes, of course. I understand. Do I need to dress up on Saturday?"

Chrissy looked at her and smiled. "You look lovely as you are, Clare. Us women need to look classy and in control. Never wear anything to appease these lot, darling, you remember that. Us ladies hold all the cards, not men."

Clare couldn't help but be impressed by Chrissy. She was a powerful presence.

"You don't ever need to come to work with a skirt up the crack of your arse to work in our places. Well, not unless you want to. But as my old mother-in-law Molly used to say," As she spoke, she leaned down to take a glass from the shelf and began pouring a pint before a customer had arrived at the bar, already knowing his regular order. "If it ain't for sale, don't put it in the window."

Both ladies laughed and Chrissy handed the man his beer. He smiled at the laughing women, with no idea what their conversation had been about.

"What are you drinking, Clare?" Chrissy asked. Before Clare could reply, she added, "Ray wants to speak to you."

Clare looked over to see that Ray had left his bar stool and was sitting at a table, looking directly at them.

"Hmm, just half a lager, please," she said, still looking over at Ray.

"Good girl. Pour yourself a half, and a pint for Ray, and go join him," Chrissy instructed. Clare did so without speaking.

"So, you split with your boyfriend and was laid off from your job, and just decided to move to this area, of all places?" Ray asked, looking directly into Clare's eyes.

"Yes. Believe it or not, I actually closed my eyes and put my finger down on a map of London and decided wherever it landed I would rent a place there and just go for it. A totally clean break."

Ray laughed. "Good on you. Why not? It's as good a place as any, I guess, particularly if you're a flexible worker with no real ties to anywhere and you're going for acting auditions."

Clare looked at Ray's handsome face, silently considering how much nicer it was to be investigating someone she couldn't deny she found attractive. But she remained totally professional. She couldn't allow herself to forget that, as handsome as he was, he was a dangerous criminal and she had a job to do.

"Yes, well, to be honest, Ray, I think the acting thing is a lost cause now. I hardly ever hear from my agent. If I'm honest, I'm somewhat of a free spirit, so I like the flexible work I do. I think a nine-to-five would never suit me, certainly not while I'm single. I've done all kinds, and picked up skills along the way, so I'm handy to have around." She smiled and knew he had noted the cheeky sales pitch.

"So, where you renting?" Ray enquired.

Clare took a small sip of her lager and replied, "A little flat on a road called Spencer Way."

"Yeah, I know it well. I know every street, every house, every building in this area," he said with a notable air of authority. "Shame we rented a flat out to someone last week. You could have had that."

She feigned surprise and looked impressed, but of course she already knew about his legitimate businesses. "Oh wow, you own property to rent out?"

Ray smiled at her and added confidently, "We rent out a couple of flats and a couple of houses. We own a gym, this pub and we own Nightingales night club. We also have a security firm supplying door staff to pubs and clubs in the area."

"I notice you say we a lot," Clare pointed out, which again made Ray smile.

"Yes, us Lanes are a team. There is no I, only we. What's mine is theirs and vice versa, that's how it's always been and always will be." He paused, his face taking on a more serious and reflective tone.

As he spoke, she had to admit she was not only attracted to him, but begrudgingly impressed by him. They were the same age, twenty-eight. She was always intrigued by criminals like the Lanes and the way they had a natural ability to run legitimate businesses, yet always found themselves attracted to funding them via crime rather than within the boundaries of the law. There was absolutely no doubt in her mind that these men, with their entrepreneurial talents, could do it all without risking arrest.

Ray's eyes suddenly diverted towards the main entrance and a broad smile lit up his handsome face. "Here he is, the main man."

Clare looked across to see a man she recognized as Harry Lane, dressed, like Ray, in a bespoke suit with neatly cut grey hair and brightly polished shoes. He certainly cut a dashing figure. Both men shook hands and smiled at each other. The bond between them and the respect these two had for each other was clearly evident.

Harry looked over at Clare and offered his hand before Ray could even start the introductions. "Harry Lane, at your service. And who might this pretty young lady be?"

As she shook his hand, she felt that warm, strangely comforting feeling come over her again. The same feeling she felt in Ray's company, which made her pause temporarily.

"Clare Reynolds. Pleased to meet you, Mr Lane."

Harry smiled. "Harry, please. No need for Mr Lane. And what's my son here filling your head with?"

Ray cut in quickly. "Clare's going to be doing a trial shift with us on Saturday, Dad. She is new in the area and looking for a fresh start."

Harry studied Clare for a few seconds, then smiled. "You sure you are up for working in this nut house, Clare?"

She nodded and smiled.

"And have you passed the Chrissy test, yet?" he added.

"Only a quick one, Harry. So it's all or nothing on Saturday."

"You'll be OK, kid. You'll soon get the swing of it," he replied, then turned to Ray. "Quick word, Ray. I want to run something past you." He turned back to Clare. "Excuse us, Clare, I just want to sort some business out with Ray."

"OK. It was lovely to meet you, Harry. I can see where Ray gets his looks from," Clare answered.

"Oh, don't say that to him, or he will be murder!" Ray said, laughing.

"Oi, I'll have you know, when I was a young man I was often referred to as the local Paul Newman." Harry smiled and winked at Clare.

"More like Nanette Newman," Ray quipped and all three laughed.

On first impressions, Clare liked the Lanes' personalities, although she was yet to meet Denny. It was funny, she had found in her experience of policing these characters that they were often quite agreeable company if you discounted their crimes.

She sat back down and took a sip of her drink whilst watching Harry and Ray, who were now deep in conversation. She then looked across at Chrissy, who was expertly serving drinks and bantering with her customers.

"Right. Well, I'm in the door. Now let's not make any silly slip-ups with this lot," she said to herself.

39.

As Clare neared the entrance to the Green Man, she could already hear the noise of the revellers and the music playing inside. It was only four in the afternoon and as she walked through the door, she was taken aback by the sheer amount of people all looking merry and in the party spirit. She surveyed the room and mumbled to herself, "Sodding hell, you weren't joking when you said you were throwing me in at the deep end. This is going to be an experience."

She weaved her way to the bar. As she was about to speak to a lady in her early twenties, who was just about to ask her what she wanted to drink, her eyes made contact with Ray's. He was sitting at a large table with all the Lanes, including Denny and various other faces she was as yet unfamiliar with. Ray signalled for her to come over. She glanced at the lady behind the bar, smiled, then headed over to the table.

"Afternoon, Clare," Ray said as all the others at the table clocked her arrival then went back to their conversations. All except Denny, who was staring intensely at her. And Chrissy, who had stood up and was now by her side.

"Hello, Mrs Lane," Clare said, handing her a greetings card. She noticed with embarrassment that the envelope had damp patches from being in her hands. Usually, she was excellent at concealing her feelings under pressure, but the pressure of the moment was making her hands sweat. "That's a birthday card for Harry."

Chrissy smiled. "That's very sweet of you, darling. Please call me Chrissy. Mind you, if you make a balls up behind that bar tonight, you can go back to Mrs Lane again." She winked at Clare and they both smiled at each other. "Right, come on, I'll introduce you to the other staff."

Chrissy held Clare's shoulder and walked her behind the bar. First, she was introduced to the lady she had seen when she first walked in.

"This is Debbie," Chrissy said and Debbie smiled as Clare introduced herself. "Show her the ropes, Debbie, and work it out amongst yourselves."

"No problem, Chrissy," a cheerful Debbie replied and turned to serve someone.

Chrissy shouted to a man who had just returned back behind the bar. "Pete?" The man approached and could not contain his obvious pleasure at the sight of the attractive new addition to the bar staff, smiling broadly. "This is Clare. She is starting tonight."

Pete and Clare exchanged handshakes and smiles. "You've not seen the cellar yet, Clare. We will be busy, so any barrels go, that's Pete's job. You just shout him up." Clare nodded back. "I'll be in and out as well, darling, so don't stress. Also, it's the old man's big night, so you're all involved. I'll come and grab you later so you can all have a break and some grub and drinks, OK?"

As Clare served customers, she took as many opportunities as possible to glance across the room at Harry, who was moving slowly around the building, greeting well-wishers. From the reaction of the punters, you would honestly think he was a celebrity. She was also keeping an eye on Denny, who was in conversation with a man by the main entrance. Denny had caught her eye a few times and was obviously as curious of her as she was of him.

Clare had a lot of previous experience of bar work and her famous memory was helping her as she was already fully aware of the lay out of the beer taps and optics and prices of most of the orders she was taking.

"Oi! New girl!" a loud voice shouted. "Any danger of service down this end, or have I checked into a drying out clinic?"

Clare looked down the bar at a man in his mid-twenties, grinning at her and waving his empty glass in the air.

"Yeah, you, darlin'," he shouted drunkenly.

As Clare walked towards him, she looked across at Denny, who was watching her while simultaneously chatting to the man he was standing with. It was evident to her from his facial expression that he had heard the way this man had addressed her.

As she served another customer, she watched Denny as he moved with some speed through the crowded pub. The man who had been brash towards her had just disappeared into the toilets and Denny had followed him in.

Clare had to admit to herself that she was thoroughly enjoying the atmosphere in the pub. She loved her undercover work as it differed so much from normal police work. It was totally unique, giving her the chance to gain an insight into the lives of the people she encountered. Of course, there were many challenges and emotions she needed to deal with, but she couldn't deny it was rewarding.

"Excuse me, Clare."

She looked up again to see the ignorant man from earlier staring at her. He was now extremely subdued and it was obvious to her that he had been crying and was noticeably shaken up.

"I'd like to apologize for the way I spoke to you earlier. I've had a bit too much to drink and I was out of order."

"Thanks for your apology. It's OK," Clare responded and asked the embarrassed man what he would like to drink. As he went to reply, she heard a voice behind her.

"I'll pay for that."

She spun around to be met by Denny's dark, intense eyes. He extended his hand. "I'm Ray's brother, Denny."

She shook his hand and stared at him. Like Ray, he was a handsome man, but his features were harder, his gaze dark and intense and his whole demeanor made her feel uneasy.

He smiled, which made her feel less threatened. "When you have served him…" He paused momentarily and looked over at the man. Clare followed his gaze and saw the man bowing his head to avoid Denny's glare. "…come and join our table. Debbie has finished her shift now, and Jenny will be in shortly. You and Debs can grab some food and drink and join our table."

As Denny left the bar area, she felt the warm glow come over her again, just like she had with Harry and Ray. What was it with these men, she thought. She felt weird around them, as if she already knew them, which she found very bizarre. She couldn't quite decide if these feelings were comforting or unsettling. Either way, she had never felt anything like it before and would certainly have difficulty explaining to others how she felt in their presence. As usual, she decided to follow her instincts and keep it to herself.

Everyone at the table was merry and in good spirits. Clare had been introduced to family members and friends. Ray's wife, Georgie, had been very pleasant towards her and had invited her to come into her salon. Denny's wife, Dannielle, was a totally different person to Georgie in every way; looks, size and attitude. She had been slightly off with Clare when they were introduced. Denny stating loudly to Clare that she was not to worry about her, as she hates any woman who is more attractive than her, which meant she hates ninety-nine percent of the women in London, hadn't helped the situation.

It was obvious that Ray and Georgie were in love and that Denny and Dannielle merely got along. They were somehow strangely compatible and loyal to each other due to the Lanes' strong belief in family. Little Carmen and Tommy Lane, their children, were with their babysitter, as was Ray and Georgie's daughter, Grace Ellen.

"There you go, get that down you, girl," Chrissy said and handed her a flute of champagne.

Clare took the glass and thanked her. Chrissy smiled at her. "How did you enjoy the shift, then? The locals seem to like you, especially the lads."

"Good, thanks. I really enjoyed it. Lovely people and lovely pub," she replied.

"Yes, Denny told me you're very good with the customers and you certainly know the bar, so drink your bubbly, girl, the job is yours. You deserve a drink after all those men slobbering over you," Chrissy added with a chuckle and exaggerated roll of her eyes.

"How many chatted you up, then?" Ray asked.

"About ten of them." Clare smiled. "I think that table over there were taking bets who could get a date. That one in the blue top never stopped trying." She pointed to the lad at a table with his friends.

Ray laughed. "Oh, that's Paul. He is in an open relationship with his right hand. Only time he gets a bunk up is if one of the clock sisters takes him home."

Clare laughed and asked, "Who are the clock sisters?"

Ray pointed across the room. "See those two over there? That's Mandy and Tracy, otherwise known as the clock sisters."

Clare looked across at the two women, both mid- to late-thirties, with the obvious signs of alcohol and tobacco having taken a heavy toll, skirts not much longer than a belt, both caked in makeup and in the highest white heels, both sporting little pot bellies. Far too polite to comment on their appearance, she asked, "Why do you call them the clock sisters?"

A straight-faced Denny spoke. "'Cause, when those two start looking attractive, you know you have had far too much to drink and it's time to fuck off home."

A smiling Harry returned to the table. He had been speaking to the singer, Gary Driscoll, who was now crooning a rendition of a Tony Bennett song. A regular at the Lanes' functions, Driscoll was a fantastic act and certainly looked the part in his tuxedo, working through a set of Matt Monroe, Frank Sinatra and all the classic singers.

"I hear you've joined the team, young Clare," Harry said with a smile and announced to those in earshot, "Clare's a trained actress and singer, you know."

An unimpressed Dannielle remarked, "Oh yeah? What part's she playing? A poxy bar maid!"

Denny looked at her and she scowled, then turned to speak to another lady.

"I've done a bit of acting myself," Denny said.

A grinning, and now slightly merry Debbie, obviously used to his banter, said, "No you haven't, Denny, you liar! What have you been in, then?"

"You, later, if you play your cards right," he replied, grinning.

"No, it's true," Harry said and waited for Clare and Debbie to look at him. "Yeah, years ago my Denny auditioned to play the part of John Merrick. They wanted someone to play him in his later years, when he was losing his looks."

As they laughed, Ray cut in. "Hey, Clare, if you've done singing and acting, how do you fancy going up and giving us a number?"

All three Lanes' eyes were on her and she knew if she indulged their suggestion it could only enhance her cover. So she agreed.

All eyes were on her as she walked up on stage and launched into a rendition of *Secret Love*. Everyone seemed amazed at how good her voice was. Harry was back sitting with Chrissy and Ray had sat next to Denny.

"Blimey, Ray, she has got some voice on her," Denny gushed.

"We've got more than a barmaid there, my son."

Ray didn't reply at first. He just stared, unblinking, at Clare as she performed.

"There is something about her, Denny. I don't know what it is, but I feel like I know her or something. I just can't put my finger on it."

Denny held Ray's gaze with a dead straight face. "I know what it is about her, Ray. I've sussed it."

"What? What is it Denny?" a wide-eyed Ray asked.

"She is a right good-looking woman and you want to shag the arse off her," Denny countered and burst out laughing.

Ray tutted then laughed himself. "You're murder, Denny." He returned his gaze back to the stage where Clare continued singing.

Denny looked down and saw Clare's handbag on the seat next to him, her purse poking out of the top. With his brother's attention elsewhere, he leaned down and lifted the purse out of the handbag and placed it between his thighs. After a quick glance back up at the stage, he clicked the purse open.

"What you doing, Denny?" Ray finally clocked what his brother was up to.

"I'm checking out who we are employing, mate."

They both eyed the cards as Denny pulled them out, one by one. Clare Reynolds, Equity. Clare Reynolds, Spotlight actor's membership. Clare Reynolds, Lloyds Bank. He placed the cards back in the purse, then placed it carefully back into the bag.

"There you go, Ray, you don't know her, you just fancy her."

Clare replaced the microphone, smiling broadly, as the room erupted into applause. Both Harry and Chrissy were walking towards her, clapping appreciatively. Harry directed the room with an encouraging wave to prompt them to cheer even louder.

"That's a fantastic voice you have, Clare, and an old song you chose. Reminded me of the good old days at Nightingales in the sixties."

"Yes, I love the old songs. I grew up listening to all my mum's records."

Harry held her gaze and both him and Clare seemed to register something that, again, she just couldn't fathom. "How do you fancy singing one more for us? A nice slow one, so I can dance with my lovely wife for my birthday?"

Clare looked at his blue eyes as they creased into a lovely smile. "OK, one more, just for your birthday," she answered. How could she say no to that smile?

Harry and Chrissy glided slowly across the floor as Clare sang her way through a slow ballad, watching the couple in fascination.

"Thanks for a lovely birthday, Chrissy," Harry said as they finished their dance and headed back to their seats. "I must be getting old, love. I feel shattered. Mind you, I've felt like that for a while now. I reckon I must have picked something up that I can't shake off."

Chrissy smiled at her husband. "Well, this lot can sod off to Nightingales soon, then you and me will have a night cap on our own."

40.

Three months later

Clare found Harry a fascinating man. He was quite unlike any other she had met. She felt so comfortable in his presence and had done since the first day they had met. She still couldn't explain the strange feeling of familiarity and warmth that emanated from him when she was in his company and nor had she mentioned it. She felt it from both Ray and Denny too, but the feeling was not nearly as strong as when she was in Harry's company.

She had unintentionally become very close to this family. Well past the stage of just liking them. And she knew full well the feelings were mutual. Particularly with Ray, who she had become very close to. In fact, Ray spent more time with her than his own wife, who seemed permanently busy in her salon. Ray's days were always full of activity. Activity that Clare had somehow become more and more involved in. In quieter moments, she often mused that despite being an undercover police officer investigating this family, she actually enjoyed working with them.

It was obvious to both her and Ray that they were attracted to each other. But luckily, so far at least, Ray had not tried to act on his feelings. He was clearly still in love with, and respectful of, Georgie. Clare had asked herself the question many times: if Ray did make a pass, would she give in to her attraction and just use the fact she was undercover as an excuse? After all, any measures were acceptable in the call of duty, weren't they?

Luckily, though, for the sake of all involved, the situation hadn't arisen and, from a job perspective, the trust and closeness she had garnered could only be a good thing. After all, the local community seemed to be very reluctant to say anything negative, or give anything away about them. Which was making finding any evidence of crime, past or present, impossible.

Her reports back to the increasingly frustrated Burt Roswell were so far totally fruitless, leading to increasingly frequent rants. She had explained to him that investigating the Lanes would be a marathon, not a sprint. They were just too clever.

Roswell's mood had lifted when she had informed him a new face had started to be seen regularly in the company of Harry, Ray and Denny. A man called Bobby James. Roswell had exclaimed excitedly that Bobby James was a notorious and seasoned South London villain. He had connections, businesses and properties in Spain, a well-known haven for notorious criminals. Roswell's frustrated dejection had been replaced, at least for now, by a vigorous energy. He had told Clare that if Bobby James was on the radar, something big was being planned and she had an even more important job to do.

In the space of a few months, Clare had somehow managed to go from just being a barmaid at the pub, to working at Nightingales, babysitting both Ray and Denny's children, to jumping up and singing with bands on stage. She had even been Ray's driver when he required it.

She had continued the façade of being a struggling actress as cover to check in with her superiors and had even arranged to attend genuine castings as she was aware on a couple of occasions Denny and Ray had arranged to have her followed. She had also arranged for a work colleague to come in to the pub when all the Lanes were present, masquerading as a former drama student from her college who was passing through the area and fancied a drink and a bite to eat. He had played the part to perfection, feigning surprise at recognising her brilliantly.

Now, as she chatted away to Harry, she became acutely aware of how drawn his appearance was becoming. She could see something was wrong, that he wasn't a well man. Although he was as cheerful as always, she could see how his face and body had altered. He had lost some weight and his interest in Lane functions and outings had diminished. He had even pulled out of the last boxing event, leaving his sons to oversee the whole proceedings. She had observed the family sitting together quietly, privately, and although she had felt the desire to outright ask Harry if everything was OK, she had held back, thinking it may be out of place. She didn't want to jeopardize the confidence she had gained and come across as unduly nosey.

"Sounds like it was fantastic in Nightingales in the sixties, Harry. I've always been fascinated by that decade, from the music and fashion to the movies and stars. I'd have loved it," Clare said as she reminisced with Harry.

"You certainly would have, kid. We had some fantastic acts at the old place. I must dig out some of the old photos we had of all our singers. They used to adorn the walls, but Ray and Denny took them down when they took over and stuck them in storage."

With that, Chrissy entered the bar. "Do me a favour, Clare, would you? When Hans Christian Anderson has finished telling you tales from yesteryear, can you nip down the shop and pick up these bits for me?" She handed Clare a shopping list.

"Yes, of course, Chrissy." Clare smiled and took the list.

"Good girl. Me and his lordship have got to go out. Very important meeting." She paused and looked at Harry and Clare registered her look of concern. "You can open up and sort everything, love. We will be back by mid-afternoon. No doubt the boys will be in later and Ray will probably have you running around for him."

As Clare left the shop with a bag full of Chrissy's shopping, she walked straight into Denny's path, which made her jump slightly.

"Hello Denny. Just grabbing some bits for your mum," she said. "She and your dad are off to a meeting."

Denny just stared at her for as few seconds, rather vaguely, then murmured, "Yes, let's hope it's good news."

She caught what he said but didn't comment. She turned to see a woman heading towards the shop door with a dog on a lead. The dog snarled at the emotionless Denny and tried to lurch towards him, much to the embarrassment of the lady.

"I'm so sorry. He won't bite you. He is just a bit excitable."

Denny looked at the dog then the woman. "He'd better not, or I'll bite you. Mind you, looking at you, you'd probably enjoy that." He grinned at her as she tutted, shook her head, and turned away in disgust, pulling the dog lead forcefully.

Clare burst out laughing, which then made him laugh. The tension broken, he said, "I'm off to Valentines for some breakfast, then off to sort out some business."

"Anything I can help with?" Clare inquired. She never got much contact with Denny, so gleaning any possible information from him was difficult, if not impossible.

"No, I'm good thanks, Clare. No doubt Ray will have work for you, and I know just how much you two like each other's company." He smiled knowingly, which made her blush.

"Yes, Ray is good company and a lovely boss," she affirmed.

"Oh, turn it in. You fancy each other like mad." He laughed.

"He is a married man, with a daughter, and I think you are seeing something that isn't there," she lied.

"I'm married as well, but if your eyes were permanently locked on me like they are on my brother, I'd have you in my bed like a shot."

She felt totally exposed as he held her gaze, smirking. Then, finally, to her relief, he changed the subject.

"Right, let's go see the Vitals. I'm peckish." He laughed again. "Tell you what, I had a massive crush on the Vitals' daughters when I was a boy. Particularly Anna. I tell you, those two were like Italian models back then."

"They're both still very attractive ladies now," Clare countered.

"Yeah, not like back then, though. They were stunners." He paused and looked at Clare with a dead straight face. "That's the trouble with Italian birds, soon as they hit middle age, they put on ten stone and grow a tache."

With that he turned and walked away. Clare could not help but laugh.

"Are you lip syncing, or is that bollocks really coming out of your mouth?"

Ray stood, looking down at the man now squirming behind his desk.

"Honestly, Ray, if I had it, I'd give it to you."

"Listen, you prick, it's called a loan, not a gift. This is the third time I've been to collect. I don't go past a hattrick for no man. You're arsehole lucky it's me and not Denny, or your head would be through that window."

The fidgeting, sweating man tried to make excuses as Ray's eyes scanned the small office. He looked at the keyholder on the wall and removed two sets of keys. "Where's the deeds to these two flats?"

The man looked at Ray, pleadingly. "Not them, Ray, those flats are my only income."

"Deeds, or next visit you get the Denny treatment." Ray clicked his fingers. "Come on, come on, I ain't got all day."

The man gave Ray the relevant documents. "Them apartments are worth more than I owe you."

Ray shook his head nonchalantly. "Call it interest, son. You're a draught piece on the chess board of life. Don't come to men like me to borrow money if you can't pay it back in the time agreed."

Clare watched from behind the bar as Ray entered the pub and walked over to a group of locals at a table.

"You working this week, Robbo?" he asked one of the lads.

"Not much on, Ray. Why?" he replied.

"Good. Go round these two flats tomorrow and price them up. I've had a look, they just need toshing through with some white paint."

"OK, Ray, nice one," Robbo said as he looked at the address on the paper Ray had handed him.

Ray went to walk away then turned back. "Get your mate to help you. Get them done quickly, I want to rent them out."

"Which mate?" Robbo asked.

"That geezer with the pock-marked face. He's a painter. Can't think of his name. Looks like the singing detective."

Robbo's face creased into a smile. "That's Dave Taylor." He turned to the others, laughing, and repeated what Ray had called Dave. They all burst out laughing.

Chrissy squeezed Harry's hand tightly as they both looked in silence at the doctor opposite them.

"Come on, doc, out with it. Trust me, things I've seen and done, I can handle it," Harry said, smiling.

"I'm sorry, Mr Lane." The doctor diverted his gaze to Chrissy, who looked at him expectantly. He then acknowledged her, speaking gently.

"Mrs Lane." He looked down at his paperwork, cleared his throat, then eyed them both again with a genuine look of sorrow. "I'm so truly sorry, I really am, but it's terminal. The cancer is too far gone. It has spread through your body to your lungs and your bones. There is absolutely nothing we can do except give you medication to ease the pain and make you comfortable as your condition deteriorates."

"How long, doc?" Harry asked, still in a rather cheerful, unfazed manner.

"Difficult to say, Mr Lane, but realistically you should get any important things done as your condition will only get worse from here on in, to the point where you will need to be cared for."

Harry absorbed the doctor's words as Chrissy sat in complete silence.

"Better get my jacksy out of this chair and out amongst it then, doctor, hadn't I?"

41.

Bobby James looked at the men in front of him: Ray Lane, Denny Lane, Ian Lambert and John Wright. Bobby was in his late fifties, average build, suntanned face, dark, swept back hair. He was a seasoned career criminal and had masterminded some of the country's biggest heists.

Bobby had been a good friend and associate when collaborating with the Lanes over the years, and now he had come to Harry to see if he wanted in on a job he had been planning for quite some time. Lambert and Wright, both in their late forties and also with extensive criminal experience, had been recruited first, followed by Harry and, of course, the young blood of Ray and Denny.

"Right, this is it, men. We are at the point of no return. Months and months of diligent planning have gone into this," Bobby said as he eyed the men one-by-one. "Each and every one of us has done our graft, especially your dad, boys." He paused as he looked at Ray and Denny, then sighed, before continuing. "Unfortunately, Harry has had to pull out due to ill health, but his input has been invaluable."

All four men bowed their heads in quiet contemplation of Harry's diagnosis.

"Now, I know just how much you wanted to do this job with your dad, boys, but it's not to be. But I say this, lads: we owe it not only to Harry but also to ourselves, for all the time we've put in to execute this job. Harry arranged the canal escape and my man in Hemel Hempstead is unmatched in the disposal and safe keeping of large amounts of takings." Bobby said nothing for a few seconds, then smiled. "This is a big one, lads. We pull this off, not a man among us will need to risk a day behind the door again. Ray, Denny, as per usual, all contact with you will be via Valentines café. John and Ian, your usual channels of contact."

All nodded in acknowledgement, without speaking.

"Under no circumstances contact each other via any other means." He laughed. "Then, all being well, while the old bill are flying about like lunatics on the road, blocking everything off, we will be relaxing at a slow pace, carrying our cargo up the Grand Union canal from the Smoke to the leafy Hertfordshire countryside."

All the men stood silently, focusing their thoughts on the job they had planned. Then Bobby broke the silence again.

"Soon as I get the whisper that the unit is holding its largest deposit, we are on a green light."

As Clare emerged from the back of the bar at Nightingales, she was surprised to see Harry walking across the dancefloor from the main entrance. Ray had asked her to come in and do a stock take and it wasn't much past nine in the morning, so the sight of Harry in the otherwise empty building had startled her slightly. To her embarrassment, she was singing along to the radio, somewhat loudly and rather enthusiastically.

"Don't stop on my behalf, you know how much I love your singing voice," Harry said, smiling.

"Morning, Harry. Didn't expect to see you in so early," Clare returned, brightly.

"Was taking a morning stroll and fancied a look around the old place. Lots of memories for me in this building." Harry quietly scanned the room.

He silently turned on his heal, eyeing the stage wistfully then spoke under his breath. "Yep, some good memories and fantastic times, that's for sure."

As she watched him survey the room, she suddenly felt an unexplainable wave of sadness come over her. She could almost feel the emotion as he remembered all the nights over the years in this building: the characters from the past; the many singers and acts; the London faces, good and bad; the relationships that may have turned into future marriages that started out as a cheeky smile from a shy young man at the bar, trying to look the part with his mates, coyly returned by the girl he would then bravely ask for a dance on that famous old ballroom floor. So many lives, past and present, changed in so many ways by this old structure, under the watchful eye of the ever-present Harry Lane.

"Are you OK, Harry? Would you like a cuppa?" Clare asked.

He didn't turn around, but answered, still in a dream-like state, "I'm dying, girl."

Clare knew the statement wasn't in jest, but had no immediate reply, so said, "Ah, overdone it with the drink last night, did we, Harry?"

He turned slowly, then walked towards her with a calming smile on his face. "No, that's called a hangover. I'm dying."

She felt stunned. She looked into his still lovely, blazing blue eyes and was instantly overwhelmed with grief. She simply couldn't control it. No police training, no drama school, could stop the flood of emotions. Her eyes welled up, her lips began to tremble and then, there in front of the man she was sent undercover to investigate, she burst out crying.

"Hey, hey, let's have none of that old nonsense," Harry said as he wrapped his arms round her and cuddled her tightly. He gently stroked her head. "Don't cry, darling. It's all part of the process of life. We are all only passing through this place."

She allowed herself to melt in his arms. She took in his smell and could feel his heart beating, slow and gentle in his chest. She suddenly felt like a little girl again, safe in his arms. She hadn't felt grief like this since her father had passed away and she had no understanding of why Harry's news had evoked such a devastating reaction, or indeed why she felt no embarrassment at her breakdown or the fact that this man was holding and comforting her. For some reason, resting her head in Harry's comforting embrace, in that very moment, felt as natural as breathing.

After her tears had subsided, Harry and Clare strolled slowly around Nightingales as he reminisced about various events and people. She felt mellow in his company, thoughts of policing and the job in hand were a distant memory as they chatted away like two long-lost friends. They stopped at a large, framed black and white picture up on the wall. Clare stared at it intently. It read, 'Nightingales, 1965'.

Her eyes fixed on Harry and Chrissy. They looked so glamorous, she thought. Like old-time movie stars. They were dead-centre, and to

Harry's right, he informed her, was his friend, now in Australia, Ronny Piper. To Chrissy's left was a huge man called Big Tony Parish, now deceased. There were about twenty other characters in the photo, all of them looking fantastic, emanating an aura, but none quite like Harry.

Harry pointed to himself. "See him, Clare?" She looked at his image, smiling out at her. "That's Harry Lane, up there. Harry Lane was never meant to grow old." He laughed. "Oh, alright, Harry Lane was never meant to be really, really old. Just a little bit old."

They both began laughing. He looked at her again for a few seconds. "You remind me of somebody. Have done since the day we first met. Can't for the life of me think who." His voice trailed off slightly. "Met so many people over the years, you see."

He suddenly snapped from his reverie, wrapped his arm gently around Clare's shoulder again and said, "Shall we go grab that cuppa, then?"

She looked up at his smiling face, her eyes still showing the signs of her tears, and replied, "Yes, lets."

Clare watched Burt Roswell pace his office. "So, as yet no leads whatsoever, past or present, on the Lanes, Detective Hendshall?"

"No sir, certainly nothing substantial worth pursuing," she answered.

"And how about our notorious Bobby James? Is he still a regular visitor to the Lanes' establishments?" Roswell asked, raising an eyebrow.

"Not over the last week, Sir, no. I've not seen him," she replied.

He paused and held her gaze. "They're ready to hit somewhere, any time soon. I can feel it, and my instincts are never wrong."

She looked at him and resisted the urge to say, "Is that why you have been chasing him for over thirty years, because your instincts are so good?"

"You must dig deep now, Detective Hendshall, because trust me, they will be on the move soon."

"Well, the bugs I've planted in Denny's and Ray's houses, and the pub and Nightingales, have revealed nothing so far, Mr Roswell," she said.

His eyes narrowed and his expression took on the familiar

frustrated, defeated look he often displayed when dealing with the Lanes. "When in God's name do they speak on the phone? I've had to sit through hours of tapes listening to all kinds of rubbish from the latest goings on at Georgie Lane's hair salon to what their children are having with their bloody Rice Chrispies." He turned away and then suddenly burst out in a raised voice, "Nothing, absolutely nothing! That bastard Harry Lane will pull a job with Bobby James right under my nose. Again!" He suddenly remembered his company and turned around. "I do apologize for my outburst, but Lane has managed to do this over and over again."

Clare spoke quietly, almost under her breath in thoughtful contemplation. "Harry is dying."

Roswell walked towards her. "I beg your pardon, Detective?"

"I said, Harry is dying, Sir. Terminal cancer. Trust me, he is in no condition to rob anything."

Roswell laughed and shook his head dismissively. "I wouldn't put it passed him to fake his own death so that his wife could claim on the insurance."

He could see the look of distain on her face. Her general demeanour confirmed his worst fears that the famous Lane charm had worked its magic on her.

"I do hope you have not compromised either yourself or our case in regards to the Lanes. Because my years of experience are telling me you are becoming less focused on the job in hand and becoming more emotionally attached to this family." She glared at him and he saw that his statement had angered her. But before she could react, he interjected, "Please remember who the senior officer is in this room before you answer, Detective Hendshall."

For the first time since walking out of Hendon Police College, Clare found herself contemplating whether she had chosen the right career after all. Even if she was on the right side, she thought of Harry and, of course, Ray who, against all her better judgement, she was falling for. She then thought of her lovely mum and her wonderful, deceased father who had encouraged her to join the police and she snapped back into police mode.

"Trust me, Sir, my mind is one hundred per cent on this assignment, exactly like all my previous ones." She took in his reaction then decided to let him know, regardless of his status, that he was out of order. "I'm undercover, Sir. It's what I do. With all due respect, it's me at risk here, mixing it with dangerous criminals. I'd also appreciate it if, on our future meetings, you could address me by my cover name and not by my real one, as it really does throw my mind game out."

She smiled to herself.

"Yes indeed, and forgive my impatience. I'm very confident in your ability. I just get the general feeling from above that they're not prepared to subsidise my investigations into the Lanes for much longer, so I fear your undercover operation is in jeopardy."

Clare lay on her bed, mulling over her conversation with Roswell and thinking about the bugs she had planted. His voice was ringing in her head: "Where do they speak on the phone?"

"Oh my God, of course," she said out loud. "Valentines! How did I not think of it? All the times I've been there and Ray has taken calls on that little phone in the corner of the room."

42.

Three months later

Burt Roswell listened to the nurse as she explained that Harry was in a bad way now and would quite possibly drift in and out of consciousness. He was on extremely strong painkillers and his nutritional intake was pretty much solely liquid meal replacements. Despite the nurse's description, he nevertheless expected to see the same old smiling man slinging banter and insults at him when he walked in and he was already preparing to give as good as he got as he walked down the corridor.

As Burt entered the room and caught sight of Harry, he was stunned to his core. People say it's rude to stare, but Harry was sleeping, so had no idea Burt was standing at the end of his bed in utter shock at the sight before him.

Harry had his head back on the pillow, mouth wide open. His once powerful frame was now just skin and bone. There was nothing left of him. His once muscular shoulders and arms hung loosely from the hospital gown, his handsome face now gaunt, with no colour to it and his thick head of hair now thin, wispy and grey.

As Burt pulled a chair up to the side of the bed, without taking his eyes off of Harry, he was overcome with sadness. After all these years of cat and mouse with this man, he could see without doubt it was now all over and he felt nothing but a deep loss. He wasn't entirely sure why, but after all these years of pursuit, of games, of ridicule and banter, suddenly there would be no more chase and no more frustration involving Harry.

Maybe the loss Burt felt was something else. Deep down, did he actually like Harry? His sharpness, his wit. Could he possibly admit a begrudging admiration for him? Had he been, for all these years, somewhat jealous of this man's looks, his swagger, his aura and his attitude? Whatever he felt for Harry Lane, looking at him in that hospital bed was absolutely gut-wrenching, and although Burt had encountered cancer before, losing family and friends to it, nothing ever prepares you for the rapid decline and wasting away of a person in front of your eyes.

As Burt sat silently, contemplating all the years that had passed and the many ups and downs they had shared, Harry's eyes suddenly sprung open, almost as if in shock.

"Afternoon, Harry," Burt said gently. Harry turned and looked at Burt, somewhat vaguely for a few seconds, before his sunken eyes seemed to focus in on his old foe. The dark circles under his eyes and the jaundiced skin slowly broke into a lovely smile that even warmed Burt's heart. Unconsciously, he returned the smile.

Harry's voice came out slightly croaky, weary and weak. "Hello Burt. You come to finally read me my rights and take me away, have you, mate?"

"No chance, Harry. You always were too bleedin' smart by far, weren't you?" Burt replied, smiling warmly.

Harry tried to lift himself up in the bed but couldn't manage it. Burt stood up, leaned across and placed his hands as gently as he could under Harry's armpits and slid him up. He could feel Harry's bones and wondered at how frail he had become. He hardly weighed anything.

Burt knew that Harry had registered his look of shock at his appearance, which suddenly saddened him. He asked Harry if he wanted some water, which he nodded to in response.

Burt pressed the button on the handset to raise Harry's bed, then tilted the beaker of water to his parched lips. Harry swallowed the much-needed liquid and their eyes locked on each other.

Harry let his famous smile brighten his sunken features again. "Who would have thought it, Burt, after all these years you would be my nursemaid."

Burt let out a chuckle, but inside he felt nothing but sadness and sympathy. Whatever Harry had done over the years, and whatever Burt was convinced he was involved with, he didn't deserve this. Such an impressive man reduced to being cared for in hospital.

"Do me a favour, would you, please?" Harry asked.

"Yes, of course, Harry, what is it?" Burt returned in a friendly tone.

"Retire," Harry croaked. "Look at the state of me, and how quickly it's happened. Take early retirement and go and enjoy your life. You never know what's around the corner." Exhausted, Harry leaned his head back on his pillow, staring at the ceiling.

A reflective Burt looked at his old nemesis and knew that his comment had been both genuine and correct.

The two men chatted away in the friendliest way they ever had in over thirty years. Harry even told Burt he'd always liked him in a way and respected him for always being incorruptible and a good community man, impressed with his charity work and, of course, the boxing.

"Can you explain something to me, Harry?" Burt asked. "And don't insult my intelligence after all these years by denying all the robberies and crimes you got away with. Why did you do it, when you could easily make a comfortable living with your legitimate businesses?"

Harry looked across at Burt and, although weary, still maintained that sarcastic grin and a sparkle in his eyes. "If I'm really honest, I liked the excitement. The planning, the execution, and getting away with the prize."

The words would normally have annoyed Burt, but today he just smiled as Harry continued.

"No one knows more than you, Burt. Long hours and honest work don't always pay that well, especially in fluctuating economies. I liked to get a very large return for the least amount of effort and I was prepared to take the risks. I was always certain I'd get away with it, or I'd not have done it, particularly when the boys were born."

Under normal circumstances, at the mention of his boys, Burt would have made a snide remark about them following in his footsteps. But today, he had no desire for bad feeling.

"Some women sell their bodies and risk their dignity. And some men commit crime and risk their liberty. They both do it for one reason. Money. But you know what, Burt? My kind, the ones prepared to take the risk, are very small in number. Luckily for you, most are far too scared of doing time." Burt listened intently as Harry continued. "How many murders and crimes of all sorts do you think there would be if we relied on people's moral compass? Trust me, it would be a lot higher than you think. If they thought they could get away with it, they bloody well would. So, your job is important. The reason these guys don't do it is because they fear arrest."

Burt smiled gently in acknowledgement. "Speaking of murder. Before I go…George Parker?"

He looked at Harry, who just stared blankly back.

"And Vince Street."

Again, nothing. Then Harry smiled.

"Burt, give up the ghost. Piss off and retire and let me sleep."

Burt smiled. "Bye, Harry. You kept me on my toes. It was certainly never boring."

"Bye, Burt. Enjoy your retirement, mate."

As Burt got to the door, he turned back. "By the way, Harry, I know you always called me the Human Blue Bottle. Those two charming sons of yours repeated it many years ago in the back of my car."

Harry rested his head back on the pillow and laughed as he slowly drifted back into sleep.

Harry smiled at the nurse as she handed him a notepad, two envelopes and a stamp. He had asked her if she would do him a favour and get them for him on her lunch break. Harry then proceeded to write a letter, telling the story of that evening back in 1955 and George Parker's demise, then going into detail about the disappearance of Vince Street. When Harry had finished writing, he placed the letter in one of the envelopes and wrote across it, TO BE OPENED AFTER MY DEATH. Then he placed the envelope inside the second one, sealed it and addressed it to Burt Roswell.

Clare listened to Burt and couldn't quite take in what he was saying. He was taking early retirement. In fact, he had already handed in his notice, pending agreement from higher up. More importantly for her, he was withdrawing her from her undercover investigation of the Lanes.

Her emotions were all over the place.

There was some relief now that whatever it was she had going with Ray would not be able to develop further. There was also relief that she just didn't have enough evidence to convict them of anything. She was, of course, in no doubt that they were all guilty of serious crimes, but she was happy that it would not be her work that would produce the evidence to turn a prison door lock on them.

But the hardest part of being pulled out of the investigation was that she would never be able to make contact with the Lanes again.

"I can see your disappointment, Detective, but after visiting Harry myself, I can say it's now a fruitless cause, and quite frankly my superiors were constantly going on at me about their damned budgets and targets, looking for any excuse to end the operation." He went very quiet for a while, then spoke very softly. "To be honest, I've done lots of soul-searching since my hospital visit. Makes you wonder what life is all about in the end." He smiled and offered her his hand to shake. "I've sent in a glowing report about your excellent work. Harry is dying and I'm far too long in the tooth to start again, chasing Ray and Denny. I'll let someone else suffer that unenviable task."

As they shook hands, Clare felt empty inside, but covered her disappointment.

"You have been given a two-week grace period to hand in your notice with the Lanes and cover yourself. I'll leave you to decide how you want to walk away. But of course, should you uncover any fresh evidence in that period, then the case may be re-evaluated." He sighed. "I think my hunch in regards to Bobby James may have been wrong, or perhaps Harry's condition made whatever plans they had come to nothing."

Ray and Denny looked on at their father as he spoke to them.

"Promise me, lads, it ends with you two. No passing it down to them kids of yours. I want a straight life for them grandchildren of mine, including any future ones you may have when I'm gone."

Both brothers agreed. No more crime. It stops with them. Ray then spoke.

"Once Bobby green-lights that job and we execute it, it's the last one for me, ever."

Denny agreed and leaned in, kissing his dad on the forehead. Ray followed.

"Who do you think I am, the bleedin' God Father? Maybe you should both kneel and kiss my hand."

They all laughed, but as they left the ward, they both felt deeply sad as they knew his condition was worsening by the day.

They were both also determined to pull off the final job their father had helped plan with Bobby.

43.

One week later

Clare looked on as Ray and Denny entered the Green Man, both smiling and still in full conversation as they headed towards her. She felt unusually anxious about their arrival and apprehensive about how they would react to her explanation as to why she would be handing in her notice, and indeed, whether it would arouse any suspicion.

"Two pints, please," a smiling Ray said. Both he and Denny were both slightly merry already and seemed in good spirits.

"Alright Clare?" Denny added, smiling.

"Afternoon," Clare replied, somewhat solemnly as she started to pour the first pint. "I'm glad you're both here together, as I have some news to tell you."

"Oh yeah, good or bad?" Denny asked as Clare handed him a pint and began pouring Ray's.

"Bit of both, really. Good because it's what I've always wanted, but bad because it will mean leaving my work with you. And leaving the area." She glanced at Ray as she said this and noted the obvious disappointment in his eyes.

Ray suddenly smiled, his face lighting up instantly. "Good girl, you got that acting job you went for, didn't you?"

She returned his beautiful smile with one of her own. "Yes I did, Ray. I won the audition against all the others," she lied.

As Ray and Clare were conversing, a young local lad came to the bar and stood next to Denny. He was a regular at the pub and often sported a black eye. Today's looked even angrier than usual. Denny looked at him, tutted and held his face, inspecting him.

"You been talking when you should be listening again, son?"

The lad looked at Denny sheepishly and took his beer. Denny

clipped him playfully round the ear.

"Go on, put your money away and sit down. I'll pay for that. Keep your guard up next time." He turned to Clare. "Me and Ray just been given the green light on a job we've been waiting on as well. So, we're all in the same boat in regards to new work."

Ray cast Denny a sharp look, raising his eyebrow slightly, then turned to Clare. "Yes, me and Denny have to go out to Hertfordshire for a couple of days to sort this job out. When we get back, I'll take you up the West End to celebrate your new job."

Denny began laughing. "Well, our new bit of work could be very lucrative indeed, so if you and your actor mates want to make a movie, we could invest." He then stared into the optics, thoughtfully. "Always fancied getting into the movie game, me. See myself as a movie producer, I do."

Ray rolled his eyes, which made Clare laugh. She then looked serious. "I feel happy I got the job but terrible for giving just a week's notice, especially with Harry the way he is. Makes me so sad."

Denny smiled at her, his face uncharacteristically soft. "That's a lovely thing to say, Clare, but he is our dad and there is nothing we can do, let alone you. You go, girl, and take your opportunities in life. Trust me, you staying here and missing out and being sad would not be what our dad would want. He was always upbeat about life and a go-getter."

Clare was somewhat taken back by Denny's comment and moved by the whole situation. She simply replied, "Thank you."

Ray stood next to Denny, laughing as he watched his brother in his element, steering the long canal barge slowly along the water. The weather was beautiful, as were the surroundings as they headed along the Grand Union Canal to Hemel Hempstead, carrying their huge take from the London cash depot. They had cleared it into their van, onto the barge, and whisked it away without a trace.

Denny turned to Ray. "I'm the captain of this vessel and bringing us safely to our destination. I'd be grateful if you would return to your quarters, able seaman Lane," he said before taking a large gulp of his beer.

"You just make sure you do get us and our cargo safely to our destination, without smashing off them banks," Ray replied. "And take it easy on them beers. Don't forget we have the locks to open and close so we have to keep our wits about us. Don't want anyone falling in and drowning."

Denny cheerfully waved to a couple walking their dog along the path and in a mock posh accent, called out, "Morning! Beautiful day, isn't it."

Ray laughed and headed back inside, muttering, "You're my brother and I love you, Denny. But you ain't well, mate."

Clare stood, watching the television in her flat as the newsreader spoke.

"A gang of robbers are still at large after committing what is now believed to be the UK's largest ever cash robbery. As yet, police have no clues. The gang have simply disappeared into thin air."

She switched the television off and, even though it was officially her last day investigating the Lanes, she decided to listen to the last recordings from the listening device she had planted in the small phone booth in Valentines.

She was getting ready to go out. She was off to visit her mum down in Surrey. After that, Ray was taking her out to the West End to celebrate her new job, as promised. As the recordings began, she dwelled on the thought that it would be her last night with him. As Clare blow-dried her hair, the phone calls clicked through the usual monotonous repetition of customers ordering cabs or phoning home.

Then, she heard Ray's voice and also recognized Bobby James's as they discussed how the barge had been tested for every possible scenario and they were good to go. The cash depot would be stuffed to the rafters.

She sat down, in shock, on the edge of her bed and listened in total disbelief to Ray and Bobby's conversation. Finally, after playing it a dozen times or more, she removed the cassette from the machine. Her mind was in utter turmoil as she placed it in her handbag.

Katherine Hendshall could see the anguish in her daughter's face and heard the distress in her voice as she explained to her mother the situation she had somehow found herself in. She was falling in love with a member of the family she was investigating and now, on her final official day on the operation, she had found evidence of his involvement in Britain's largest ever cash robbery.

"Oh mum, it's all such a mess. I can't stop my feelings for him. I think I love a man that I can't possibly ever have a relationship with."

Katherine felt her heart breaking as she sat opposite her daughter. She knew only too well the devastating emotional trauma the desire for impossible love could cause. The shame, the guilt, the fantasies.

"Does this man feel the same as you, my love?" she asked.

Clare looked at her mother and contemplated the question before replying, "Yes, he does, mum. But whether he does to the same extent or in the same way, who knows. He is a man. Who knows what goes through their heads?"

This made Katherine laugh, which raised a smile from her daughter. "Have you slept with him?"

Slightly surprised by her mum's direct question, she felt her face flush. "No, we haven't, mum." She then became slightly angry and frustrated. "How the hell could I? He is a career criminal and I'm a police officer, not to mention the fact he is married with a daughter. Oh God, I miss dad so much, mum. He would know what to do."

Katherine looked up at the picture on the sideboard of her with her husband and sighed. "I know, love. So do I."

"This is meant to be my last day on this case, and would you believe it, he is taking me to the West End to celebrate me leaving for a job that doesn't exist. And now I have evidence that it is my duty to hand in."

Katherine felt so sorry for her daughter and the stress she must be feeling. "What will you do, darling?"

Clare looked utterly shattered and confused. "His father is in hospital, dying as we speak, and if I hand in my evidence, the man I love will go to prison. And if I don't hand it in, I've failed in my duty as a police officer." She paused, reflectively. "Either way, he will find out I've been undercover, trying to nail his family."

Clare suddenly jumped up as she caught sight of the time on the mantelpiece clock. "Oh my god, mum, I've got to go. Ray will be expecting me. I need to get back to London."

She kissed her mum before dashing out of the room. "I'll tell you all about it and who they are in a couple of days, although if I hand my evidence in, you will know soon enough from the news."

As she grabbed her handbag off the bannister, and ran for the door, she didn't hear her work diary fall from her bag.

"Bye mum, love you."

It all happened so quickly. Katherine slowly got herself up from her chair and walked from the living room into the hallway. She glanced down at the floor and spotted the diary. She picked it up and as she did, it fell open. As she stared at the page, her heart thumped in her chest, a wave of nausea causing her to feel faint. She staggered backwards and leaned back heavily into the wall, then slumped onto the stairs, still clutching the diary.

Still in shock, she looked at the names and numbers. Ray Lane, Denny Lane, Harry Lane, Chrissy Lane, Nightingales, Valentines café. As she tried to take in what she was reading, she suddenly remembered her daughter's words: "Ray will be expecting me."

Suddenly, she leaped up from the stairs. "Oh Jesus, for the love of god, no!"

Katherine climbed in to the back seat of the black cab and instructed the driver to take her to St Paul's hospital, north London. She had found out from the diary that was where Harry was. She had tried calling all the numbers she could find, and tried all the avenues she could think of to contact her daughter, but had had no luck.

She needed to prevent her meeting Ray. Although she knew that they hadn't slept together yet, Katherine also knew, from her own experience, that her lovely daughter could be about to make the biggest mistake in her life.

And the reality was that it would all be Katherine's fault.

The secret she had vowed to take to her grave was now going to shatter her daughter's life and destroy everything she had ever known and believed in. But Katherine knew she had no other choice. The other scenario was too terrible to contemplate.

As the taxi headed towards the hospital, Katherine opened the scrapbook she was holding and tearfully looked at the photos and newspaper cuttings of herself as a young woman.

Kathy Kane is a big hit with the crowd at Nightingales! A star in the making, says proud club owner Harry Lane as he makes Kathy Kane his top entertainer! "I just love to sing and perform," the talented Kathy

Kane tells our reporter!

As Ray walked Clare back to her apartment she looked down at his shoes.

"Your laces are undone, Ray."

Without looking, he casually replied, "No, it's just that I'm so cool, as I approach my destination, my shoes start undoing themselves in preparation for my arrival."

She looked up at him and laughed. "Oh my god, you are so full of yourself."

He smiled at her and wrapped his arm around her. She leaned her head in and rested it on his shoulder. Regardless of what tomorrow would bring, she was relinquishing any responsibility or thoughts of police duty and enjoying this last evening with Ray.

When they reached her building, she walked up the steps and opened the door. Without a word to each other, he followed her inside.

"You never said how your trip to Hertfordshire went," she enquired softly.

He grinned slightly as he replied. "I'll tell you about it one day. But it turned out very lucrative indeed."

Clare handed Ray a glass of wine. "Thanks so much for a lovely day, and for your company, Ray. It was fantastic," she gushed.

Without saying a thing, he leaned in to kiss her. She closed her eyes but before their lips met, the phone in her apartment rang.

Her eyes sprang open and she pulled her head back impulsively. Somewhat embarrassed, she let out a gasp. "I'd better answer that."

In that split second, the moment was gone. Ray's conscience remained intact. Clare's career was equally undamaged.

"It's the hospital, Ray," a now alert and concerned Clare said. "Apparently, your dad has been trying to get hold of us everywhere. He wants us there straight away. It's an emergency."

As Ray and Clare hurried into the ward, the room fell silent and everyone stared at the new arrivals.

Sitting to the right of Harry's bed was Chrissy and Denny. To the left, Katherine.

A stunned Clare looked at her mum. "Mum? What are you doing

here?"

Before Katherine could speak, Chrissy intervened. "Sit down, darling. Sit down, son. We have a lot to discuss."

Clare looked at herself in the hospital toilet mirror. She felt the panic overcome her and went to the window, opened it and gulped in the fresh air, taking in far too much and making herself feel even dizzier. She stared out at the dark sky and down towards the hospital forecourt, weakly bathed with sodium light. Nurses and visitors milled around in the gloom.

A knock at the door made her jump. As she came round from her reverie, she heard Ray's voice. "Are you OK, Clare?"

She held her breath to make the room as silent as possible. She couldn't face him. She couldn't face anyone. She couldn't take any of it in.

The woman she loved and trusted more than anyone had lied to her. The man she had believed to be her father, who brought her up and who she had grieved, wasn't her father after all. Her real dad was next door, dying. The man she thought she was in love with was her brother.

She was shocked again from her reverie by Ray's knocking. "Come on, Clare. We are all stunned by this. Me, Denny, mum and dad. Come out, please!"

Clare looked at herself again in the mirror. She then opened her handbag and removed the cassette containing Ray's conversation with Bobby James. She paused, looking at it briefly, then slung the tape down the toilet pan, pulled the chain and flushed it away.

She looked down, and watched as the gushing, frothing water dispersed and settled.

Happy the evidence was gone, she left the room.

Epilogue.

Burt Roswell looked at the newspaper headline.

*POLICE STILL NO CLOSER TO FINDING
THE CULPRITS FROM BRITAIN'S LARGEST
EVER ROBBERY*

He then looked at the letter from Harry Lane resting on his desk. He picked it up and read the message on the envelope. 'Not to be opened till I'm gone. I'm watching you Burt and I'll know.' He smiled and slowly slit the envelope open. As he removed the letter, a twenty-pound note fell out.

Burt slowly read the letter, taking in its contents and slowly shaking his head.

"I knew it was you that killed George Parker that night," he said out loud. "I was on my beat and I knew you was there, Piper! And you, Antonio, you lying old sod."

As he read Harry's explanation of Parker's bullying behaviour, Burt felt no sympathy for George but allowed himself to feel happy that after all these years he had been right all along.

He then read how the Quinns had dumped Vince Street's car, together with his corpse, on Harry's door step, leaving him to take the blame.

"Jesus, Harry, you lived dangerously. So that day in the car park when I was questioning you, you had a body in the car behind you all along." He laughed out loud. "Christ Almighty, and I thought my job was stressful." He shook his head and tutted. "Well, Johnny and Jamie, you two are right where you deserve to be, festering in prison, you no good pair of sods. You're proof there is no honour among thieves."

He read the letter again, taking in the dates and details and his mind flashed back to all those moments. He smiled. "Blimey, Harry, you certainly lived on luck and your wits, old son."

He read the final sentence and roared with laughter.

> *Dearest Burt, my old friend and foe, please*
> *enjoy your retirement and the rest of your life and*
> *have a pint on me and Barclays Bank, 1974.*
> *All the best,*
> *Your old mate Harry Lane.*

Burt folded the twenty-pound note and placed it in his wallet. He then took the letter and placed it through the office paper shredder. He went to the door, switched the light off and as he walked down the corridor, he chuckled.

"You were a one off, a total one off. Right, let's go and have that pint on you and to your memory, Harry Lane!"

Acknowledgements.

Bringing the Lanes to life in print has been a lot of hard work, and not just from me. This book would not be possible without the help and support of a number of brilliant people. Not least, my mum, Eileen, who not only kept me sane while I wrote, but also undertook the thankless task of typing up my illegible handwritten script so that it could be read without translation tools. To my good friend Sedge Swatton for creating a brilliant cover for me at short notice and with fantastic results. And to Mike Harris for all his editing skills and patience putting it all together.

My dad, Bern, is no longer with us, but his voice was in my head all the time that I was writing, and a lot of the humour no doubt comes from him.

Lastly, I'd like to thank you, the reader, for taking a chance on an unknown author. I hope you enjoyed getting to know the Lanes as much as I did. I'm always happy to hear from readers, so please do get in touch by email timothybthomas166@yahoo.com.

Printed in Great Britain
by Amazon

45389097R00139